Knocked Up by the Bad Boy

Vanessa Waltz

ISBN: 1512054666
ISBN-13: 978-1512054668

CONTENTS

ACKNOWLEDGMENTS

Thank you Kevin McGrath and Faith Van Horne for your excellent work..

JOHNNY

Smoke shifts in front of me in a gray haze, obscuring the bodies surrounding me. Desaturated shapes move behind the smoky background, and I search through them. It's hard to tell what makes my veins burn with the need for *more*—more wine, more cigarettes, and more pussy.

Music pounds into my chest like a second heartbeat, mirroring the vicious desire thrumming through my veins. Cocktail waitresses whisk the smoke-filled room like apparitions. Their clothes cling to their bodies like Saran Wrap.

Scantily clad girls are magnets for my cock, and being the boss means I can have my pick of any of them. It's a free-for-all. Hard to choose one. Their eyes follow me wherever I go, and I look back, gauging their interest. Do I want to fuck her? How far will she let me go?

A warm, female body slides against mine. Her torso shifts so that she stands right between my legs, the deep neckline of her shirt giving me a nice fucking view of her tits, pressed against her too-small t-shirt. No bra.

Blood seems to drain from my head, feeding the rush

to my groin. She sets down drinks at the bar. They make sharp raps as the glasses hit the counter, one after the other.

I recognize her.

It's the second time she's rubbed against me like a cat in heat. My cock stirs when she leans into my shoulder, strands of her blonde hair just dragging my shoulder.

Fucking broads. If you want my cock, just ask for it.

Is she hot though? Those big tits distract me, just hanging there without a bra. She leans over the bar counter, chatting with the bartender. I look up her slender legs, all the way to the curve of her ass when her short skirt rides up slightly. Her arm presses against mine as if she's oblivious, as if she isn't aware that she's touching me. One set of deep-blue eyes flash at me as she meets my gaze briefly, smiling through those pink lips.

There are two types of women in this world: those who want to fuck me because I'm the boss, and those who want to fuck me because they've heard of my reputation between the sheets.

Not to brag, but I'm a pretty great fuck. I never leave them disappointed. Even the ones who think they can get something out of fucking the boss always beg for seconds. I rarely indulge them. Why try the same thing when I can have any flavor of the week?

My attention turns back to the cocktail waitress, who is still hell-bent on teasing me, leaning over to shove her ass in my face. *Maddon*, I want to grab the backs of her thighs and pinch that perfectly round, bubble ass.

Her, my cock says. *Fuck her.*

I love getting it wet, hearing them scream my name, night after night. I fucking need it because it's not easy being me.

The waitress finally pulls away from the bar, her warmth disappearing from my shoulder. A rush of energy makes me reach out and grab her wrist before she can take two steps away. Her pulse jumps into my fingers. She whirls around, her blonde hair clinging to her neck.

I'm disappointed to realize that she's not as hot as I thought she was. But she hit on me pretty blatantly, and that's enough to make me want to fuck her.

"Where the fuck do you think you're going?"

An uncertain smile twitches. "What do you—?"

"That's the second time you've done that." My fingers circle around her wrist tightly as I feel the burn from her skin.

"Done what?"

Playing coy, are we? I hate that shit.

Pink flushes her face as she sucks in her lip, my cock stirring as I imagine the wet heat wrapping around my dick, her tongue sliding up and down.

"Don't play dumb, sweetheart."

"Okay, *fine*. I just wanted to get your attention."

A smile widens my face as she allows me to slide my hand down her arm and anchor securely over her elbow. I pull her close. Close enough for her hair to flutter from my breath, and to see her vein jumping in her throat. She parts her lips, her eyes batting as though I'm about to kiss her, and her hands touch my chest.

"Just ask me."

"Huh?" She barely whispers it.

I spot her name tag. Alyssa. "Alyssa, tell me that you want my cock, and I'll take you into that VIP room right now and fuck your brains out."

My words run through her like liquor. A sudden, hot burn flashes over her face. She doesn't flinch at the word—she's drawn toward it. "But—my job—"

A deep chuckle from my chest cuts across her words. "Who do you think hired you?"

Her eyes widen in recognition.

"*Oh.*"

Oh.

She might not have brains, but my cock stirs again when her hands suddenly clench my sides.

"I'm sorry, Mr. Cravotta. I didn't know who you were."

"You didn't offend me, hon."

It's not every day that a girl blatantly hits on me. People who know who I am avoid me like the plague. No one wants to run into the boss of the family. They're afraid of pissing me off. As if I would get offended by a girl asking me to suck my cock. Jesus Christ, what has the world come to?

I take her waist and guide her to the VIP rooms. They're a series of black leather booths with enough privacy for someone to get in a quick fuck—or a blowjob—as I'm judging by the sounds.

I lead her through the doors, the men parting to give me space. She wraps her arms around my waist, her tits flattening against my chest. My blood boils as she reaches down with a sly smirk, grabbing a fistful of my cock.

Fuck.

Yes.

The noise of the bar slightly drops away as the door closes. Then I slide into a leather booth and look up her trembling legs.

"Take off your clothes."

Without a split second of hesitation she pulls the flimsy tank top from her head, and a thrill shoots into my heart. Creamy tits bounce on her chest, the pink nipples contracting slightly from the cold. Platinum-blonde hair falls on her delicate shoulders. My hand curls around my cock, feeling the blood pounding through it already. It screams for me to fuck her—to get on with the show.

The flimsy skirt and nylons are next. She watches my hungry gaze with a knowing grin that I'd like to wipe off her face. I beckon to her, blood rushing to my groin as I see her thighs glistening, her pink pussy already flushed. I reach up and yank her naked waist so that she tumbles into my lap, big tits rammed against my face. I'm addicted to that red flush that spreads across her chest like a fever when my mouth opens wide and I tongue her hard nipple, flicking it. Alyssa wraps an arm around my neck, still wearing that smirk.

I don't like it.

I grab one of her tits and pinch her nipple hard. If this little cunt is going to play games with me, I'm going to torture her with my tongue.

"I don't believe that you didn't recognize me the moment you saw me."

My dick tells me to shut the fuck up already, but what I like more than spreading those lips apart is making them come for me. Manipulating that little pussy to do what I want. She looks down at me with a slightly dazed expression—halfway between lust and fear. All I can think about is that she's positioned right over my cock, her thighs gripping my waist, and the warmth of her skin under my hands.

"Lie down."

She obeys, lying faceup as my hands knead her perfectly round globes. Her knees draw up together and my hand rips over her thighs, her face cringing with the sting.

"Spread your legs for me."

"But, Johnny—"

"It's 'sir' or 'Mr. Cravotta.'"

I suppress a small grin as she flinches at the growl in my voice.

Her cheeks blush as I stare down at her, my hand spreading over her stomach as her thighs spread apart, trembling.

"I swear, I didn't know—ah!"

My hand engulfs her glistening pussy, the middle finger riding against her clit. Her blush deepens, and her lips part. Fuck, it gets me hard as a rock. The way she begs me with her eyes. My fingers curl into her wet cunt and she lets out a sharp moan as I grab her tits with the other hand.

"Just admit it. You wanted to know what it was like to fuck a boss."

She's so fucking wet. I pulse my fingers slowly inside her, slamming them home as she arches her back.

"Admit it."

"Yes, okay," she says, out of breath.

She must be able to feel my thick length just under her head. With her head in my lap, she turns to the side. Desperate fingers grasp my jacket as I slam into her cunt. Over and over again. The obscene, wet sounds and her shallow breaths fill my ears. Her greedy hands try to grasp my tie, but I yank it away from her.

No. I'm in control.

I stop for a moment to give her a rest, my fingers deep inside her as her chest pulses.

"Please, I want you inside me."

Maybe it's because I've heard the words so fucking often, but they fail to thrill me. Of course she wants me, but there's something that turns me off about this broad. She tried to play me. Manipulate me. The idea makes me laugh. Yeah, everyone knows that I'm constantly banging a different girl. That doesn't mean that you can flash pussy in my face and get me to do what you want. I fuck them because I want to fuck them, because it's how I manage to keep breathing.

She tugs at my slacks, her fingers plucking at the fabric as her lips shape into a bratty pout. Hunger claws my insides. My dick doesn't give a fuck that she's not what I want. I know that if I bang her, I'll still need to find someone else.

I'll finish her off quickly.

My hand twists inside her, and I feel my cock twitch as she fists my slacks and lets out a groan.

"Mr. Cravotta, *please.*"

"Please what?"

I stop for a moment, and she cries out as if I slapped her. Fuck, it turns me on to see her so hot for my cock. Her pussy contracts over my fingers, and I grab her tits with my other hand, kneading one after the other.

"I want you."

I'm hard enough to pound nails into the wall, but I've already decided that I'm going stick my dick into someone else.

"Please, sir!"

She's begging you to fuck her. Just do it already.

No.

I look into her heavily lidded eyes. "I want you to come for me. Understand?"

She nods, and I ram my fingers back inside her. My other hand massages her clit, and she arches her back in a soundless gasp. Fuck, it's taking everything in me not to flip her over and drive my cock deep inside her. I slide in and out, unable to not think about that tight warmth around my throbbing dick, which is uncomfortably thick in my pants.

"Oh my God—!"

Alyssa grabs my tie and yanks my head down. I snake my hand through her tangled hair and yank her head back, my teeth finding the delectable flesh on her throat. I kiss her, flicking my tongue over her skin as my hand locks inside her.

"Oh, *fuck me*!"

My mouth smiles against her raw skin as she reaches up, gripping my hair. Her body arches into me as her pussy contracts on my fingers. It clenches over and over, sending shaking moans out of her chest. Then I slide my hand out and lift my head, giving her a second to breathe.

I pull her upright, her head lolling to the side as I stand up from the booth, my hard-on still on perfect display.

"How was that, sweetheart?"

"*Fucking* amazing."

A glow of pride hits my chest as she stares at me, her chest still heaving.

"I'm glad you enjoyed yourself."

"Wait—where are you going?" She grabs my hand, stopping me.

"Back to the bar."

Her face falls as I slide my hand out of her grasp, but she doesn't say a word. She can't complain. I just got her off.

Energy pulses in my chest as I leave the VIP room and enter the bathroom to wash her juice from my hands, looking up into the mirror at my scowling face. The need to have a naked girl in my arms still blazes under my skin like fire. Fucking her would have been like eating the shitty chocolate bars I used to get as a kid. They crumble in your mouth and by the end of eating the whole thing, you're left with the same craving.

The cloud of smoke blasts my face as I walk back into the bar, scanning it briefly. Women—so many fucking women. None of them catch my eye, and I'm headed back to my seat before I see a girl who makes the one I almost fucked look like a wilted hag.

I don't recognize her. This is supposed to be a closed event—just a little celebration for my men—but I've never seen her before. I know everyone's girlfriend, but not her. Fuck, who gives a shit how she got here?

The first thing I notice is her body, wrapped up in a skintight lacey black dress that shows off her curves. I can make out the faint line of a G-string under the fabric, and my mouth waters just thinking of pulling it right off her thighs. She crosses her legs, exposing a length of tantalizing flesh. Then my eyes travel up that body I can already see naked, all the way to the tits nearly popping out

11

of her dress. It's fucking sinful. A sliver of her bra peeks out, and she keeps pulling the top of the lace over it, only for it to slip back down.

No, don't do that. By all means, let your tits go free.

She has a haughty-looking face, like a girl who usually gets what she wants. Her eyebrows arch high. Dark. Dramatic. That's what I'm getting from this chick. She's gorgeous. Makes the place burn a little brighter.

Only, there's a problem.

François is already hitting on her.

How the fuck did he get here so quickly?

He leans beside her, his body turned toward her. She laughs at something he says, a beautiful smile lighting up her face, and a surge of jealousy burns in my chest. She moves suddenly, her eyes roaming through the crowd. They fall over mine. They jump back and hold me. And a grin hitches on her face as she studies me.

Good thing I'm the boss.

I make a beeline for François, trying in vain to think of something nicer than telling him to fuck off, but let's face it. I didn't become boss by being a nice guy. There comes a point where you stop giving a fuck. Taking what I want, whenever I want has served me pretty fucking well so far, but there are rules, of course. I can't fuck around with anyone's girl, but she's not his girl. She's fair game, except nothing is fair when I'm involved.

She notices my approach before I even get there, and a small blush fills her cheeks as I approach her. Damn, she's gorgeous.

But I have to get rid of him first. I touch François' shoulder and lean in slightly, talking low enough so that the girl can't hear a word I'm saying. "I need you to check the VIP rooms. I don't want anyone doing drugs in my bar."

He blinks at me.

It's a bullshit request. He knows it. I know it.

The faintest glint of resentment shines in his eyes as he nods in affirmation. "All right."

I can just hear his thoughts: *Fucking cock-block.*

It's a dick move, but I wouldn't be what I am today if I just stood aside and let people take what I want.

He moves away from the girl, giving her a second glance as if wondering if he should ask her for her number, but I smile at him.

Don't even fucking think about it.

He keeps walking and I take his seat.

She turns her head toward me, a seductive smile on her pretty face. "That was a pretty epic cock-block."

A smile stretches my face. "I guess I couldn't help myself. I mean, look at you."

"What about me?"

Blood rushes to my chest when she brushes her fingers across my knee. Heat blazes through her fingertips into my slacks, and for a moment I don't know what the fuck she just said. Now that I'm close to her, I see that she's young. At least ten years younger than me. It doesn't seem to bother her one bit. She looks me up and down, sucking in those plump lips.

Jesus Christ.

"I hate to break it to you, but your tits are popping out of your dress."

She lets out a frustrated sigh and notices that her dress slipped down again. It distracts me. She tugs at the lace, and her tits bounce, and I think about just yanking it down.

"Guys will come after you like flies on honey when you look like that."

"Are you saying that I look nice?"

"I'm saying that I'd like to fuck you."

For a moment her eyebrows lift in surprise, but then her chest shakes with laughter, her light-brown hair hanging in front of her face.

I fucking want her.

"Is that your opening line with all women, or do I get the special treatment?"

"You get the special treatment."

"Why's that?"

"Because you're wearing that dress, sweetheart."

Her face burns a light shade of pink. "I borrowed it from my cousin."

"You look hot."

"It's not my size."

I smile as she fiddles with her empty drink, watching how her pupils dilate as I lean in closer. "I'll let you in on a little secret: guys don't give a shit what the dress looks like. We care about how *you* look in the dress."

Hunger blazes in those dark-brown pools even as she withdraws her hand from my knee. "Can you actually use that cock of yours? Or is this alpha-male posturing compensation for something else?"

"You have some balls to insult me in my own bar."

"It's an honest question."

She does not know who the fuck I am.

"You must not be familiar with my reputation."

"How am I supposed to when I don't even know your fucking name?"

This could be interesting.

"I'm Johnny."

She uncrosses her legs as she gives me a scorching look, and I'm tempted to grab her thigh just to make my

15

cock shut up.

"Maya."

Beautiful name. Exotic.

I grasp the strands of hair around her face and slowly push them across her soft skin, tucking them behind her ears. A barely suppressed shiver runs through her body as I take my hand away.

She wants me.

"You should come home with me, Maya."

An unspoken need simmers just beneath the surface of her skin. She trembles as if she waits for me to touch her again, but her voice strengthens. "At least buy me a fucking drink."

I almost laugh at the hostility in her tone, but she's right. My manners flew out the goddamn window the moment I laid eyes on her.

I signal the bartender for another drink, but Genevieve lets a glass fly from her grip when I catch her gaze. The glass shatters on the floor at my feet and causes a small commotion—a couple raised voices and a smattering of applause. She looks at the broken pieces and then at me, her cheeks burning.

It's a fucking glass. Who cares?

Jesus.

"Clean it up."

Red-faced, Genevieve nods and steps around the bar, apologizing profusely.

For the life of me, I don't understand why people think I'm going to shoot them in the face for an accident. Maya's hand touches my knee again, and it's like a lure for my cock. *Jesus Christ control yourself.* She looks at my with a flirty, little smile.

"Everyone acts like you're some kind of tough guy."

I am a tough guy.

The bartender sweeps the pieces of glass into a dustpan, the crinkling sound distracting me.

"What gave you that idea?"

"That bartender looks like she's going to cry."

Maya raises an eyebrow at her. The bartender hurries into the employees-only area even though there's a trash can right behind the bar. Maya gives me an accusatory stare, and then I'm struck with the fact that she really, *really* doesn't know who I am. She just thinks I'm some run-of-the-mill asshole hitting on her in a connected bar. Fuck, she might not even know it's connected.

Jackpot.

"So you own the bar?"

It's rare to bump into someone who doesn't know who I am, especially at places that I own. I search her eyes for any hint of sarcasm, but I don't see anything but polite curiosity. There's no point in enlightening her, so I decide to keep her in the dark.

"Yeah," I say with laughter in my voice. "I'm the owner."

It's more like I own the entire city.

Maya takes the drink from the other bartender, sipping it. She swivels in the chair, her legs bumping into mine. Fuck. She's a fucking tease. To prove my point, she crosses her legs, exposing another mile of skin.

"What's it like owning a bar?"

What *is* it like?

"Ah—you know. I sit around and bullshit with customers. Hit on beautiful girls. It's not bad."

"Yeah?" She grins. "Are you on the clock right now?"

"We can leave anytime you want."

"Always with the sex." Although she hardly looks offended. The way she keeps eyeing my cock, it's as though she's screaming for me to fuck her.

"It's taking everything inside me not to throw you over my shoulder and bring you into my office."

She sucks in air, the sound sharp. "And then what?"

I'll tell you and then what.

I lay my hand right over her knee, and she doesn't move a muscle, but a red flush fills the skin right above the swell of her tits. We're so close that I can smell the

18

perfume she wears. It's light and refreshing, like spring flowers. I want that smell all over my sheets, clinging to my naked skin. Her legs part ever so slightly as I knead her skin.

"And then I'd bend you over my desk and fuck your tight cunt until you came all over my cock. I'd take you home and shove my tongue deep inside that pussy until you moaned loud enough to wake up the neighbors."

Maya can't look away from me. Her gaze lingers on my mouth, my body, and the hand touching her knee. "You really know how to talk to a girl, huh?"

"That's how I talk to girls who dress like that. I'm sorry, did you not come to this bar looking for a good time?"

I squeeze her knee again and she makes another small gasp. A series of emotions cycle through her face. She's offended, scared, turned-on. Christ, the innocent act gets a rise out of me. The more she reacts, the more I want to push her. Fuck, I just want to shove my hand all the way inside her dress and feel how soaking she is.

"I *am* having a good time."

Fucking tease.

I'm surprised that I'm enjoying this. When's the last time I flirted with a girl? It's usually very cut-and-dried. I take their hand, give them a look, and they're mine for the night. Low effort. There's a part of me that really gets off on that, but I like this even more.

Her skin glows like a heat lamp. I inch up her thigh and knead her with my thumb. The sounds she makes cut the air between us, and then finally she takes my hand off her thigh. She turns it over and runs her fingers on my calluses. It's not as though she's touching my dick, but it's intimate. The space between us feels comfortably warm and the sound from the bar disappears to a low murmur. She smiles at me, and my heart pounds hard, making my chest jump.

Good God, I want to fuck her.

"What's your story?"

"I'm just a girl at a bar."

She squeezes my hand and I twist it around so that I'm covering her. The relentless beating against my chest slows down, and then I think about filling my hands with her tits and it starts up again.

"Everybody's got a story."

"You don't want to know mine."

"As long as it ends with you in my bed, I'm okay with it."

I wish I could drag her off her stool and onto my lap.

Her head turns toward the door, which seems a million miles away from us. She doesn't say a word, but I know what she's thinking: *I should leave.*

"*Stay.* Have a drink and talk to me."

Something in my voice reels her back in. Her eyes lock with mine. Heat builds up in my chest.

"You don't want to talk to me."

I want to fuck you.

"Yes, I do."

She pulls her lips into a smirk.

"There are just other things I'd rather be doing with you. *To you.*"

"*Shit.*" She seizes her drink and sips as if to give herself a reason to avoid looking at me.

I won't let her.

I stand up from my stool and get close enough so that I can slide my hand over the back of her chair, my fingers tickling her arm. She takes a huge gulp of her drink and a bright flush fills her cheeks as the booze works its way through her veins, or maybe it's the fact that she finds me irresistible. She takes my tie in her hand, starting at the knot at my throat. Then she slides slowly down the long length. What would it feel like to have her hands do the same thing to my cock?

"I shouldn't."

My finger glides under her jaw and she follows the pressure without even thinking. Her nerves are all over the

21

VANESSA WATLZ

place. A strong heartbeat jumps into my fingers, and it surprises me for a moment. This is a girl who looks like she's down to fuck, as if she does it all the time, but she shakes in my hands.

"You really, *really* should."

"Do you always get what you want?"

"Almost always."

I reach around her head and tighten my fist in her hair. My lips crash against hers right before she whispers, "Fuck." She sighs into my mouth and leans into me, her hands gripping my waist. Then her tits crush against my chest, and my cock strains against my slacks as if it's about to bore a hole into the fabric.

Sweetness swirls in my mouth, like the drink I gave her. Her tongue is even sweeter, and yes, I'm shoving my tongue down her throat in the middle of this bar. I don't give a fuck. It's instant chemistry between us. A surge of heat straight to my cock makes me curl my fingers in her hair. Fuck, I could sweep my arm across a table and bend her over right now.

Her hands push my chest suddenly, and I break away from her briefly to see red, parted lips.

"You all right, hon?"

"Y-yeah."

"Then let's continue this in my office."

"No, I can't. I need to go."

Sounds like bullshit.

She takes a step back and suddenly her eyes go wide as her huge heel slips on something, and then she falls to the ground before I can catch her. Her cry of pain makes me stoop down quickly.

Oh Jesus Christ.

My guys wheel around, offering to help her up, but I bend down and grab her skinny arm. She gets up painfully, and that's when I notice a shard of glass sticking out of her knee.

"What the fuck, Genevieve!"

The bartender snaps her head around, looking mortified.

"I told you to pick up the fucking glass!"

"I'm so sorry, sir!"

I turn back toward the girl in my arms. "Maya, I have bandages in my office. Come."

She hesitates but looks at the line of blood trickling down her skin and nods. I bend over and yank the glass from her skin, hurling the bartender an ugly look as I walk Maya to my office.

I'll fucking deal with you later.

I open the door for her and usher her inside, unable to stop the jump of excitement in my cock as I close it, shutting the noise of the bar away.

"Here, sit down."

She takes a seat in one of the leather-backed chairs and I grab the first-aid kit under my desk.

"I'm really sorry about this."

"It's okay. It doesn't really hurt."

I rip open the kit and grab some gauze and Neosporin. Maya tentatively extends a hand to grab it from me, but I shake my head.

"I'll take care of it."

She cocks her head. "I think you just want your hands on my leg."

You're not wrong.

"I want a lot more than that."

Her cheeks are stained with red. For the life of me, I can't pin down this girl. She dresses like a slut but she acts like a blushing virgin. What the hell is that about?

Shaking my head, I take her leg in my hands. It's hard to concentrate as I glide them up her smooth skin. I extend her leg so that it lies across my thigh, and then I spread the ointment over the cut. She closes her eyes as I wrap my hands around her. Then I take the gauze and press it firmly over the cut. Her thigh shivers when I smooth my hand over the bandage.

"Thanks."

No problem, sweetheart. Now suck my cock.

Her leg is inches from my dick, and I imagine her straddling me in this chair. Blood rushes to my groin and I can't help spreading my fingers around her flawless skin. Her chest pulses faster with my movements, but she draws her leg away from me.

"Let me take you home and give you a night you'll never forget."

Her eyes blaze. "Tell me what you'd do to me."

"I told you."

"I want to hear it again."

The headiness in her voice makes my lips tug into a smirk. "First, I'd take a pair of scissors and cut that dress from your body and free those tits. Then I'd lay you over my couch and spread your legs so that I could lick your pussy."

"Why?"

Why not?

"I want to make you come with nothing but my tongue thrusting inside that wet cunt."

"Jesus."

"Then when you're nice and wet, and shaking from your orgasm, I'll fuck you so goddamn hard and good your pussy won't ever be able to enjoy another man's cock again."

"How would you fuck me?"

She's driving me crazy with all these questions. I sweep my hand along her calf and grip it. "I'd take this leg and put it over my shoulder, and then I'd take the other and do the same thing so I could fuck you nice and deep."

Maya's dress vibrates right above her heart. I can see the fabric fluttering with her heartbeat, and I can feel my own thrumming hard. Like a goddamn jackhammer through my cock.

I get up from my chair and her eyes widen as I stoop down to kiss her again.

She places a palm against my chest and shakes her head.

"I can't."

What?

"Why the fuck not?"

She bites her lip viciously. "You're Italian, aren't you?"

"Yeah, so?"

"I can't." This time her tone is resolute. She stands up from the chair and gives me an uneasy look before she heads toward the door.

What the fuck?

"Whoa, sweetheart. Talk to me. What happened?"

I grab her wrist, and haughty eyes flick down at my hand and back at me. I'd like to fuck the insolence out of

26

her gaze.

"I'm going home."

"You can't fuck me 'cause I'm Italian? What kind of prejudiced bullshit is that?"

A sad look wipes the pride from her face. "My dad would kill me. I'm sorry."

She pulls away from me, and frustration boils in my veins. Jesus fucking Christ, she's the biggest cock-tease I've ever met.

"Let me talk to your dad."

Maya suddenly bursts into laughter and throws back her head as if it's the most hilarious thing she's ever heard. It's fucking insulting, and I want to tie her up and fuck her anyway, father or no father.

"Lets just say that my father could make life very miserable for a bar owner."

She pushes open the door, leaving me stunned in the office. I have to remind myself of two things. One, this girl has no idea who I am and how far I'm willing to go to get what I want. Two, I need to restrain my anger.

But I can't.

I barge out of the office, back into the noise of the bar, and grab her shoulders, whirling her around to pin her against the wall. A slight gasp leaves her throat as her back bumps the wall, and I feel a stab of guilt for the fear

27

widening her eyes.

"No one walks out on me."

Her eyebrows narrow. "You think very highly of yourself, don't you?"

"I don't tolerate disrespect from anyone."

A smile flickers on her face. "Look, you're hot and all, but I can't date Italians. My father would kill me."

"Are you fucking shitting me? You're what, twenty-two, twenty-three, and you're going to let Daddy tell you that my Italian cock is no good for your French-Canadian pussy?"

Her eyes narrow dangerously.

Too far.

"Let me go."

Fine. Get the fuck out of here.

My hands slide down her arms, which sprout with goose bumps. She reaches for the hem of her dress and pulls it over her tits, my cock hardening at the sight of them bouncing right in my fucking face.

"Come home with me," I say in a deep voice. "Daddy doesn't have to know."

The effect of my words slides down her throat like a hot drop. Her lips tremble as she stares at me.

"Can't. Sorry."

Then she gives me a quick peck on my cheek.

"Thanks for the drink."

Thanks for the drink.

Like I'm some fucking chump. This has to be a joke.

"Are you fucking kidding me?"

She gives me a scathing look. "I never promised I'd go home with you."

Her hair feels like silk in my hands. I let her strands glide through my fingers as I watch her inhale deeply, trying to hide how much she wants me. "I don't like being teased."

A blush rises in her cheeks. "I didn't—"

I back her against the wall. "No, you just wanted to *fuck* with me. That was the plan, wasn't it? Some harmless flirting, and then you give him blue balls and go home to Daddy without finishing what you started."

She doesn't back down. A light blazes from her eyes as she clenches her jaw shut, clearly bursting to tell me off. I step back from her, and she throws me an ugly look before walking away.

"If I see you in this bar again, I'll throw your ass out. Don't come back here."

I say it to her back, but she hears me. She slows her step and then walks out of the hallway, disappearing into the bar.

My cock's still rock hard and I want to hit something.

I walk into the bar, ready to smash my fist through the drywall, to beat in the first person's face who looks at me wrong. What's wrong with being Italian? It's not like she was Irish.

Tabarnak de câlisse, it pisses me off.

I look around the bar, tempted to find another broad to bang and forget about the hot one still burning in my mind, but none are half as beautiful.

François, my captain, gives me a curious look as I return to the bar counter. "Did you get her number?"

My arms cross over my chest. "She doesn't fuck Italians."

He chokes with laughter. "Well, she picked the right place."

It's a connected bar. Everyone knows that. It's my bar—and I'm the boss of the Cravotta Crime Family.

He beckons to me, leaning in to talk close in a hushed whisper. "Listen, me and the guys have an idea for getting a copy for the guards' keys for the heist."

I don't feel like talking business. My desire for the party evaporated the moment that girl walked out on me.

"We'll talk about it later. I'm going to head out."

And jack off furiously when I get home.

* * *

That girl simmers in my head the whole weekend. The

rage boils over, mingling with burgeoning lust. The fact is, I get around. I score a lot of easy pussy, but none of them ever fucked with my head like this. Rejection is not something I deal with as a boss of the family. Period. Women are eager to please me just like everyone else.

"Chris, let me out here."

My driver stops the car in front of my mother's house and I step out of the sleek Audi, shutting the door hard enough to make the windows rattle.

God, I need to get it together.

The last thing I want is to visit my ma, but I'm supposed to be a family man. It's important to respect your family in this business, even if I don't care for mine. At the end of the day, I do whatever the fuck I want, but it's hard to shake off that feeling of duty to your family.

I knock on the door, my fist banging against the dense wood. Seconds later, Ma wrenches it open. She's well kept, my mother, and that's always something I admired about her.

"Johnny!"

She wears an apron over her yellow dress and looks at my suit, her eyes widening. "Look at you, looking so handsome. Do you have a date?"

Jesus Christ. This again.

I step inside her house. "No, Ma. This is how I always

look."

Her eyes wrinkle. "I wish you would get a girlfriend and settle down."

"I did, remember? Twice?"

Married twice. Divorced twice. I married Stacey when I was too young, and all we did was resent each other. Karen, my second wife, left me. That part of my life is over. I guess you could say that I gave up on having the perfect family life. Fuck it. I like being able to go out whenever the fuck I want. I like fucking a new piece of ass every night.

Which inevitably reminds me of the piece of ass who teased me a couple nights ago. Who I can't get out of my goddamn head.

"When am I going to get grandchildren?"

"Did you just invite me over to give me shit about this again?" My angry voice echoes in the small apartment as she guides me to the kitchen.

"Johnny, I don't like hearing you curse."

Mange d'la marde.

"Sorry."

"Come, you need to eat. You're too skinny."

I'm always "too skinny" for her. She expects me to bloat like a beached whale, like my old man. He was a fat fuck.

She flaps her hands, motioning me toward the bowl of *spaghetti alla Bolognese.* Ma serves me at least a pound of pasta. The steam rises from it in spirals, the spices from the meat failing to distract me from my two ex-wives.

It's really the only thing I've ever failed at in life. I have all the money and pussy I could possibly fucking want. The only thing I don't have—a family—I failed at. Twice.

I'm not going for a third. I just won't.

Besides, living a bachelor's life isn't bad at all. Tony did it, before he knocked up that girl.

I pick up the fork and wind the pasta around and around.

Then I think about how Tony talks about his baby girl all the time with a look in his eyes that I don't understand, and my chest tightens.

I shove the feeling away.

Who needs a wife?

"So how's work going?"

"Pretty good."

Work is always a tricky topic to navigate around my mother. She knows exactly who I am, but I wouldn't tell her, for example, that I'm planning the biggest heist in history. Millions of dollars in cash. That's what fucking drives me. Nearly every restaurant, casino, and racetrack in this city gives me a piece of their action in exchange for protection from other gangs. If this heist goes as planned, all of us will be fucking rich. We won't need that shit anymore.

She looks up at me from her plate of *Bolognese*, her eyes evasive. "I just find it hard to believe that you can't find another wife."

My fork clatters on the plate as I throw my head back and close my eyes.

Keep it together. Don't fucking yell at her, or she'll cry and you'll be stuck here even longer.

"Ma, marriage isn't for me."

"I thought I would die of shame when you got divorced the first time. It's a sin, Johnny. Marriage is a sacred vow—"

"Oh will you *fucking please* stop with this shit!" The chair crashes to the floor as I stand up abruptly. "Every fucking time I come over, it's the same thing! I'm not getting married again. I'm not having kids. Get the fuck over it. I am."

I'm stewing with the rage of being reminded of this failure *over* and *over* again, but then she bundles the tablecloth in her hands, and her face screws up.

Shit.

"How can you talk like that to your mother?"

Seeing her tears would be a bigger punch to my gut if

she hadn't done it a thousand times already. I shove my hands deep inside my pockets, filled with a rush of self-loathing.

She's right. You don't disrespect your mother.

"I'm sorry, Ma."

"You're all I have left. Your father left us."

Oh, fuck him.

A fresh stab of anger hits me right in the chest as she looks at a family portrait hanging on the wall. I want to smash it, or at least cut him from the fucking photograph so I don't have to see his rotten face staring back at me.

"He's been dead a long time, Ma. You should meet someone else."

"I can't. I loved your father."

I didn't.

I don't dare say that out loud.

"I'm so proud of you, Johnny. I just want you to be happy, and I don't think you are."

I *am* fucking happy. Aren't I?

What the fuck is happiness? Is it whistling to yourself as you walk down the street without a care in the world? Is it being able to fuck gorgeous women, night after night? I search inside myself, but I only feel vague annoyance and that stirring need for more stimulation.

Bending over, I pick up the chair from the floor,

avoiding my mother's gaze. "I gotta go."

"Already? But you just—"

I take a few steps toward her chair and give her a kiss on the cheek. "Yeah, thanks for the food."

"Wait—I have to give you leftovers!"

"No, really. I got to go."

I finally breathe the moment I'm out of that fucking house, and for some reason that girl pops into my head again, shoving all thoughts of my exes away. She was a fucking tease, and she talked to me as though I were just a regular guy. Hell, she acted as though she was better than me. It's so rare that I meet a beautiful girl who is self-confident.

Then I think about how hot those haughty lips would look wrapped around my cock, and I hope she returns to the bar.

I'm not taking no for an answer.

MAYA

For a while I was content to sit there in my cousin's badly fitting dress, surrounded by men I didn't know as conversation and music boomed around me. It felt familiar and yet different from the obnoxious beat of the clubhouse. It was just as loud, but without my father's men treating me like a princess. It was nice. Now it's like nails on chalkboard, like an unpleasant shrieking sound, growing louder and louder. Kind of like my heartbeat, slamming against my chest.

Shit. What did I almost get myself into?

My chest rattles from my heartbeat as I totter in my heels, trying to look dignified as I focus on getting the fuck away from this bar as fast as possible.

That Italian guy in the bar had me wrapped around his finger. He just wanted to fuck me, to use my body. My father's dire warnings against them ring in my head: *Never ever let me catch you with an Italian, Maya. They're no good. They'll just use you for your body and dump you when it's over.*

Damn, I almost made a decision I would've regretted.

Don't kid yourself. You would have loved stripping off your dress for him. He was sex on a stick.

He was. Fuck, the way his hands glided up my legs, just brushing my upper thigh. I was ready to give myself to him there, to let him smooth his hands all the way up my thighs and make me come the way he said he would.

Daddy will never know.

I shiver in the warm June air as I think of that desperately sinful smile, those dimples curving into his face, the small wrinkles near his eyes. Just having his hands on me in the office was almost enough for me to get wet. They felt so strong and confident, as if he'd held a woman many times before. There was no lack of confidence in that hot gaze, even when he told me to let him talk to my dad.

Hah. As if.

I've never met such a ballsy bar owner, but then again, I didn't tell him who my dad was.

"You're thinking about that hot Italian guy, aren't you?"

"What?" I say in a voice that's way too high-pitched. "No, of course not."

My cousin gives me a sidelong glance, the corner of her lip tugging into a smile.

"You are."

"Fine. So what? He was hotter than any guy in the MC."

Beatrice shrugs one bare shoulder. "I don't know about that."

"Are you crazy?" My voice rings down the street. "What, you like those bearded, nasty assholes who get drunk every Thursday with those strippers my father always hires?"

She throws back her blonde head and laughs, the golden highlights harsh under the streetlights. "Oh come on, they're not all like that."

I stare at her wide smile as we walk back to her car, unable to understand her levity. We both grew up behind the same walls—both have restrictions on our comings and goings from the compound. Fuck, we're not even supposed to go to bars without an escort. Let alone a bar rumored to be connected. Dad would flip.

How can she be happy about this?

"So what happened when you went into his office?"

My insides seize up as she walks past me with a shrewd grin. My hand slips on the door handle of the car as blood careens inside my veins. "I—I didn't do anything with him."

The sound of the doors unlocking makes me jump, and her grin widens. "Right."

As much as I like Beatrice, I could never trust her with something like this. All it would take was one word from her to my father and I'd be fucked. She needs to understand that nothing happened.

I wrench open the car door and slide in next to her. For a moment there's nothing but the sound of her keys as she slides them into the ignition. She won't even look at me.

"*Hey.* Nothing happened."

I touch her shoulder and finally she turns her head around. "I came with you here because you seemed determined to piss off your dad, and because you needed someone to watch over you."

Anger rustles in my chest. "I have enough of that at home, Beatrice. I don't need it from my cousin."

"Actually, you do. You're the president of the MC's daughter. Every time you step outside, you put yourself at risk—"

"We're allied with the mob!"

"That doesn't matter!"

Her sharp voice rings in my ears, bouncing within the walls of the car. I look down at my lap and clench my hands.

"They're no good, Maya—and whatever you did in that office with that guy—"

"*Shut the fuck up!*"

I lean over my seat, raising my fists as Beatrice backs

up against the car door, looking at them with widened eyes.

"You're right, I'm the president's daughter. I told you that nothing happened and that should be good enough for you."

I'll pound her fucking face in if she makes another stupid comment. Beatrice eyes my hands, a scowl twisting her face. "You don't have to be a bitch."

"If you say a word to anyone, I'll beat your fucking face in. Understand?"

She says nothing as my heart pounds against my chest. Threats are a way of life in the MC. There's no getting around the fact that we both grew up knee-deep in violence. I watched my mom beat the shit out of some poor girl she found in my dad's bed. As the president's daughter, I've had to flex my power a few times to keep the other girls in line.

I do whatever the fuck I want, and you're not going to stop me. Bitch.

Beatrice backs down, the fire disappearing from her eyes as she starts the car.

It's important to watch their eyes for the change. She needs to respect me, and for that, she needs to fear me.

And I can see her hair trembling around her face.

I won.

* * *

My cousin and I glance at each other as we gaze up the concrete walls of the bunker we call home. Getting back inside the compound isn't too hard. It just takes stopping at a gas station and changing out of your slutty clothes, so that your dad won't know you went out partying instead of shopping like you said you were.

She lays on the horn, and I wince at the sound. The guards walking the walls recognize us and wave their hands. The massive steel doors shriek as they roll to the side, and Beatrice pushes on the gas pedal to move us inside.

"Your dad would freak out if he knew about that Italian guy."

Just the mention of him sends a rush of heat to my skin that suddenly makes me feel sick. Yes, Dad would fucking flip out. He would march over to that bar and put a bullet in his head, all for the crime of being Italian and hitting on his daughter.

"I thought I told you to shut up about it."

"Relax. My ass is on the line, too."

My ruffled feathers settle down somewhat as we park in the compound and step out of her car. I imagine how odd the sight of this place must look to an outsider. Reinforced steel and concrete, barbed wire, and men patrolling the borders with guns big enough to shoot you in the ass a mile away. They wear their leather cuts with "THE DEVILS" emblazoned in a white font.

We walk together over the paved concrete toward the clubhouse where we both live. It's always loud in there, filled with smoke and drunk assholes. Whores occasionally fill the entire place when my dad thinks that his men need another fucking party where everyone gets wasted. Then it's inevitably the women's job to clean up the mess. The puke. The beer bottles. The cigarette butts. Jesus Christ, I'm sick of it.

Sounds like there's another party going on. The walls rattle with rock music and I'm greeted with the sight of scantily clad women. They wear pasties and G-strings as they strut around the club, grinding on the members as the prospects keep watch or pour drinks.

I've seen so much shit that it hardly fazes me, but the irony doesn't escape me. I'm surrounded by sex, and yet I can't have any. Daddy won't let me date any outsiders, and because he's president I have to do what he says.

Everyone does what he fucking says.

Beatrice spots Paul, one of the prospects she has a crush on, and joins him at the bar with a wide smile on her face. Unlike me, Beatrice doesn't have a burning desire to leave this fucking place. In a few years she'll get married to one of these assholes and spend the rest of her life trapped in this concrete hellhole.

I make my way through the maze of the clubhouse, finding my room in the back, which is across from my dad's. Of course. I open the door and shut it, wishing that I had a lock. Then I grab the too-small dress from my purse. I borrowed it from Beatrice, and a hot blush fills my cheeks when I realized how bad the fit was on me. Even Johnny said so.

"Your tits are popping out of your dress."

Instant heat spreads across my chest. He looked at me as though I was a piece of meat. I was *desirable*. I can't remember the last time a man expressed interest in me. The only men I hang around with are part of the club, and they don't dare hit on the president's daughter. Not that I'm interested in any of them.

The door bursts open, swinging inside as I fling the dress away from me in surprise, looking up into the eyes of my livid father.

He stands up straight, but I can tell that he's already fucked up. Red-rimmed eyes bore at me as he clutches the frame of the door.

"Maya, where the fuck have you been? Julien tells me that you just got in."

"I told you, Beatrice and I went out for shopping and a

movie."

He stares at me for a little longer and nods, almost accepting the lie, and then his eagle-like eyes fall on the discarded dress.

"What the hell is that?"

I try to stuff it out of sight with my foot, but he reaches down and snatches it.

It would almost be funny to see the horror transforming his face as he lifts up the skimpy dress, imagining it on me.

Almost.

"You fucking lying bitch. You wore this and went out to party, didn't you?"

"I—I didn't—"

My father's grizzled face comes within inches of mine as he inhales.

Is he sniffing me?

His nostrils flare as he catches a whiff of my perfume and smoke and God knows what else.

"You went to a bar, didn't you? Wearing this thing?"

I hate how he makes me feel ashamed just for putting on a stupid dress and feeling alive for once in my goddamn life.

Yes, I did, and I met an Italian I almost had sex with.

"What the fuck is wrong with you?"

45

The acidic tone cuts right through me. He acts as though I committed treason.

"What, I can't go out like a regular person and have a good time?"

"You're not a regular person!" he bellows. "You're my daughter, and I won't have you acting like some fucking *slut*!"

How dare he?

"So *you're* allowed to fuck strippers behind Mom's back, but I'm not allowed to go on a date with someone I like?"

His biceps ripple over his leather cut as his knuckles turn white, clenching the dress so hard that I'm sure he'll leave holes.

Fuck him.

Fuck the MC.

His hand blurs in front of me, too fast to follow, and suddenly my cheek burns with a vicious slap. My body falls over my bed with the weight of the blow. I'm too stunned to sit back up.

He *hit* me. Dad never hits me.

Heavy boots creak the floorboards as he walks to the edge of the bed, venom spitting from his mouth. "Don't talk to me like I'm your fucking friend."

Believe me, I don't think you're my friend.

"Your job is to stay here and look after the kids. *That's*

it."

A boiling feeling makes me sit up abruptly. "I don't want to look after someone else's brat. I want to go on dates."

Even Dad can't ignore that I'm a twenty-two-year-old woman. That I'm going to attract male attention, and that every cell in my body is screaming for a man's touch.

I want sex.

Is that such a crime?

The hard lines in his face don't fade. I can see it in his eyes: the bastard thinks I'm asking for too much.

"There are plenty of good men here for you to date."

Good men? You mean the ones that peddle crack to kids?

"And I've *told* you that I'm not interested in them."

"I won't have a daughter of mine dating an outsider."

The unfairness of it all seethes in my chest. I'm *not* a submissive person. I buck against authority and do whatever the hell I want. Always have.

Fuck, do you know what it's like being horny as fuck, but having no way of satisfying yourself? I can't even masturbate because my door doesn't have a lock.

"You can't keep me here forever, Dad. I'm going to go to beauty school—"

He wipes his hand over his face. "Waste of fucking money."

"I'm going to do what I want, because it's my life and only I get to choose what I get to do. Not you. Not Mom. *Me.*"

He stands in the middle of my shabby room as at least a decade's worth of hostility hangs between us like an electric cloud.

"You're a stubborn little *bitch*, Maya. You know you can't leave the club. The Popeyes, hell, the mob would love to get their hands on you."

Maybe I want their hands all over me, Dad.

I think of Johnny and how much I enjoyed his hands all over me. Desire simmers in my stomach. He was slim and handsome—almost too perfect looking in his fitted suit, his hair gently slicked back. He caught my attention the moment I saw him walking toward me, that small smirk tugging at his lips, which were just begging to be kissed. Then he got rid of the guy hitting on me. I don't know how he did that, but damn. The balls on that guy.

It was fucking hot.

Everything about him felt intoxicating, and I had to work really hard to appear in control. Johnny seems like just the type to take advantage of any weakness. His hands on my waist made me so wet that I was afraid it would soak through my panties. Then his hot lips touched mine and he actually shoved his tongue into my mouth, right in front of anyone.

It's all I'll ever think about again.

It's stupid, I know. Beatrice and I heard rumors the bar was connected with the Mafia. It might be true, but I convinced her to go anyway. I didn't expect anything to come out of it. Maybe I was desperate for a bit of harmless flirting, but every dirty word that flew out of Johnny's mouth turned me on.

The side of my face still burns as I sit on my bed, forced to a sitting position as my dad takes a step closer, flinging the dress at my face.

God, I hate him.

I'll take classes at the beauty school I picked out and upgrade from my job at the café. I'll become a hair stylist and finally get enough money for my own place.

Then I can get the hell out of here.

"Are you done? Can you get out of my room?"

Don't fucking push it.

Dad's bushy eyebrows narrow even farther. I can't suppress a shiver when he turns his face, that horribly pitted scar like a crater in his skin. I've never been afraid of my father. All my life it's been push and pull. Seeing how much I can get away with. He smacked around my mom enough to make me hate him. Sometimes I hate myself for being too much of a coward to try to stop him from laying

49

one more hand on my mom's face. He stopped doing it years ago, when he became president and wanted to clean up his image. It was enough to stop him from hitting his wife, but not enough to stop his bikers from peddling crack to kids at school.

"Tony wants a haircut tomorrow."

"Tony can cut his own goddamn hair."

"What the fuck did you just say to me?"

"I'm not cutting anyone's hair for free anymore. My time is not a fucking charity—"

"You'll do what I say, or you'll get another hand across your face."

I stand up from the bed, knowing that he won't do it. He's already regretting his words. Doubt flickers in his eyes.

"I want in-and-out privileges. I don't want to ask you permission to go to the store or to my work."

Someone crashes through the hallway, stomping noisily. I catch a flash of a half-naked stripper clinging to a patched member, and my blood boils.

His smiling face turns back toward me. "No."

* * *

No.

It's a word I've heard my whole goddamn life: no.

No, I'm not going to buy that for you. No, I'm not

taking you to practice. No, I'm not paying for fucking school. No, no, no.

I fucking hate that word.

Even worse is that smug look on my father's face when he denies something that I really want. Something I've been saving up for a long time, like the beauty school classes.

I used to cry my fucking eyes out. Scream with rage and pound my fists on the walls so that everyone in the club could hear how much of a spoiled brat I was, but I didn't care. Mom would argue with him, would try to take pity on me—to allow me this one, *small* thing. No.

Then I swallowed it down over the years. Did whatever Dad said, because it was easier. Pretending not to care and building up walls around myself was easier than letting myself feel how powerless I am.

But I just can't take it this time.

I pace inside the small room Dad cleared up for me in the garage. It's a quartered-off space with a couple sinks for washing hair, a chair, and a giant, old mirror. I yank open the drawers, looking at the scissors arranged neatly side by side. They rattle as I slam it shut.

All of it is fucking useless if I can't go to beauty school and get the hell out of here. Otherwise, what's the fucking point?

What's the point of practicing on these douchebags?

Blood pounds through my limbs as I seize a heavy hair dryer. I look at myself in the mirror. A girl with widened eyes and shaking lips stares back at me.

She looks weak.

I hurl the dryer at the mirror. It shatters and swings from the nails on the wall, crashing to the concrete. That's not enough. I stomp on the shards, grinding them to dust under my boots. Fuck him and this place.

"Are you out of your fucking mind?"

Mom's shrill voice stabs my ears before I feel her hand seizing my shoulder roughly.

"He's trying to keep me here like some fucking pet!"

Mom crosses her arms over her low-cut black t-shirt, tossing her head to shake the dark hair from her eyes. "Everybody has a place in this club."

I grit my teeth. "I never wanted this. Since I was a kid, I wanted to be normal."

She reaches up and cuffs the side of my head like a bear swatting one of her cubs. "That's enough."

It's not nearly enough.

"He's a piece of shit—he thinks he can just lock me inside—"

"*Go*, then. If you want to live out there so badly, just leave. Leave and see what happens."

The hollow feeling in my chest gapes open. Everything falls inside. Every hope I have for myself drowns in that emptiness.

"You know you can't leave, baby. I know it's hard, but everything he does is for your protection. He loves you."

Mom touches my face and pushes back my thick hair, looking at me under dark lashes. That's how she always is: a rising tide or a gentle lull. Crashing down on you one moment and then kissing you on the cheek the other.

"He doesn't love me. He just wants to control me."

I brush past my mom, the broken pieces snapping under my boots. The satisfying sound doesn't quite take the edge off my anger, but it helps.

I'm going back to that bar, and I'm going to fuck the shit out of that guy.

I decide it the moment I step into the sunshine. If Dad's determined to keep me imprisoned, I'm going to make his life hell, starting with giving myself to the hottest Italian guy I've ever seen.

* * *

Sneaking out twice in the same week isn't hard, but it requires a little bit of finesse. And guile.

I shove my hands deep inside my pockets as I approach Julien at the gate, the sunshine glaring through the thick steel bars and casting long shadows on the ground. They crawl up my body in long, dark strips like the bars of a prison cell. How appropriate.

He's a newly patched member, and he's eager to please. The older members are used to me pulling shit, always trying to run a scam by them, but not Julien.

I lay my arm across my face to shield my eyes from the sun and he turns around with a little jump.

"Hey, um—listen, I need to go outside for a while. Just for a bit."

His thick arms cross over his chest as he watches me. "Why?"

I bite my lip. "Um—I'd rather not say. It's really embarrassing."

"I'm sorry, but I need to know why if you want to leave."

Then I lean in, my hair hanging around my face. "Well—I just got my period and we're out of tampons."

It's the magic word.

Julien's face immediately burns a bright shade of red as he wraps his arms around himself, taking small steps backward. "Uh—well—"

Poor, poor Julien.

I adopt an uncertain tone. "You could get them for me, I guess. I was just going to pop off to the store and get some."

"No! I mean—yeah, I'll open the gate. Give me a second."

A grateful smile spreads across my face as I thank him and head to my car.

Sucker.

I don't plan on coming back. Not for a very long time. Daddy will just have to deal with the fact that his daughter likes to have sex. With men. I know, it's a shocker.

Parking at the nearest subway station, I take the train into Montreal. I don't want to deal with the parking in the city, and taking the metro is just another snub at Dad. Even using the subway was forbidden to me.

My stomach churns as I think about what I'll say to Johnny when I finally meet him. He told me not to come back to his bar.

I feel lighter than I have in ages when I get out at a stop with a bunch of shopping. There's not much in my bank account, but I splurge so rarely that I don't really feel guilty for trying on new dresses.

Maybe he'll change his mind if I look like this.

In the department store, I look at myself in a sexy little summer dress. It's a bright-red knit with an art deco design, and it clings to my every curve. Dark eyeliner makes my eyes pop, and my hair shines with the new ginger conditioner that I bought. I look sexy, damn it. No,

I'm not model-thin, but who gives a shit?

Fuck yes. I'm buying this.

I walk out of the dressing room still wearing the dress, my black gladiator heels clicking on the floor.

My confidence is blazing when the girl at the register compliments how it looks as I buy it, even as I walk out into the dim early evening as men whistle at me from across the street. It feels different to be free, and I'm too angry to care about the shit I'll have to deal with when I return home. The summer night is nice and balmy, and everywhere there are couples.

I pass by that bar, already bustling with people, and my heart slams into my chest so hard that I feel dizzy. All of a sudden my confidence bursts like a needle to a balloon.

A group of handsomely dressed people stream out of the bar and dig through their pockets to find cigarettes.

This is stupid. I can't go back in there. He'll laugh in my face. Besides, I don't even know what to say—

You're going to give up now? Coward.

I imagine myself turning tail and heading home, of making up some excuse to Julien why I was gone so long, and my stomach sinks. Failure isn't an option. I *want* to go home with that man. Christ, I want to feel him inside me. The last time I had sex was years ago. Years of pent-up, unsatisfied urges, unable to touch myself in my own bed.

The thought of another few years of this is too depressing to contemplate.

It'll just be one time.

Yes, one wild night to remember.

I march through the open doors of the bar, straight into the thick of conversation and music. I wipe my hands on my dress and wade through the crowd of testosterone. Male heads whip around at me. There are so many here to choose from, but I only want one man.

The man who promised me that he'd make me come hard over his cock.

Is he even here?

I belly up to the bar, avoiding the gaze of the pretty bartender. A chorus of deep male laughter captures my attention. Four dark-haired men in suits hang near the bar, and the breath catches in my throat as I recognize one of them.

Johnny raises a shot glass to his wet lips, throws back his head, and swallows the clear liquid. My heart skips a beat when he licks the salt off his hand. His tongue drags on his skin, and a line of pleasure runs straight to the space between my legs. Goddamn, he makes drinking a shot of tequila look sexy. I want that tongue on *my* skin.

So what now? Do I just go up to him or do I puss out and order a drink?

If you don't approach him, someone else will.

The thought sends a jolt of electricity through my legs, and I head straight for him. Even though the bar is crowded, it's easy to navigate this place. I watch as his head turns, staring at the cocktail waitress' ass. She sets down drinks for them and walks away.

Don't look at me.

Don't look at me.

Scorching black eyes pass over the heads in the bar, and then they crawl up my figure. They flicker back.

Fuck, he looked at me.

I can't begin to describe the intensity of his eyes. They're like some kind of personification of a lion's stalking gaze. Everything about him doesn't seem entirely human, from the perfectly slicked-back hair to his spotless appearance. He's too perfect to believe. Then it suddenly hits me: no way this guy is just a bar owner. And my palms sweat as that realization drops into my head.

I want to bolt in the other direction, despite the fact that I just don't get nervous around men anymore. Why's he so different? I can't figure him out.

I'm still shaking as I weave in between his men, inserting myself into that circle of testosterone as Johnny's eyes lock onto my face.

He looks gorgeous as he lounges on that bar stool.

KNOCKED UP BY THE BAD BOY

Clean shaven, not a stray strand of hair, and that tantalizing V of skin right below his neck, revealing his tanned skin and a sprinkling of dark hair. He looks at me, recognition dawning on his face as a slight frown knits his eyebrows.

"I thought I told you not to come back to this bar."

Oh fuck.

My pulse races ahead and I almost want to take a step back from him, that's how forbidding he looks.

"Relax, hon. I'm just joking. I knew you'd come back."

Heat rises in my cheeks as deep dimples carve into his face.

Cocky son of a bitch.

He turns his head, addressing the guys around him. "She told me she didn't fuck Italians."

Laughter explodes around me. I knew it would happen—I expected it. Hell, I deserve it for turning him down.

He sits with his hands on his knees, grinning at me like the Cheshire cat as his friends laugh and *laugh* their asses off. "Some balls!" one of them yells.

Johnny's speech is a bit heavier than usual from the alcohol, but his eyes look just as sharp. "Couldn't resist a bit of Italian sausage, am I right, sweetheart?"

I roll my eyes at the crude banter. If he thinks he's

going to offend me with that shit, he's wrong. I've heard worse. I've heard a thousand times worse. Hell, I grew up around a bunch of foul-mouthed bikers. This is child's play.

Still, that deserves a brushing off.

"You know what?"

The corners of his lips pull, and I hate how my heart does a little flip when I see it directed toward me. "What?"

"I think you're right. My pussy is too good for your cock." I flash a grin at his stunned face. "Bye."

Then I turn around and walk about two feet before my body stumbles backward into something solid and warm. A hand grasps my arm and yanks me back.

The air from my chest disappears as his strong hands turn my body around so that I'm facing him, crushed against his chest. Still smiling, he leans in until his lips are brushing my ear. If I thought I was uncomfortably warm before, it's nothing compared to now. My whole body heats up like a furnace, responding to his touch.

"Where do you think you're going?"

The growl in his voice takes me aback for a moment. I wonder if it's another joke, but it doesn't feel like it when his fingers are pinching me. Jesus, I've never met such an intense person in my life.

Despite the fact that I'm just waiting for him to turn

his face and brush his lips against mine, I push his chest. "I'm going to find someone else who won't humiliate me in front of his friends."

"You started it."

Whatever.

His eyes light up with mischief. "That's the only reason why you're here, isn't it? You're pissed off at Daddy, and the greatest revenge you can think of is to suck my cock."

Yeah, that's about the size of it.

"You want me thrusting inside you, filling you up with my cum. You want to be defiled by me. Don't you?"

Sweet Jesus, yes.

I want to have one wild night with him. Not because he's Italian. Not because I want revenge. Because I haven't gotten laid in years, and he's the most seductive, sinful man I've ever met. He's just a bar owner, but he acts as though he's larger than life. The confidence. The sexiness. Trash flies from his mouth, and my pussy gets wet. I don't understand it.

I want to strip off my clothes right now.

"I want—I want a good time. You look like you're good."

He takes my chin between his forefingers, and I feel like some kind of pathetic puppet. Dark eyes dance at me. "You bet your sweet ass, I am."

Warm breath mists over my face, and I'm waiting for him to kiss me. All train of thought halts to a standstill as he touches my waist. The warmth from his hand burns through my dress as though it were made of silk. His hand. On my waist. Oh, he just squeezed me.

Fuck, he's talking.

"Maya?" he says with laughter in his voice. "Did you hear a word I just said, or were you thinking about how badly you want my cock inside you?"

No, you're letting him get overconfident.

"Do you kiss your mother with that mouth?"

"Yes," he says, eyes flashing. "I can do many things with my mouth. I think you'll find that I'm very talented."

His arms wind around me slowly, like a snake coiling around its prey. I'm slipping into some kind of coma, trapped in this guy's arms. His jacket smells like cedar, but there's not a hint of cigarette smoke, despite this bar being full of it.

"Talented at what?"

But I already know the answer. I already know it from the smile on his face, as he drops closer and closer, his hands locking me into place now. His lips hover over mine, and I stand still as if paralyzed.

"*Eating out your pussy.*"

I can feel it clenching tight at his words. Eating me out?

I've never experienced a man's tongue and mouth down there, but now I'm imagining his dark head bobbing between my legs.

Then his hands unwind from my hips and he steps back with a pleasant smile, the warmth gone.

What the fuck?

"Want a drink?"

The suggestion makes me angry. He stands in front of me, humor in his eyes as I cross my arms over my chest. His guy friends are still eyeing me, but I don't give a fuck. I've been waiting way too long for this, and if he won't give me a one-night stand, I'll find someone else who will.

My voice erupts in the middle of the bar. "*No*, I don't want a drink. I want you to take me home and *fuck me*."

My raised voice catches the attention of his friends, sitting nearby. One of them looks at me with a slack-jawed expression as the bar goes suddenly silent, the patrons wheeling around to look at the crazy girl.

"Jesus Christ, Johnny," one of them says as he eyes me. "If you're not banging her, I will."

A smattering of laughter rings out, and the noise returns to normal levels.

My very ears are burning.

Johnny's voice darkens as he shoots the man a warning look. "Don't be an asshole."

It's weird. The man gives Johnny a cowed look and mumbles an apology to me. Johnny turns his attention back to me, hitching up a smile on his face. He tries to act cool, but I can see the hunger blazing in his eyes.

"Why the fuck should I? You insulted me last night."

My laughter chokes my throat. "What are you, the Godfather or something? I insulted you because I didn't want to fuck you?"

"You're a real smart-ass. You know what you did." His grin widens. "I could have any piece of ass in this room. Why should I waste my time with you?"

I take a bold step forward, showing him that I'm not afraid of him despite whatever the fuck he thinks he has to prove. I take his tie in my hands, watching how his eyes flicker over my lips.

"Because I'm the hottest piece of ass in the room."

A smile tiptoes over his face, and there's real laughter in it, unlike the condescending grin he keeps wearing.

I pull his tie slowly, his head inching toward mine, and he lets me draw his face in. His lips crash against mine, tongue darting inside my mouth to taste me. A shock zaps through his lips into mine, running all the way down my back in a delicious line. He still tastes like tequila. Fingernails slightly dig into my scalp as he fists my hair and forces my mouth against his. I lean into him as every part of me starts to heat up. It's as though my body's waking up after a long sleep, and he feels amazing and it's just kissing. I'm not going to regret this.

When he pulls back, it's not because either of us wants to. It's just to breathe. He takes a deep, shuddering breath. "All right. Let's get out of here."

He pulls away from me for a moment to whisper something in that guy's ear, and then he returns to my side, wrapping his arm around my waist. He digs his phone out of his slacks and makes a call.

"Chris. I need you to pick me up. All right."

Then he ends the call and shoves it back into his pocket.

There's just so much that doesn't add up about this guy.

He pulls me toward the exit, never letting me go for a second. A black Audi pulls up to the curb and Johnny lets me go to open the door for me like a perfect gentleman. Man, he's so different from the guys back home. I feel heat emanating from him as I walk past him and slide into the backseat. He joins me, his thighs pressing against mine.

"Take me home, Chrissy."

The driver, a young guy wearing a leather jacket, nods and pulls the car away from the curb. How strange. The driver isn't wearing any kind of professional clothing. For some reason it makes me a little nervous.

Fuck it. Who cares?

I want to think about his hand casually resting on my leg, his fingers wrapping around my knee, and the thrill that it gives me. He looks at my legs, my thighs, my tits, as if he's deciding what he's going to do with me. It's a bit awkward with the other man in the car, but Johnny doesn't seem to care.

We drive back to his place in silence. It's a bit unnerving, and the closer we get to his home, the harder it is to ignore my frantic heartbeat. He kneads my thigh, inching up higher, dragging my dress over my skin as I turn sideways. He tips my head back with a single finger under my jaw and his lips fall over mine. They start out soft, at first, oddly restrained, and then they're hard and biting. He slides one of his hands up my waist and grabs me roughly, as if he can't decide which part he should focus on. I gasp into his mouth as his palm slides between my breasts. He grabs one of my tits—just groping it roughly, sliding his thumb over my peaking nipple.

"*Tabarnak*, your tits."

My face burns scarlet, or I imagine that it does. Suddenly I'm reminded of the driver's presence and I pull away from Johnny, returning my hands to my lap. His arm stretches behind my head, his fingers tickling the back of my neck. I burn at the sight of amusement on his face.

We finally arrive at what looks like his high-rise apartment.

"Thanks, Chris."

"No problem."

He doesn't pay the guy. Huh.

I take Johnny's hand and climb out of the car as he waves goodbye. The car rolls away, and a jolt of fear suddenly hits me as he guides me toward the lobby.

I can count on my hand how many times I've had sex, and never before have I had a one-night stand. I want him, but I still feel racked with nerves. He's too gorgeous, too slick. My confidence can barely keep up with him.

It's too late.

The elevator doors slide open, and I'm lulled into a false sense of security.

"I'm starting to think that you're not just a bar owner."

Johnny leans his back against the mirrored wall, grinning wickedly. "Yeah? What gave you that idea?"

"Everyone treats you like you're a king."

This time he really does laugh. It rebounds sharply in the elevator, and he pushes himself off the wall, advancing upon me like a predator. Until my breaths get short and I have a hard time focusing.

"Maybe I am."

Oh God.

"Ever think about that?"

He's connected. No fucking way.

An icy feeling spreads inside my chest as he pulls me against his body roughly without giving me any time to respond.

This is what you wanted, remember? You went to that bar because you knew Dad hated Italians, and what's worse than an Italian?

A *Mafioso*.

It all fits—the bad-boy attitude, acting as though nothing in the world can take him down, his fucking ego, and the guys sucking up to him.

Oh *shit*. Oh God.

I've no idea how high up he is, but he's a soldier, at least. He's a made member. I'm sure of it.

Dad would fucking kill him. And me.

The elevator pings open and I'm half-tempted to think of some kind of excuse to bail, because this is nuts. I'm the daughter of the president of the Devils MC, and he's in the mob. I almost want to laugh at how panicky I am right now. The other, louder part of me wants to do it anyway. It's wrong. It's exciting. I've already gone too far.

He leads me down the hall, and still I haven't made a move to suggest that maybe we should call this whole thing off. Save my fucking skin and his.

Instead I let him pull me into the darkness of his apartment. Into that horribly terrifying silence that simmers with desire. It's always the most awkward part of first dates. The *whens* and the *hows* are torturous. When should I kiss him? I could handle him if he was an ordinary man, but he's the opposite.

He's a predator.

Like a black hole, he's the brightest thing in the universe. I could pick him out in a crowd instantly. Get too close and you're dead. You're gone.

He shuts the door and locks it. The moment I hear the locks slide home, I know I'm fucked.

Johnny's face seems different in the darkness. There's no levity, just a humorless look and a predatory stare. It makes my heart jump in my chest. Then he flicks on the light, illuminating a vast, gorgeous apartment.

Ok, he's definitely not just a bar owner.

"Wow."

I turn around, impressed by how richly decorated the place is. He's not some kind of rich frat boy. He's got style. A blood-red abstract painting hangs near the entrance. I walk deeper inside, checking out the modern furniture. And what's more, the whole place is pristine. I can't see a speck of dust anywhere. It's fucking creepy.

No guy on earth is this clean.

I wander around his living room and sit down on one of his couches, to see him still standing near the door, half-hidden in shadows.

My chest deflates.

I expected my clothes to fly off the moment we walked through the door, but he takes deliberate steps into the living room, turns toward the stocked bar he has, and pours us both drinks.

Ice clinks in the glasses as he walks to where I'm sitting, balancing the drinks in one hand, giving me a strange look. He offers me mine and I take it just to do something with my hands. The drink slips down his throat as he eye-fucks me, standing close enough to touch me.

It's unsettling.

"What's that look?"

"I can't figure you out."

The glass table makes a sharp sound when he sets his drink down, and then he plants his hands on either side of my head. I sink into the fabric as his face comes within inches of mine. Heart pounding in my ears, I can barely make out what he says to me.

"You really have no idea who I am?"

His breath mists over my face and I'm so tempted to lean the few inches forward and catch his lips in mine. I lick my lips.

"Are you going to fuck me, or what?"

A smile flickers. "I asked you a question."

"No, and I don't want to know."

Puzzlement makes his eyebrows knit together and I take a gulp of whatever drink he brought me, the amber liquid burning down my throat.

He slides into the couch next to me, the sound of the leather fabric oddly loud in my ears. He doesn't touch me. It drives me crazy. The alcohol spreads a flush over my chest, and I'm just about out of patience.

"I don't trust easily. I don't trust at all—and I feel like you're hiding something from me."

"What makes you say that?"

A snort leaves his nostrils. "It's my job to sniff out people trying to pull a fast one on me. The world's filled with people trying to fuck you over."

I have no idea what he's talking about.

"I don't want to fuck you over. I want to fuck you."

He looks forbidding, but I ignore his body language, which tells me to stay the fuck away. I get up from the couch and stand between his legs. He watches me with the air of a wolf scenting a prey animal, and my blood pounds in my neck. My fingers take the hem of my dress and I pull it right off my body. It slowly drags over my thighs, exposing my black silk panties. His face goes slack as he watches the edge of the dress rise over the swell of my breasts.

Yes, look at me.

Desire pounds between my legs as I reach behind myself and unclasp the bra, a thrill shooting through me from rendering Johnny speechless. His eyes are glued to my tits and then my hands, gently tugging at my panties. They snag over my hips.

Something snaps in his eyes. Suddenly he leans forward and grabs my waist, yanking me forward. The panties are halfway down my thighs, but he makes me straddle his legs. There's a ripping sound and I realize the panties have a tear in them. I gasp as he takes them in his hands and rips them off my body with one quick jerk.

Fucking hot.

Warmth floods my pussy as he wraps his arms around my naked skin. I arch my back, and his face bumps against my tits. His tongue darts out, sending a shock through me as he swirls around my nipple. Then he bites down on the hardened nub.

I've never done anything like this before with a man I barely know. I've never wanted to strip away all my vulnerabilities. He thinks I'm hiding something from him, and he's right, but I'm not giving that up. I don't want to ruin this night. If he finds out who my father is, he'll ends things now. That, I'm sure of.

My thighs rub against the coarse fabric of his suit as I wrap my arms around his neck, burying my fingers in his thick, dark hair. His hot mouth takes my breast and he bites down on the flesh, letting out wicked laughter when it pops out of his lips. "You think you can distract me with tits?"

"Yeah."

His eyes are fractured. There's a battle in them. Pride versus lust.

The hand cradling my ass suddenly disappears, and reappears in a loud slap. My skin burns as the sound cracks across the room as Johnny looks greedily at my body.

"Fuck, you are gorgeous. And right."

I'm temporarily paralyzed with the sensation of being naked in his arms. Hard fingers grope my tits, making me arch against him. He grabs a hunk of my hair and pulls me toward his lips, and they devour me.

It's carnal, as if he hasn't fucked a woman in years. I love it.

"I'm going to make you mine tonight. Just for one night, sweetheart."

Then his hand dips from my breast down my stomach, all the way to my aching core. He cups my pussy and rides his middle finger over my clit.

"Already wet, huh? When's the last time you've been with a man?"

My face burns and I consider lying for a moment, but what's the point? "Years," I mumble.

His middle finger doesn't pause. It slides inside me. "Jesus. No wonder."

I tighten my arms around him, uttering a small moan when I feel my walls tighten around the two digits, aching for something thick and hard. His cock is right there. The outline of him grows in his pants. Jesus, he's huge. I reach down and wrap my fingers around him, and it twitches inside my grip.

I lean forward and grasp his head, brushing back his hair and running my fingers along his stubble as I kiss him. Every ounce of passion and need explodes out of me. He just keeps fingering me calmly, the wet sound driving me insane. I want him naked—I want all of him.

"Please, Johnny!"

He smiles against my lips. "I'm going to give you a night you'll never forget. First, I'm going to fuck you really hard. I'll make your cunt numb, just like you wanted." His fingers twist inside me and another jolt of pleasure rips through me, making me yell out loud. "Then I'm going to make you come with my tongue. I'll fuck you again, and again, and when you go home tomorrow to your daddy, you can tell him that Johnny Cravotta fucked his little daughter."

Oh Jesus. The things he's saying. It's so—*wait a second*. I know that name.

Who fucking cares?

"How does that sound?"

His smooth voice invades my ears, the only noise I hear besides my own wetness sliding around his fingers.

"Tha-that sounds—ah!"

His fingers slam into my pussy, a third one inside me. Johnny's soft laughter rebounds around his living room.

Finally he pulls out of me and wipes his fingers on my thigh. Then his hand splays on my neck and pushes me down so quickly that the air is knocked out of my chest. My back sinks into the couch cushions as he stands up, gazing down at my naked body with unmistakable greed.

"Touch yourself. I want to watch you."

A blush creeps up my face as my hand tentatively curls around my thigh.

He puts a hand on my knee and pulls it apart from the other. "Spread those gorgeous legs apart so I can see your pussy."

It's rare that a guy gives me orders. Even rarer that I follow them, but the authority ringing from his voice is impossible to ignore. He's the first man who has ever made me want to obey him.

I spread my knees farther apart as I lower my hand over my pussy, sliding my fingers down the slick skin. Johnny sits down on the glass table, feet from me. He touches himself, and another bump of excitement adds to the fire. I've never seen a guy do that before. He curves his hand around his thickening cock and strokes it through his slacks, which are uncomfortably tight.

"I want you to imagine me inside you."

But I don't care about me. I want him. And I've never been good at listening.

I slide off the couch, ignoring his angry commands as I kneel at his feet and wrap my hands around his belt.

Redness flushes his skin as I grab him through his slacks, tugging the belt out of its loops as Johnny loses the fight to get me to do what he wants.

"Please. I want to suck your cock."

I want him to lose control. I want him to forget who he is and what he's doing. Wild, unbridled desire.

His hand cups my cheek, his thumb caressing my bottom lip. "Some fucking day, you're not going to get what you want."

But I always do.

He lifts his hips and I drag the slacks from his waist.

They pool at his feet. Damn, Johnny is hiding an amazing body. He's lean and all muscle, but not bulky, which I like. His dick sticks out of his black briefs like a flesh-colored flag. I pull his briefs off his hips, and then that delectable cock springs free. I grip it in my hand, marveling at the warmth.

He clucks with sympathy, running a hand through my hair. "You must be starving for cock."

Yes, I am.

"I'll let you have a little taste."

Then he shoves my head down, his fingers digging into my hair as my lips bump against his head and open wide. He passes through them, so thick and firm. It's been fucking years, but I grip the base of his cock, taking him all the way inside me. My lips suck hard near the tip and I look at Johnny's face as I do it. His eyes close in rapture and he wets his lips, keeping his hand fisted in my hair.

"Ah, *fuck* yes."

He lifts his hips in a thrust as my lips glide down his length. Holy shit, I can't believe how turned-on I am. His teeth clench as I take him all the way inside me, his balls flush against my lips.

"*Criss.*"

I feel his cock twitch inside me, and I wrap my other arm around his thighs, his hair tickling my palm. I anchor solidly over his ass, feeling my core clench as his moans hit the ceiling. His breathing deepens as my lips tighten around him, gliding up and down, swirling my tongue over his swollen head. It turns me on to see his red face trained on mine, lust burning through his skin. I let him pop out of me and slide his cock over my lips.

In a few swift movements, Johnny picks me up and hurls me over the couch. He tears off his jacket with an animalistic growl. My heart leaps as his body falls over mine, my legs wrapping around his solid waist.

Fear careens through my veins, battling with the aching need to be fucked. It's been too long. I can't wait anymore.

He reaches back and I feel the head of his cock sliding against my folds and an overwhelming blaze of lust almost makes me scream.

He sinks inside me with a grunt. The head pushes through my slick walls, and ecstasy washes all over me. I forgot how amazing it felt to have a man inside me. How did I wait this long?

It throbs inside me, so big that it hurts to feel him thrust. His tie dangles around his muscled neck and I spread my hands underneath his shirt collar. I want to touch every inch of his skin.

"Your pussy feels so good."

The ragged voice sends a rush of excitement to my

chest. He slides out and ruts me deep, all restraint forgotten. My clit hums with the pleasant burn of his cock riding up against it. I've never felt something so amazing in my life, but I don't want to come—not yet. I grab the tie dangling in my face and pull his grinning face down. He knows exactly what's going on.

He thrusts hard as my lips crush against his. He kisses me back in a frenzy as I groan into his mouth.

"That's it, baby. Moan for me."

My fingernails dig into his back as he takes one of my tits and roughly squeezes it, pinching the nipple as his cock hammers my cunt.

"Johnny, you should stop."

"Why?"

"I'm about to come. *Please.*"

But of course the bastard does the opposite. The grin on his face widens as he wraps his arms around my shoulders and fucks me for all I'm worth. I try to fight against the building pressure inside my core.

His mouth seals over mine, his tongue forces down my throat, and I arch my back.

"No," I moan into his mouth.

"*Yes.* Come for me. I want you to."

I can't ignore the thick cock pulsing through me, hitting all the right nerves as his body, which is covered in wicked tattoos, fucks me like a battering ram. The breath knocks out of my lungs and my hands reach around to his ass, urging him on. I scream as the last thrust shoves me over the edge and I clench hard around him. My nails dig into his flesh as I come hard, the wave of relief knocking me down flat. Johnny silences my moans with his mouth, his breathing frantic. I melt into the couch, but his hips crush against mine, ramping up the pleasure again, until finally he breaks off the kiss and groans loud enough so that for a moment, I wonder if something is wrong.

His hips thrust hard, jamming his length into me as his warm cum explodes from his cock. He thrusts a few more times, each one jarring me back into lust.

Jesus.

The dampness of his skin makes him stick to me. I'm covered in his smell, my pussy full of his cum. Hot lips find my neck as his breath mists over my skin. He kisses me over and over, down my neck, teeth nipping at me before he takes my breast in his mouth and bites hard. Shit. Something so painful shouldn't feel so damn good. He raises his head, his wicked grin adding another sharp bump to the need pulsing inside me.

A growl issues from his throat. "I can't keep my hands off you."

My heartbeat is still sprinting, but then it does a little

flip when he gives me a small smile. The glow of my orgasm slowly fades away, and for one horrible moment I feel doubt clinging to my shoulders. The post-sex awkwardness makes my cheeks burn.

"What's the matter?"

He fixes me with an intense stare that makes my insides tighten.

"I'm just—shy," I say finally.

"*Shy?*" he says with a small laugh. "I'm balls deep inside you, and you're shy."

I look away from the laughter in his eyes.

"I'll give you something to be shy about."

The steely look in his eyes makes my breath catch in my throat.

"*What?*"

JOHNNY

"What?"

The surprise widening her eyes makes me want to laugh. If she could only see inside my fucked-up head.

I palm her flat stomach, loving the way her skin shivers under my touch, and curl my fingers over her mound. The slickness of her cunt clings to my skin, and excitement burns through my veins.

This girl has a gorgeous body. Way better than all my recent lays, and she's hot for me. Of course she is. She hasn't gotten laid in years. I can't in good conscience let her leave my apartment without her being thoroughly fucked.

She yelps as I lift her off the couch. "What do you mean?"

"Stop talking."

I bring her to my bedroom, my cock stirring back to life as I think about the box of toys in my closet. Then I roughly drop her onto my mattress. She falls down with a loud bump, and I enjoy the view of her tits bouncing on her chest. Her high, arched eyebrows narrow dangerously at me. So the princess isn't used to being talked down to?

Too fucking bad.

Control just isn't something I give up easily. I take it from people all the time, but this broad was hot enough to wrestle it out of me. I fuck girls all the time, and I never come inside one without a condom.

Talk about Russian roulette.

Maya did that to me.

I take her delicate throat in my hand. "I told you I would make you mine tonight. I don't want to hear you talk, unless it's to ask me permission for something."

Laughter dances over her dark eyes.

I'm going to fuck the pride right out of you.

"I've got you pinned down. You're not used to taking a man's orders."

"You're damn straight."

Heat flashes over my face as I glare at her. "I told you to shut the fuck up."

My words slap her across the face. A beautiful red pricks her already flushed cheeks, but she stays silent. Finally.

"I'm not your daddy. I won't let you walk over me." I take her shoulders in my hands and push them back so that she lies flat on the bed, her hair splayed behind her. Her vein jumps in her neck and I bend over her, my lips touching her ear. "Give me the respect I deserve, and I'll make you come over and over again. Don't listen to me, and I'll throw your ass out."

I have to remind myself that it's not entirely her fault. She doesn't know who I am yet.

Maya's pink mouth parts slightly. She looks as though she wants to speak, but she doesn't dare piss me off. Good, it's working already. There's nothing but the sound of her quick breaths in my bedroom. I don't know if I could handle it if she walked out on me, because I'm not satisfied. Not in the least.

Her mouth twists in anger, but I place a finger over her swollen lips to silence her.

"Don't. Accept the fact that you don't know me. This is how it's going to be."

She sucks in her lip and bites down hard as she thinks it over in her head. I see the struggle behind those proud eyes. She wants to fuck me, but her pride won't let her.

Then finally she swallows. "Okay."

There's a slight edge in her voice that I don't like to hear. As boss, I'm always on the lookout for any hint of defiance in my men. I'm always searching for the one who will challenge me, so that I can crush him. Mock execution. Most of the time, it's just a bullet between the eyes. I like to send the message that I don't fuck around. Second chances? Fuck that. You get one chance with me.

Smiling, I turn my back on her and enter my closet, looking for the stash of toys I rarely get to use on the women I bring home. This one's different. She's desperate for cock. She'll let me do whatever the fuck I want.

I pick out a nice leather blindfold dyed in a wine-red color and curl it around my hands. She glances at the blindfold around my hand and tries to look unconcerned, but her hands tighten over the comforter.

"Sit up."

She obeys quickly, her dark eyes flicking to the blindfold and then to my face. Blood rushes to my hands as I touch her neck, feeling her fluttering heartbeat. The blindfold wraps around her eyes in a tight embrace, and I slide the strap through the buckle until it's snug. She can't see a fucking thing.

I touch her shoulder, and she jumps a little. It gets my blood going like you wouldn't believe. She doesn't expect where I'm going to touch her, and her head lifts, her lips searching for me. I trace my finger around those beautiful lips.

"I told you I'd make you mine tonight," I say, pinching that succulent bottom lip. "I meant it. Just one night as my fuck toy, and then you go back to Daddy."

Her lips tremble as I take my hands away, and then I grab her wrists, tugging them. She follows the pressure unsteadily, standing up from the bed. Her brown hair swings wildly as she stumbles forward into my chest. She inhales a small gasp, and the pink blush spreading over her cheeks makes my dick hard enough smash diamonds.

"Hands behind your head."

She tentatively raises her hands, a question forming on her lips that she swallows.

A smile tightens my face.

Good girl.

Her tits look amazing with her hands behind her head. They stick out like two perfect orbs, her nipples already hard. I watch as the breath catches in her throat when I take one of those nipples in my forefinger and thumb and pinch hard. Fucking beautiful. I love the way she gasps and bites her lips. Then I lower my head and take that hard bud in my mouth.

The sharp sound of her gasp cuts the air. I love watching her reaction. It gets me so fucking hard. Her nipple hardens around my tongue and I move it in slow circles. Then I pull back and blow air over her wet skin. I do the same to the other one, taking more of her tit in my mouth, sucking hard over the creamy skin so that a bright, red mark burns on her skin. The blood pounding through my cock makes the ache almost painful.

My power over her is like a heady, seductive scent. It

makes me feel drunk, makes my veins run with fire. I say, "Jump," and she obeys. I crave that kind of control. Fucking need it. But I need this even more.

I sit down on the edge of the bed, turning her trembling body around.

"Kneel."

My command rolls over her body like silk. Maya's thighs tremble. "Why?"

I reach around her legs to rip my hand across her gorgeous ass, the sound cracking through the room. Maya jumps and moves her hands down her head. Anger rustles in my chest, and I slap that ass a little harder so that she shrieks.

"I told you to keep your hands behind your head."

Her chest pulses for a few seconds as she stands there, humiliated but unsure. Then they rise back behind her head.

That's better.

I can't help but stroke the red burn blossoming on her ass. An obedient girl deserves a reward, right? I take her hips, and she follows my pressure, kneeling with her tits sticking out.

Fuck, I could make myself come with the sight of her sitting there, her legs tightly pressed together as if to hide her arousal. I wind my fingers through her hair and I pull her head forward. She follows blindly, right into my lap. Then the warm head of my cock brushes over her lips.

"Suck my cock."

Her tongue darts out in an experimental taste. Fuck, her little tongue just wets my cock, and I push myself between her lips. It feels incredible. So smooth, warm, and moist. She might be a daddy's girl, but she's a champ at sucking cock.

She works her mouth, bobbing her head with her hands behind her. Her slick tongue works magic on my prick, rubbing the underside and making me jump in her mouth. My breathing quickens. Heart pounds. I can't think about anything except the noise she makes when she moves her sloppy mouth up and down me. It makes me feel as though she's in control.

Has she been fucking with me this entire time? I pegged her as some kind of uptight broad with an asshole for a father, but the vigorousness of her mouth—fuck—I didn't expect this.

"Tell me how it feels to have me balls deep in your mouth. Go on, give your mouth a break."

I pop out of her mouth, but not before she gives my head a kiss with tongue. Wetness gleams from her lips, and it's a sexy sight.

"It feels nice."

She says it in a shrugging tone, and I pinch her chin. "You feel how hard I am?"

"Yeah."

That fucking grin.

"How is it that a girl who hasn't gotten laid in years can suck cock like that?"

Her shoulder lifts in a shrug. "I watch a lot of porn."

A girl that watches porn. Dirty. I always aimed for traditional girls. I fucked sluts to get my rocks off, and dated girls who were good candidates for marriage. Traditional Italian women. The girls I dated would've never been into porn. Karen called it "disgusting."

It makes me realize that I can't go much longer without fucking this broad.

"Up."

We switch places; I gently lead her to the bed so that she's lying down. She drops down cautiously, still blind, flinching when I touch her legs.

I promised her I would make her come with my tongue, and I intend to keep that promise. My hand slaps her inner thighs, and she bends her knees and spreads them apart, only parting them about an inch.

"Spread your legs."

"I—it's—"

It's wrong. It's dirty. I don't care what she's about to

89

say.

"Do it." My voice cuts hers off, louder than ever. She spreads her legs as if she's fucking hiding drugs in there, and then I just take her knees and roughly pull her apart.

Her gleaming pussy calls to me like a Siren's song. I fucked her already, but I've forgotten what it felt like. I can't imagine it, and my dick is driving me crazy trying to remember. She inhales sharply as I kiss her inner thigh, leading a trail right to her swollen cunt. Maya throws her head back when I kiss her outer lips.

My laughter hits her face like a slap. She burns.

"Maddon, so that's it, huh? That's your sweet spot."

"Please, Johnny." Maya arches her back as I reach all the way back with my tongue and lick her, swimming in her musk. She screams to the ceiling, and my heart rams against my chest.

"I told you what I'd do to you."

She makes a desperate sound as I close my mouth over her sweet pussy, sucking hard and flicking my tongue inside her to feel her squeeze.

Maya fucking loves it. She forgets all about staying quiet and obeying me. Her legs wrap around my head, and then I sink my tongue inside that cunt as far as it'll go.

Her screams lift to the ceiling as if I'm killing her.

"No!" she screams, face flushed. "I can't—I don't

wanna—"

"You don't want to come?"

"It—it makes me lose control. I need to feel—oh!"

"That's exactly what I want, baby. I want you to fall to your knees and beg me to fuck you."

She clenches her teeth. "I don't beg."

Stubborn bitch.

I curl my fingers inside that slick pussy, watching her eat her own words as she fists the sheets and cries out to the ceiling.

"You're begging right now."

But I still need to hear her say it.

My tongue swirls around her clit, nudging that little nub as I put my face between her thighs and lick her pussy for all I'm worth. She arches into me, pressing her body into my lips. Then I pull back, leaving her panting.

"What are you doing?"

Giving you a taste of your own medicine.

I smile against her pussy, giving her thigh a harsh slap as I kiss her clit, thrusting my fingers inside her. I wait until her breathing reaches a crescendo and then I pull back. It's the hardest fucking thing I've ever done in my life.

She lifts her head and looks at me like I'm a god. I am a god compared to the men she's been with.

"Just do it already."

"Yeah?" The need in her voice gives me a high. This beautiful girl wants me so badly that she's ready to beg for it. "I'm sorry, sweetheart, but I'm not done eating my fill."

My mouth smothers her steaming cunt, and she locks her knees around my head and screams. I mean, the bitch sounds like she's being murdered in my apartment. Her pussy juice slides in my mouth, and I fuck her hard with my fingers.

Then her legs rub against my face, and I turn my mouth to kiss her calf. And it hits me. The memory of having those silky legs sliding in my hands in the office. Wanting to fuck the shit out of her.

Then I can't take it anymore.

I flip her around by the waist and nearly drive into her when I see her bent over on all fours, her ass high in the air for me. I grab a fist of her hair and yank hard, forcing her to arch back. She tenses when she feels my thighs pressing against hers.

My cock is flat against her ass, pressing into her like a gun. My prize is so fucking close. Instead, I smack her ass. Hard.

"You know what I think? I think you like this shit."

"I—"

"Any normal girl would've walked the fuck out."

She doesn't know who the hell I am. If she knew I was

boss, she'd be on all fours, sucking my cock until I said, "Thank you." Fuck that. I want to take her submission.

The blood rushes to her skin as my palm cracks over her skin.

"You want to be dominated by a real man, don't you?"

I loop my hand around her hair and tug it hard, forcing her head back. Then I run my lips over her ear.

"I just want to get laid."

"Why pick me out of all the guys there?" I hiss against her ear. "Why go to all that fucking trouble to buy a new dress?"

Her face turns, burning red in the dim light. "I wanted you."

"Yeah, you chose me. You saw that I was an alpha male—just your type—"

"Yeah? So?"

I smack her ass against that insolent tone.

"Put your hands against the headboard."

Maya shuffles forward and extends her thin arms, placing her palms flat on my headboard as she sticks her ass out, begging for my cock.

"Just fuck me," she says with a growl in her voice as I edge up behind her, smoothing my hands over her thighs.

I ignore her plea. "First, I'm going to spank you. You're going to count how many times I do it."

She nods, still facing the headboard.

Just fuck her already.

My hand drapes over her ass and her muscles tense. I let her feel my fingers spreading over her skin, my thumb right on the edge of her ass. I pull her skin and see her glistening pussy, which is just waiting to wrap around my cock.

God fucking damn it. Fuck the girl, will you?

Gritting my teeth, I raise my palm from her skin. Crack. The sound splits the air. Blood rushes to her skin and I feel the heat underneath my palm.

Her voice trembles. "One."

Again, on the same round cheek. The sound gets me every fucking time. She gasps a bit and then her voice hardens. "Two."

Her arms shake as I bring my hand down on her raw flesh, waiting for that moment to break over her eyes. With my other hand, I fist my cock, letting it slide all over her folds. She groans and pushes her ass closer to me. It couldn't be plainer that she wants me inside her, but I need her submission first.

Another slap hits the bright, red burn on her ass. This time she yells. It's painful, but it's mingled with the pleasure of my thick length rubbing up and down her clit.

"Th-three!"

"What's the matter, sweetheart?"

"I just want—I want—ah!"

I strike her left cheek, the force of it so hard that it stings my hand. Then I rub her swollen flesh. "What's that?"

Shit, I'm loving this.

"Four." The answer explodes from her. "You know what I want."

"I won't give you what you want. Not until you admit that you love what I'm doing to you right now."

I'm not sure I can keep that promise. I feel her walls trying to grip me as I slide all over her pussy, the head just nudging her in the right spots. Maya is barely able to keep her arms against the headboard. She moves her head back and I see her strain with the effort of keeping it together. Her tits hang like perfect teardrops. I grind against her and grope one of them.

"Fuck me!"

Her scream stabs me right in the fucking ears, but I don't care.

"You sure you want me to fuck you?"

Still groping her tits, I give her ass another brutal slap, and she cries out. "Five! Yes, I'm fucking sure."

"Beg me."

All the energy roils in my stomach as she collapses over

the pillows, unable to keep herself up anymore. "Fuck me, goddamn it! I can't take it anymore!"

I want to play with her. I want to make her crawl on her knees and beg me while I'm in her mouth, but I can't take it anymore either.

I seize her hips and force her legs apart, and there's a brief moment where the head of my cock pushes between her folds, and then her warmth envelops me like a tight, warm glove.

"Hands back on the headboard."

She obeys and then her body jackhammers forward as I ram my hips against hers. My cock thrusts deep as every instinct urges me to fuck her hard and fast. So that's what I do. I grind my hips against that pussy and nail her deep, until she lets out a sharp yell.

"Yes!"

Her arms tremble from the force of my thrusts. Her voice is like a lightning bolt straight into my cock, energizing me. My vision narrows to the girl writhing on my bed, screaming for more. With every thrust, she opens her mouth in a moan and her tits swing forward. I grab both in my hands and wrench her upright, using them to hold her against me.

"Oh my God, John—"

"I need you to come, baby."

My arm snakes around her waist while the other holds her tits. As I thrust into her, I grab her swollen clit and press down hard, rubbing her in circles. She nearly swoons in my arms. Maya turns her flushed face toward mine, and I crush my lips against hers. It's too much. The fucking feeling of her tight pussy gripping my cock like it doesn't ever want to let me go, her tits in my hands, and the screams she makes.

"I need you to fucking come."

She doesn't flinch from the rough edge in my voice. She's lost in the pleasure of it just like I am.

"I am!"

I feel the explosion ripping through her body as she grips my cock hard and falls apart in my arms, sagging against me. Then I'm done, too. I'm no match against her perfect body. I ram her so hard that she screams in pain, and the ache swells like a wave. It crashes down, and I feel the hot jets of cum, and her wet thighs against mine. I let her down gently and pulse a few more times.

"Fuck!"

Yes, I needed this.

Still inside her, I lie down over her, propping myself up by my elbows. Damn, I'm exhausted.

"Oh my God."

Her mellowed voice breathes out in my bedroom as her

chest pulses. A thrill of pride hits my chest as she turns to face me.

"I've never been fucked like that. Ever."

I smile, pressing my wet forehead against hers. "I told you I was good."

She touches my chin, tracing it. "I knew you'd be. I just—"

"Didn't know how good it would feel?"

I'm amused at the slight blush pinking her cheeks as she nods, the haughtiness in her eyes finally gone.

Right around now would be the time where I'd usually invent some kind of work-related business I had to attend to because I'm an asshole and I want them out of my apartment, but I feel no desire to get rid of her. And it hits me suddenly. I want this girl again. Not just for tonight, or the next day. I want her on call whenever I want to fuck her. Why should I bang cocktail waitresses when I have a hot piece of ass who will let me do whatever the hell I want?

But it's against my rules. Fuck a girl more than once, and the next thing you know, they want a relationship. And then they want to meet your mother and tickets to the opera and fuck knows what else.

Then she kisses me. Her lips are against mine before I can even summon up an excuse to suggest that she should leave, and then that compulsion is wiped away completely. She kisses me and slips her tongue inside me, making my heart pound.

* * *

Crack of dawn. Something moves beside my bed. A shadow.

I don't even think. In seconds my hand clutches the handle of the gun stashed under my pillow. Then I lunge across the bed, grabbing a skinny wrist. A female cry of pain surprises me as I bury the gun in her temple, pressing her body to mine.

"Shut the fuck up and don't move."

"It's me, you idiot!"

Holy fuck.

My heart clenches painfully as I recognize her voice and put the gun aside, flipping on the lamp. She blinks furiously against the bright light.

"Sneaking out in the middle of the night, eh? Nice."

I should be pissed, but it's hard not to laugh at this shit. Who the fuck has the balls to walk out on me?

"You had to put a gun to my head?"

"You took me by surprise," I say, letting her go roughly.

"I just wanted to leave before you woke up."

"Classy."

Maya crosses her arms and stares at me.

No apology, nothing.

"Why? So you could go back to Daddy before he woke up?"

Her face heats up like a lamp. "You don't understand, and I can't explain."

My chest heaves in a sigh. "Fine. At least let me drive you home."

"No," she says too quickly.

No. "No" is not a word I hear very often. It makes my stomach churn to see her standing there like that, just as defiant as she was in the bar.

Now my blood is starting to boil.

"What the fuck is wrong with me giving you a ride home, huh?"

"Nothing," she insists.

"Are you embarrassed by me?"

"No!" Her face burns under my stare. "Please, just take my word for it. He can't know."

Fine. Whatever.

"You should stay the night. He's going to find out anyway."

She tenses at that. "He can't."

"It's not safe walking alone at this time."

Her lips stagger with a small grin. "It's safe for me."

What does that mean?

I slide from the bedsheets and stand up naked beside her, watching how her gaze lingers on my dick, chest, and arms.

"Give me your number so we can do this again."

"I told you, it was a one-time thing."

"Tell me I wasn't the best lay you ever had."

She reaches out with her hand, that look blazing in her eyes again. "It's not about that. I can't just do whatever I want."

I don't buy that.

I pick up my slacks from the floor and pull out a small white card with my private phone number. If she even knew how rarely I gave it out to girls, she'd be honored, but of course the dumb idiot doesn't. I haven't had a comare in ages, and I'd like to have her as one. I take her hand and gently close her fingers around it.

Then I bend my lips to her ear and I feel her shiver. "Call me the next time you feel like a good fuck."

"I don't think so."

A grin stretches my face. "Maybe the next time you fight with your dad."

She stuffs the card in her jeans without looking at it and I walk her to the door, opening it for her and giving the whole hallway front-row seats to my cock. Maya doesn't want to leave. It's all over her body. From those nipples sticking out like pins on that fuck-me dress she wears, to her eyes locked on mine.

"You're trying to tempt me back inside."

"Is it working?"

The blush spreading over her cheeks tells me yes.

"Don't you care that anyone could see you right now?"

"No."

A smile cracks her face and suddenly she takes a step forward. She bumps her lips against mine. For a moment I think she's coming back inside, but she pulls back almost immediately. It's just a cheap goodbye.

"Bye, Johnny."

I don't say a word as she backs away from me and walks down the hall.

This isn't goodbye.

* * *

Smoke curls around my fingers. I blow out a stream and watch as my cigarette makes calligraphy in the air.

A man stands above my table, waiting for me to notice him. My silence hangs over his head like an axe. He clenches and unclenches his hands.

What a moron. If he had any brains, he would make me notice him. Maybe he's playing it safe. Maybe he knows I wouldn't have a problem with blowing out his brains in the middle of this restaurant. No, he doesn't say a word. He's real quiet. Like a dog waiting for scraps.

I hiss the smoke through my teeth, and then the waiter comes to my table with my Marechiara pizza. A blood-red pie sits on my table, thin crust, the big black olives wrinkled with the heat with the pits still inside. None of that canned olives shit. Napoletana is one of my favorite pizza places in the city. It's cash only, of course. The owner fought me hard against paying me protection money, and my love of the pizza in the place kept me from torching it until he finally buckled down and gave me my money.

"Uh—Johnny?"

I don't even look at him. "What?"

"L—listen, I just wanted to apologize."

I finally flick my gaze to him. He's a strapping, young guy with at least fifty pounds on me, but he looks at me as if I'm Jesus Christ. His hands are clasped in front of his body and his head is bowed, as if in penance. I can taste the fear sweating off his body. He's waiting for a reaction from me. A condemnation or a reprieve. I won't give him either.

"Apologize for what?"

I slide a slice of pizza onto my porcelain plate and cut into it with my knife and fork. Dignified. Slow. A boss can't just shove pizza down his fucking throat like some fat fuck. The hot sauce stings my tongue. It's like fire, but it tastes so goddamn good that I can't help but keep eating. I grip my wineglass and the dry vintage slips down my throat, adding fuel to the burn.

"I fucked up, but I can fix this. Please let me fix this."

His shaking voice makes my tongue curl.

"How?" I cut my gaze over his, staring into his widened eyes. "I've been planning this heist for almost a year, you dumb fuck."

Millions of dollars of untraceable cash, just sitting in the airport. Begging to be stolen. My whole crew knows about the heist, of course.

"I can get the keys. I have a plan—"

"François told me about your plan."

The dismissive tone almost brings him to his knees. "There's a short window. Fifteen minutes. I can get copies of the keys made."

I doubt he can get anything done. "Do it."

Relief washes over his face, and I almost want to laugh at him. I'd probably kill him anyway, just to tie up loose ends. I don't trust him to keep his trap shut if anyone's busted, because he's not a member.

"Thank you, John."

"If you don't get copies of the keys, don't come back at

all."

I watch him leave, an uneasy feeling eating away at my stomach as he walks away. Then I beckon toward Chris, who kneels to my side immediately.

"I want you to follow him. And then I want you to take care of him."

Chris doesn't betray any shock. His young face freezes for a moment, and then his dark eyes slide to mine. "Take care of him?"

You know what I mean.

Then he leans back and nods, patting his front jacket pocket as he heads outside.

It takes a split second for me to make a life-or-death decision.

Like I said, I don't give second chances.

The Mafia is a family, yes, but it's mostly a business. We're in it for the money, not the fucking honor. I surround myself with people who are valuable. I don't give a fuck whether someone isn't one hundred percent Italian.

I grab another slice of pizza and carelessly tear into it with my teeth as that girl pops into my head again. It just galls me that someone might discriminate against me, of all people. All week I couldn't get that cunt out of my mind. Can't forget the way she let me fuck her. The screams she made when she came on my dick. All week I've been waiting to bump into her in that bar, like some schmuck.

Whatever. I'll find a new piece of ass to fuck. I always do. Hell, even in this restaurant. Women turn their heads to look at me, sitting with a few of my soldiers. I could ask the waitress out. She has a nice ass.

Not as nice as hers.

I swallow painfully as that truth sinks in. How can I forget her? I spanked her ass right before I sank my dick into her. Before that, she climbed into my lap naked. I can still feel her skin gliding in my palms. Her gorgeous curves bounced in front of my face. She let me put my hands all over her—she let me do things to her that I only did with hired pussy.

I smile into my wineglass as blood rushes to my cock. Fucking hell, I cannot get hard in this place.

"François, we need to head up to Sorel-Tracy. There were problems with the last shipment."

His face twists slightly, but he nods. He hates bikers on principle. Hell, we all do, but we don't have to like each other. We just have to work together.

They run all the drugs, and I handle just about everything else because I never wanted to be involved in drugs. I facilitate the shipments, and the bikers sell the drugs on the streets. Getting twenty-five years for possession is not worth it to me. Anyone in my crew caught selling drugs gets his head chopped off.

I get up from the table and my bodyguards follow me outside. I slide into the passenger seat of my car as François takes the wheel, and my thoughts linger on a certain brunette as he drives. Finally we get to that concrete shit-hole of a fortress that is like a beacon should the CSIS ever decide to raid the place. The walls are thick, and guards patrol the towers with guns.

François lays on the horn and the metal gate screams as it swings aside.

"Putain de merde."

Carlos waits just inside the community, wearing his filthy leather jacket. We roll the car into a dirt parking lot and I open my door, fixing a smile on my face.

"Carlos, good to see you."

"John."

He nods at me, and then we walk toward that shack he calls a clubhouse. I'll have to wipe the dust from my shoes when I get out of here. I walk past a lot of sullen, drawn faces. Like dogs at the pound. What a depressing place to live in.

The clubhouse has a bit of charm. Inside, there are strippers wearing pasties, gyrating on poles as those bearded fucks ogle them. Loud rock music grates against my ears. A biker grabs a passing stripper and pulls her onto his lap, groping her tits for everyone to see. I sneer at them as I walk by. These people have no fucking class. I don't want to touch any surface, because I have a suspicion that the entire place is covered with a film of cum and pussy juice.

Thankfully we enter Carlos's office, and my bodyguards wait outside. He walks behind his desk and my eyes wander over the dusty room, passing over a couple of golden frames. A figure catches my eye.

My heart jumps in my chest and I lean in, studying the picture frame. It's a photo of Carlos, and his wife and daughter.

So? What's got me so excited?

The daughter. The picture is a few years old, but there's no mistaking those pouty lips and haughty eyes. Maya. The girl I've been fantasizing about is also the daughter of the president of Les Diables MC.

Oh fuck.

My heart races and I swallow the urge to curse out loud. Everything makes sense now. Her hesitation to fuck me. No wonder.

And she had no idea who I was the whole time. She said her dad would be pissed. No fucking kidding. This could start a war.

Fuck me.

I lean back into my chair as Carlos gives me a sharp glance. "What's funny?"

I look into his suspicious eyes, wishing I could tell him:

I fucked your daughter.

MAYA

"Pick up every last piece, you little bitch."

On my hands and knees, I look up at the man who stirs a flash of rage in my chest.

You fucking pick it up.

I don't dare say it out loud, not when his men surround him and he looks as though he might knock out my teeth if I say something wrong.

But I want to take the pile of broken mirror shards in my hand and fling it into his face.

"I don't know what the fuck is your problem. I try to support your hobbies, and you pay me back by trashing your salon?"

The edges of the mirror shards cut into my palm as he kicks aside one of the broken pieces.

"It's not a fucking hobby. It's going to be my career."

Deep laughter cuts into me, his bright eyes lit with malevolence. "A career? You want to make a living out of cutting people's hair?"

"I should sell dope to kids instead?"

Screw him, acting as though he's fucking better than me when everyone knows about the drugs in schools.

I stand up and toss the shards in the garbage bin, turning my back on Dad. He grips my shoulder and the air squeezes from my chest when he shoves me against the wall.

"Who the fuck makes sure you have clothes on your back? Food in your stomach? Me. I don't want to hear you bitching about how I make a living."

His arm crushes my throat and I dig my nails into his arm. He's not going to kill me. I know that. He just wants to scare me.

You don't scare me, Dad.

"Carlos, enough."

Mom's voice cracks across the converted garage and I hear the sound of her boots snapping the broken fragments.

He releases me, and I breathe hard through my nose, never looking away from him. "You're done at that coffee place," he seethes.

The bottom drops out of my stomach.

It's my one refuge. The one place I feel normal. It's much more than just a job. It's a ticket to my freedom. I can't just give it up.

"I'm not quitting."

"Then I'll go down there and I'll quit for you, and my way won't be nearly as nice as yours."

A boiling pressure builds up behind my eyes. "You can't keep me locked up like some slave!"

"Carlos, maybe she could work there once a week."

Once a week? That's not nearly enough hours to get out of this fucking place.

"Fuck that!"

His face whitens with rage. "One more word out of your fucking mouth and I'll make you wish you'd never been born."

But I already wish that.

"You're quitting the job. Today."

He took away my freedom to date men, and now he's taking away my right to earn a living. It's too much. Tears sting my eyes, and I look away from him. *Don't fucking cry. Smash his face in, instead.* God, I really want to. He walks out of the garage, turning his head around to give me a final smirk.

And that sets me off.

With my mother watching, I take the garbage can in both hands and scream, hurling the can across the garage as all the mess slides over the room. Then I pick it back up and bash the metal against the heavy sinks. It's like a loud gong, crashing against my ears. *BANG. BANG. BANG.* I trash it until there are heavy dents in the cheap metal, and then I hurl it to the floor.

"WHAT THE FUCK ARE YOU DOING?"

Mom screams at me, her hands wrapping around my arms. I whirl around and yell at her furious face.

"I don't care! He's taken everything away from me!"

"Clean this shit up!"

"Fuck that."

I walk quickly out of the garage, my face burning as my eyes immediately seek out the gate. The tall bars seem to touch the sky from where I stand, and then I realize that in all probability, I'll never, ever leave this place.

"Hey, Maya. What's wrong?"

A timid female voice snaps me out of my trance and I quickly wipe my face when Beatrice steps in front of me, her eyebrows knitting together.

"Nothing. I'm fine."

It wouldn't do to spill my guts to my cousin. If Dad leaned on her just a little, she would blab about everything that happened in the bar.

She opens her mouth, but I quickly silence her. "I don't want to talk about it, Bea."

"I was just wondering if I could have my lights done."

"Yeah, okay."

What the fuck else is there to do?

She follows me back into the garage, where my mom is sweeping up the bits of broken glass. A stab of guilt hits my chest as I watch her, and Beatrice lets out an audible gasp.

"What the fuck happened?"

Mom glares at me as I lead her into the garage and use a rag to wipe the salon chair free of glass.

"Mom, I'll clean it up."

Dark eyes glittering, she sets aside the broom and gives me a tired sigh. "Come here, sweetheart."

My insides clench painfully as I leave Beatrice's side and join my mother's, whose arms are so firmly crossed that I think it would take a crowbar to uncross them.

"Mom—"

"You have to stop talking to him like that. You're never going to get what you want by fighting with him."

I gape at her. "He doesn't want me to do anything. Just sit here and watch after the kids and waste my life—"

Her eyes flare. "Like me?"

That's not fair. "You wanted this. I don't."

She tosses her dark hair and closes her eyes as if in pain. "Do what he says. He'd ease up if you actually listened to him."

But I don't want to listen to him. I'm twenty-two, a grown woman, for God's sake, and I have my own dreams. My own desires. And he's determined to block me from all of them.

"You have no choice. Look at who your father is."

Must I always live under his fucking shadow?

"I don't give a shit."

She lets out another sigh, brushing past me as she raises her manicured hands to her temple.

I turn back toward Beatrice, who smiles at me expectantly, and I force my muscles to return the smile.

More than anything, I want to be alone to think about him. A smile hitches on my face as I comb through Beatrice's hair. He was way too damn handsome and incredible in the sack. More surprising was my willingness to follow his orders like a goddamn slave. Do this. Do that. It made my blood boil, but there was something irresistible about the authority in his voice. I couldn't help but listen to him. I mean, Jesus, he put his mouth on my pussy and sucked me. Fuck, I can still feel his tongue lapping at my clit, his breath like steam on my pussy. I let him come inside me.

A small twist of fear drains the blood from my face. It was stupid of me. I wasn't thinking. But I can't deny how fucking amazing it felt to have him fill me up with his seed, his hands owning me, running over my body's curves and squeezing as if I was irresistible. He called me things that made me soar. Gorgeous. Beautiful. The fucking nasty shit he said—I loved that, too.

I folded the card he gave me into fours, but never looked at it. I just stuck it in my jeans pocket, and I run my fingers over the coarse edges whenever I feel like calling him.

There's no future with that guy.

A heavy wave hits me. My hands tremble and I'm suddenly glad there's no mirror, so that Beatrice can't see my eyes burning with unshed tears.

"I'm going out with him. Paul."

I can tell that she's been dying to tell me since the moment she saw me. "Oh, cool. When?"

"Geez, don't sound so excited."

"Sorry, I'm just in a bad mood right now."

"We're going out to the city tonight. That's why I wanted to do my lights."

Jealousy burns inside me like the glowing embers of a still-hot fire. "That's great."

Beatrice gives me another weird look, but I'm in no mood to act cheerful for anyone.

* * *

The smell of coffee beans saturates the air, burning my nose. I wipe down tables with my wet rag, content to just ignore the customers and fill the little sugar things while my mind lingers over Johnny's lips. Johnny's tattooed, lean body warm against mine. Johnny's dick.

116

A man looks up at me from the book he's reading, and I blush hard as if he's caught me thinking nasty things.

"Maya, I heard it's your last day!"

One of my coworkers, a sweet younger girl, bounces up to me.

"Yeah."

"You have to come out with us for a drink or something. I can't believe you're leaving."

I ball the wet rag in my fist as a sudden pain hits me. Oh God, I'm about to cry.

"I—I can't. I have to go back home."

Her face falls comically. "You can't have one drink?"

I bite my lip suddenly as I consider walking past that bar. His bar. No, I can't. We messed around once, and that's that.

"Sorry."

I turn my back on her, unable to stomach the look of disappointment and my own sinking feelings. It galls me that that fucker has so much say in my life, the man I'm supposed to call Daddy.

The door opens, swinging wide as a man in slacks steps inside, his leather shoes gleaming against the floor. I'm still bent over the table, so I don't see his face. I'm working as slowly as I can. Fucking savoring the last drop of freedom.

"*Jesus*, look at that guy."

117

I raise my head at the sound of her awed voice and my heart stalls in my chest because only one guy I know of looks that good in a suit.

Johnny.

"Oh my God, he's looking at you."

A slow grin staggers across his devilishly handsome face. He wears a blue pinstripe suit, looking as immaculate as he did in the bar. He slips his phone in his jacket pocket, looking unsurprised to see me here.

What the fuck?

Amy gives me a very curious look. "Why's he gawking at you like that?"

"Like what?" I can barely hear what she's saying. He's a dream. This can't be real.

"Like he's seen you naked." An excited gasp leaves her throat. "Do you know him?"

Before I can utter a word to make her shut up, Johnny takes a couple strides and joins my side. He's close enough to breathe in, and I smell freshly laundered clothes and the shampoo on his hair. He's way too clean, and I probably smell like coffee grounds. It's embarrassing, him seeing me here like this.

Amy slinks away to gawk at us behind the counter, flashing me a grin when I catch her gaze.

"How the fuck did you find me?" I mutter.

118

"Maybe when you left my apartment, I made sure we'd bump into each other."

My skin burns when he grabs my waist, and I'm pretty sure I've lost the ability to breathe, because my chest is paralyzed. I summon every ounce of indignation I have, but he's holding my waist. I feel the warmth of his hands through my t-shirt, and then he squeezes. God, I remember him doing that when we were naked.

Holy fuck, don't think of that now.

"You had me followed?"

"You didn't give me a choice, sweetheart. You never called."

"And now what?"

His voice deepens. "I want you to come home with me."

Another hard thump of my heart against my ribs makes me dizzy.

"You want me again?"

A little laugh shakes from his chest, and then he swallows it to give me a look that makes me hot all over. "Of course I want you again. That's why I gave you my card."

I'm surprised and flattered that he actually tracked me down. He took the time to find out where I worked, when he could have easily found someone else.

I take his hands from my waist to push him away from me, but he twists his grip so that he's holding my hand in his. Then he raises it to his lips and kisses my skin.

Intense heat rushes exactly where he kisses me, until I think that my face must be on fire. With a dark look thrown my way, he takes my elbows and yanks me into his chest.

"You have some balls. You know who my father is?"

Amusement twinkles in his eyes. "Yeah. And maybe I don't give a fuck."

What?

The confidence in his voice *stuns* me. It's like a club to my head. Logic tells me that he must be brazen or stupid, but I don't know. He's so fucking sure of himself.

Either way, it makes my panties soak in an instant.

"You're in the Mafia," I hiss back.

"I thought I was just a bar owner," he says, smirking.

He looks even hotter with that shit-eating grin.

Then, as if he expects it, as if he knows I'm just inwardly begging for him to do it, he lowers his head and catches my mouth in his. My heart rams against my chest as his lips touch mine, the kiss deepening as he clenches the back of my neck. He's softer than I've ever felt him, but then I feel his tongue, and then I remember that we're right in the middle of a fucking café.

Good thing I'm quitting.

Johnny pulls back with a primal growl in the back of his throat, looking as though he'd quite like to strip me down right in the café.

"How about it? Do you want another night—"

"—Shh—"

"—Where you scream my name as you come on my cock?" He just laughs at me when I pound his chest. "Come on. I'll take you out."

God, I can't fucking stand it even though I know it's wrong. He's wrong. I want him. Every cell in my body screams for him.

"We're a disaster waiting to happen. If my father finds out—"

"I'm not afraid of your father."

Sold.

I don't know what kind of drugs he's on, but if he doesn't give a shit about the risk he's taking, why should I?

I leave the rag on the table as I take his hand, my spirits so high that I could probably fly if I jumped in the air. There's a car waiting out front, and he opens the passenger door for me, my skin heating when he slides in next to me. I don't know why, but I feel fucking nervous locked in the car with him.

"I can't believe you're not pissed off about my dad."

Johnny shrugs as he slides his arm around my shoulders and draws me closer. I feel his breath on my face and I know that if I turn my head, he'll kiss me.

"I was pissed before, but now I understand."

Fucking slick bastard will say anything to get into my pants.

He hooks his hand around my thigh and an electrical shock runs straight to my pussy as he tilts my face toward his with just a finger under my jaw.

It was inevitable once I felt his hands on me. The spark between us is undeniable. Like flesh on flame, like tongue on steel. His lips crush mine as the stubble on his cheek scratches my skin. My heart pounds when he pulls back slightly to look at me with unbridled lust. I've never been with a man like this. He swallows my gasps as he kisses me again, grabbing my tits through my shirt. His thumb moves roughly over my peaked nipple as a wave of heat rolls over my chest.

I yank his lapels and feel the heat emanating from his skin. I palm his chest, sliding down his tie as his tongue dazzles my mouth. His tongue slipped inside my pussy that night. That's all I can think of as he kisses me. My hand settles in his lap, the burning heat now a raging forest fire. I grab his cock, which stiffens in my grip. Johnny digs his fingers in my hair as he rests his forehead against mine, a low growl rumbling from his chest.

I love that.

The car stops and Johnny pulls away from me, adjusting his cock so that his raging hard-on is not so obvious. My mouth waters as I look at it. He gives me a wink as the driver opens the door, and then I realize how fucked up my hair must be.

Oh shit.

He stopped us in front of small café: *Momesso*. Italian sausage sandwiches.

I press my lips into a firm line as laughter builds up inside my chest. This must be his idea of a joke.

"What, we're going to eat here?"

"That's the idea."

"Italian sausage? Is this a joke?"

He looks at me, smiling. "They make really good sandwiches."

I don't know. I look around the parking lot for a hint of chrome, because if one of my father's people saw me with an Italian—

"Relax. We won't be seen."

He holds the glass door open for me with a smile and I walk inside as my stomach clenches over and over. I'm already condemned.

Johnny's suit clashes horribly with the interior. It's an

ordinary-looking café, with plastic tables and chairs. Nothing special. Johnny wraps an arm around my waist and bends his head to my ear.

"Go get us a table."

I turn around to see the whole fucking establishment staring at me. Their eyes drop when I catch them, my heart pounding louder than ever.

That's fucking it. I'm Googling him when I get home.

I don't know who the fuck he is, but obviously he's someone important. High up in the family. I choose a table and watch the cash register. Johnny takes out his wallet and argues with the cashier, who waves his hands.

"Your money is no good here."

"I appreciate it."

"Of course, Mr. Cravotta."

Damn. That son of a bitch doesn't have to pay for anything.

Moments later he walks to our table with a sexy little smirk that makes my heart flip. He sits down across from me, and he looks at me as though I'm the meal even as the worker sets the plates of sandwiches down. The spicy smell of the Italian sausage, split in half in the toasted bun, makes a sudden, sharp pang of hunger hit me. I take it with my hands, but he picks up the plastic knife and fork and uses them to cut into the sandwich.

What a freak.

"So, what is this between us?"

He merely glances up at me. "It is what it is."

Well, that's a nonanswer.

"You know my dad would kill you if he found out about this, right?"

His smile widens and a stab of anxiety hits my chest.

"Oh, I doubt that very much."

I watch as he pops a piece of the sandwich into his mouth and chews, his eyes dancing with mirth.

What is he hiding?

"This is how it's going to be, hon. I want to keep fucking you, but you're right. Daddy can't know about us."

My jaw clenches shut and my teeth grind together in my head. "Would you *stop* calling him that?"

He grins back at me, and for a moment I'm perturbed by this guy's cavalier attitude. The Devils MC isn't a fucking joke. He seems to be under the delusion that he won't get hurt by my dad, and I can't figure out why. My chest freezes as I wonder what kind of motivation this guy could have for fucking around with the president's daughter. Is he trying to use me as leverage or something?

"You're not using me, are you?"

My voice comes out in a whisper, but he picks up what I said. Dark, intense eyes flash at me.

"What are you talking about?"

"Why else would you mess around with the president's daughter?"

A boyish grin lights up his face. "Because she's good at sucking cock, that's why."

"Don't talk to me like I'm some goddamn whore. I'm not one of your sluts that you fuck around with."

The amusement on his face doesn't falter. "It turns me on when you talk back to me like that."

What the fuck?

"*I don't care*. You treat me with the respect I deserve, or you can spend the night with your hand."

He sits back into his chair and cocks his head at me as though he's never seen anything quite like me. "Fair enough." Then his voice deepens. "Although, a part of me thinks that you actually like the way I talk to you. I think it's just your pride telling you that I shouldn't talk to you like this."

I can feel sweat beading over my skin as he stares at me as though he can see through my proud disguise. Deep down, I'm fucking scared that he's right. That I enjoy every filthy word that flies out of his mouth, no matter how insulting it seems. Why does that scare me so much?

He suddenly reaches across the table and just grazes his fingertips over my hand. I clench it into a fist, hating the way my body responds to him.

A sweet smile widens his face as keeps looking at me. "I don't think you're a whore. I think you're beautiful."

I inhale a sharp breath as he shrugs with an apologetic smile that makes me want to leap across the table and tackle him. *Damn it*, he's a master at seduction. He knows what to say, and exactly when to say it. Like a politician. He should be eating out of my hand. That's what I'm used to.

I don't know how to handle him.

Fuck, at this point it's clear that he's the one handling me.

He clears his throat. "Let's go."

* * *

His lips touch the back of my neck, and I feel my skin prickling into a row of goose bumps. My world is black, but I feel him. Taste him. Hear him sigh as he pushes my hair to the side. My body pulses with need, every surface of me aching to be touched.

"I've thought about you all week."

Deft fingers touch my shoulders and then slide down my arms. Christ, how does he make everything feel so goddamn erotic?

"It's not like me to get obsessed over pussy. Put your hands behind your head."

I do as he says, feeling that wonderful release as I follow his commands. The cool air makes my nipples contract, but he makes me burn. His palm touches my stomach, and I suck in surprise. Another hand gropes my breast, gently massaging. The ache grows between my legs like a fever. I feel hot and delirious.

The hand on my stomach dips down, and down. Excitement ramps up in my chest, and then he slides a finger down my clit, tutting in my ear.

"So fucking wet for me. You must have it bad for me, huh?"

The slightly mocking tone makes blood rush to my cheeks. "You going to talk all night, or are you going to actually fuck me?"

I wait for the swift blow of a slap, but all I feel is his sigh on my shoulder. "I think I've a solution to your smart mouth."

Rough fabric suddenly presses against my lips, and a musky smell invades my nostrils. Is that my fucking underwear? I open my mouth, protesting, and he shoves it inside, clapping his hand over my mouth.

"Hold fucking still while I gag you."

The terrifying sound of duct tape makes me jump, and then I hear it tear. A sticky substance presses against my skin when he uncovers my mouth and slides it over my lips. He traces them with his fingers and I groan against the duct tape.

"You want me to fuck you? Tell me."

Jackass.

Nothing escapes my mouth except for muffled groans. I can just imagine the grin on his face.

The warmth of his body disappears for a moment when I hear metal clinking together, and he grabs my arms so that they link behind my back. Then he locks the cuffs around my wrists. The coolness of the metal bites into my skin. He yanks the links, and I fall back against his chest. My handcuffed wrists find his thigh, and then slide up his muscled legs to his rock-hard cock.

The fabric that I'm sure is my underwear slowly soaks with my saliva.

"You see how fucking hard you make me? It's a *sin*, what you do to me."

Whatever the fuck that means.

His breathing quickens as his voice deepens into a growl, and his grip becomes biting. He shoves me forward and I land on the mattress. Naked, blind, and mute. His body quickly follows, the fabric rough against my skin. I want him so fucking bad. My legs slide on either side of his body, my hands uncomfortable behind my back, but I don't care about the pain. I care about the ache pounding through my pussy.

I hear the sound of his belt unlooping from his slacks and his pants hitting the floor. Then I feel his body sinking into the mattress, his bare skin pressing against my legs. His cock lies flat against my pussy. I buck against him. Feeling that hardness so close to me is torture. The ache screams for him to adjust his length slightly and drive deep inside me.

"You want it so fucking badly."

With a small chuckle, he adjusts his cock, and I groan into my gag as he barely pushes through, teasing me with his head. His hands scrabble at my ears and suddenly the world explodes with light. Johnny's mocking face hangs over mine. He gently pulses in and out of me, only burying the head of his cock inside me. It's fucking maddening.

More, I want more!

"I want to see you."

I use the backs of my heels to dig into his bare ass, but he shakes his head, refusing to budge. His cock teases my pussy, but I'm sure it's torture for him, too. His lips shake as he moves his hips and stops for a moment to stroke my tits. Bending his head, he takes my nipple in his mouth and bites down hard. It's a sharp pain, but then he draws a circle with his tongue and it's as though he's doused my ache in gasoline. I feel it fucking burning, and then his hips jerk and his bulge moves inside me. Not quite enough to make me satisfied.

"Tell me you want me."

I give him a furious look as I twist my hands behind my back. I can't say a fucking word and he knows it. I try to say it anyway, and it comes out as muffled nonsense. He laughs.

I feel as though my gasp almost hits the air when he suddenly wrenches back my body and impales me with his cock. His whole throbbing length drives into me all the way until he's balls deep. Then he hammers me. My breath is knocked out.

I'm trying to gasp, but there's a gag in my mouth so I breathe hard through my nose as my heart jackknifes into my chest. His hips slam against mine, and he nudges hard, burying that cock as deep as it'll go. He swells inside me and I'm overwhelmed by the sensations. His lips shake with the energy of holding himself back.

"You're *mine*."

I look into his frenzied eyes for a moment before he buries himself deep inside me again.

Holy *shit*.

I moan hard into the duct tape, my hands screaming with pain as he nails me against the bed. He hoists my legs over his shoulders and looks down at his cock. *Bam. Bam.*

Bam. He keeps hitting me so fucking hard that I feel the jolt in my stomach. The pleasure ramps up, and my breathing quickens, and I want to touch him, but I can't.

"I want your mouth. I want to come inside that smart mouth."

And he rips off the duct tape, wiping the saliva from my mouth as he takes my soaked panties and throws them aside. His lips crush against mine as his hips thrust, and I'm taken to a new high. I can't take it anymore.

"Come for me, baby." He whispers it against my lips.

"Fuck me harder!"

His arms wrap around my shoulders and he thrusts with his whole body, pounding my cunt so hard that I scream into the air. I jerk my hands against the cuffs as I feel the wave hit me.

"*Johnny!*"

He knows. He feels my pussy gripping his cock, and then he pulls out and hoists himself so that he's straddling my face. I open my mouth and he slides over my tongue, gripping my hair as he fucks me. Deep moans echo in the room as he gets closer, throbbing inside my throat. Then I feel his gasps shudder into a long, drawn-out moan, and his cock hits the back of my throat.

"Oh *fuck.*"

Warm saltiness fills my mouth as he comes. A thrill

shoots into my chest as I feel his legs shake, and the possibility that I make this powerful man vulnerable. I swallow his cum as he sighs, smoothing my hair over my head. He pulls out of my lips, and I lick them, savoring his taste. Something between a groan and laugh shakes from his chest as he lies down beside me.

"You're too fucking good."

My face twists. "Johnny, my hands."

Smiling, he pulls my body over his and grabs the key on the nightstand, unlocking my hands. I put them on either side of his head, and he kisses the faint pink line on my wrist. A swooping feeling makes me weak. I touch his face, sliding my hands through his thick, dark hair, and finally his restless gaze falls on mine.

"You're sexy as hell."

A pang hits me.

Why couldn't he have been an asshole?

It hurts because I want him again, but it's never going to happen. Not now that I've lost my job and the only freedom I had.

"I can't see you again."

He rolls his eyes. "Sure, whatever."

"I mean it."

"You've said that before." He grins. "And look where you are now. Hell, I can't blame you. I know I'm hot shit."

"I can't leave the compound anymore. He made me quit that job and there's no way he'll allow me to leave for hours anymore without getting followed."

A shadow crosses his face. "Your dad's a real *prick*. No offense," he tacks on quickly.

None taken.

I lower my body into his arms and lay my head over his chest, closing my eyes. His steady heartbeat pulses into my ear. I should leave, but a voice inside me keeps saying: *Just a little longer.*

A heavy arm wraps around my back and I relish the feeling of being held, that afterglow of sex when you've been fucked into exhaustion.

I shouldn't have to live up to anyone's standards but my own.

"We'll figure something out. I'm having way too much fun with you to give up that easily."

Johnny's voice is filled with confidence, but I just don't feel it this time.

It's over.

* * *

It's for the best.

Isn't that what people say when something they really want gets ripped away from them? *It's for the best.* We were a ticking time bomb. Dad was bound to find out, and when he did, Johnny would be dead. So it's for the best, really.

I sit in one of the booths in the clubhouse, too lonely to just waste away in my room, but angry enough to avoid conversation with anyone. Another week of playing with Johnny's card, folding it and unfolding it so many times that it's about to fall apart. Dad has me watched day and night. I can't go to the fucking store without a goddamn chaperone now.

No, it's not for the fucking best because if "the best" means surviving in here, I don't want to survive. I want to *live*. Fucking that mobster, however wrong it might be, made me feel alive.

The TV blares with some news story, and the vice-president's voice roars at it.

"Change the fucking channel. I don't want to look at that fucking *wop*."

I look at the bright TV screen and see a handsome, dark-haired man who looks a hell of a lot like Johnny.

"*Reputed mob boss Johnny Cravotta was sighted attending a charity dinner yesterday. He was seen entering* La Ciccia *at seven pm last evening.*"

The image flicks away as someone changes the channel, and I grip the edge of the table and fight everything inside me to scream to change it back.

He's the boss of the Cravotta Crime Family.

I fucked a boss.

Oh Jesus. *Oh my fucking God.* And he knew! He knew who I was and went after me anyway. No wonder he wasn't worried about getting caught. He's only the guy who my father worked with for fucking years. He has Dad under his thumb, just like everyone in the city.

And I didn't put two and two together.

I feel faint. I feel like I'm going to throw up.

I stand up, legs shaking, and head for my room, avoiding everybody's face.

The things I said to him. I was so disrespectful. If I had known who he was, I would have *never* approached him. Jesus, what was I thinking? He must have thought I was so cute, having no fucking clue who he was.

As soon as I'm inside my room, I burst into mad laughter.

I didn't just fuck a boss. I fucked the boss of Montreal. The most powerful man in the city, and I didn't recognize him. To be fair, I've never seen him before. I try to avoid anything related to my father.

God, I'm such an idiot. I feel so stupid.

Now you really *can't see him again.*

If it was any other guy, Dad would throw a fucking fit, but this goes beyond anything he'd tolerate. He'd take it as a personal insult.

The mattress squeaks as I sit down, twisting my hands in my lap. Another pressing worry makes my stomach twist in knots.

It's been a week since I've seen him.

My period is a week late. It's fine, really. Happens sometimes. Right? Then I think about the first night we were together, a week before the last time I saw him. We didn't use a condom.

I rise from the bed so quickly that blood rushes to my head and blackness overcomes my vision. Color pricks back into my view as I take deep, shuddering breaths.

It was only once.

It only takes one time, idiot.

I have to find out. *Now.*

My footsteps seem oddly loud as I leave my room and head toward the stockroom where we store all our pharmacy supplies. I keep my head down, as if maintaining eye contact with anyone would spill the fact that I fucked the boss of our biggest fucking rival. Everyone would loathe me if this got out. It'd be considered a betrayal.

I burst into the small pharmacy, which is manned by a sweet but inconveniently sharp woman. She smiles at me behind a small desk.

"I've a headache."

"All right, well, help yourself. The Tylenol is in the back."

I head in that direction while keeping my eyes peeled for pregnancy tests on the shelves. My eyes scour the rows, and then I see them a few rows behind the Tylenol next to all the condoms. Goddamn.

I pretend to search for the pills, and then look over my shoulder at her. Her gaze is fixed on me.

"I can't find—oh, shit."

My arm sweeps aside a dozen or so pregnancy tests to the floor, and I stuff two of them in my jacket before I shove the boxes back on the shelf. Shit, she's going to see where I was searching. Her chair scrapes the floor.

"Did you find it?"

I pretend to be replacing the toothbrushes just as she sweeps behind me. My arm pins to my side, crushing the pregnancy tests to my body. They can't fucking fall.

"They're over here." She leads me to the Tylenol and pops open a bottle for me.

"I'll just take two. Thanks."

I pop them in my mouth. I'll probably need them anyway.

"Do you want water? You don't look so good, hon."

I'm fucking fine, except for the fact that I fucked a mob boss and I might be pregnant with his kid.

"Yeah, okay."

Because I can't just swallow two pills without choking, I take the paper cup in my hands and tip the water down my throat. Some of it splashes over my lips. She takes the cup from me with a scandalized look.

"Thanks."

Good god, I must look so goddamn suspicious.

I see her walking toward the shelf I was searching as I leave, and my heart seizes.

One crisis at a time.

At this fucking place, there's no such thing as privacy. Communal bathrooms, showers, everything for those of us who aren't married. Couples get mobile homes with all of that shit. Even the president's daughter has to take a piss in the midst of ten other women gossiping about shit in the bathroom.

I squeeze into a stall and sit down on the toilet seat, trying to keep my legs from shaking. The girls saw me come into the bathroom. They can't fucking know that I'm taking pregnancy tests. I open my jacket.

I watch one of the tests slip from my hands to fall to the floor, faceup with the brazen logo.

FUCK!

The sound of the cardboard hitting the tiles grates against my ears. It's so fucking loud. My hand snatches the box immediately and I pray that they didn't fucking look at it. The voices in the bathroom simmer down and I crush the box in my hands, feeling a slow burn on my cheeks. There's a nervous giggle, and then the talk resumes.

I balance one of the tests on the toilet paper holder and carefully unwrap the other one. Fuck. It's so goddamn loud. I flush the toilet and rip the cardboard box, tearing the plastic with my teeth before dumping it in the toilet.

Okay. Just pee on the thing and it'll be fine.

I take the test and grit my teeth as I balance it on the tampon disposal, grabbing the other box. Fucking hell, now I have the same problem.

I hate this place.

The toilet's noisy flush covers the sound of me tearing the second box apart, and then I take the second test.

Now what? Do I wait here, or do I head back to my room?

I could stay here and feign an upset stomach, or I could retreat to my room where anyone could burst in at any second and see the tests lying there, plain as day.

Fuck it, I'll wait.

The minutes tick by slowly as I pick up both tests and stare at the little windows.

Please, God. Let me not be fucking pregnant.

Then it happens. Faint pink lines hover over the

window like a shadow, becoming more and more clear. Two ungodly pink pluses. Two positive tests.

Just my fucking luck.

It's hard to breathe now. I have to bite down on my fist to keep myself from crying out.

I fucked a mob boss and I'm pregnant with his kid.

Oh yeah, I'm screwed.

JOHNNY

Le Zinc is probably my most frequent haunt. It's one of my favorite restaurants, and it should be, considering I hired the kitchen staff. Good food is important to me, and that's why this place is fucking packed. They come to this restaurant in droves. I can't blame them. Everything is streamlined. Modern. The food is great. You can smoke. You can bring your own wine.

But some don't come for the great food or the service. They're tourists. They watch an episode of *Sopranos* or they read the *Montreal Gazette*, and they know that this is a connected joint. Fucking Hollywood. What a joke.

Anyway, one of those assholes sits in the restaurant with a baseball cap. *A fucking baseball cap.* And he holds his smartphone in my direction.

I'm trying to have a meeting with my captains in this place, and that jerk-off is taking pictures of me. With that fucking baseball cap on his stupid head.

It's disrespectful.

"Hold on a second." I interrupt François with a hand as I stand up from the booth, smooth over my suit, and walk in the direction of that jackass.

KNOCKED UP BY THE BAD BOY

His head perks up as he sees me coming, frowning at me. I can just imagine what I must look like to this prick. When I reach his table, I grit my teeth in an attempt to smile.

Do not make a fucking scene. Be polite.

"Excuse me." That probably never sounded so hostile. "Take off the hat, please."

His mouth opens stupidly. "It's my hat, and I'll wear it if I want."

How is this moron still breathing?

"Don't be a jerk. This is a nice restaurant."

Our eyes meet for a tense moment and for a minute I think he's going to back down, but then he shakes his head. The veins in my head are about to pop.

I reach up and cuff the side of his head. It flies off and flutters to the ground.

"What the fuck?"

The other diners look up from their meals at the sound of the commotion, and then Shit For Brains stands up with his fists raised.

"Don't touch me!"

Cute.

"Get out of my fucking restaurant."

Before I drag you out the back and beat the shit out of you.

He obviously has no idea who I am, but his friend

does. He gets up from the table and yanks Shit For Brains' arm. "That's Johnny Cravotta."

"Oh."

I almost want to laugh at his wide, horrified eyes, and the way his whole body deflates. He puts his hands behind his back and his shoulders slump, almost as if he's bowing.

"I'm sorry, sir. I didn't know who you were."

"Get the fuck out."

He nods and bends down for the hat, but I step on it, viciously grinding all the dirt and shit from the sidewalks on that fucker's hat. Then I step back.

"There's your fucking hat. Now get out."

His eyes splinter with a flash of resentment, and he hesitates near my feet. I have to hold myself back, but the cool fire inside me recedes when he puts that fucking dirty cap on his head and walks out like a beaten dog. I reach into my pocket and throw money on the table for the waitress, and then I walk back to my captains, who give me appreciative smirks.

People who know me say I'm cruel, but everything I do is necessary. Even humiliating that dumb fuck in my restaurant. I need to set a precedent. I am *always* being watched. And I am always watching *them*. I learned that from my father.

Prick.

I sit back down at the table without a fuss, and we continue our meeting, but my mind is elsewhere.

"What about the bikers?"

The question snaps me in two. "What?"

"*Les Diables*. Shouldn't we give them a taste?"

My hackles settle down and I lean back into my chair. "I told Carlos that the airport was off limits. That's all he needs to know. I'm not giving him a cent. It's our fucking territory."

François shifts in his seat, looking uncomfortable. "He has people working for him at the airport. I don't know, John."

He has the gall to question me in front of all my captains.

"I didn't ask for your fucking opinion."

The men around the table go quiet as François sits back, looking subdued.

"All due respect, John, he has a point."

My consigliere Sal mutters in my ear as blood pounds in my head. I'm not giving that fucking asshole a penny. If they knew how prejudiced he was against Italians, they'd be on my side.

"There are two kinds of heists. Ones where there are no witnesses, and ones where everybody gets caught." I grind my cigarette into the ashtray. "I don't trust bikers.

145

Not even to pay them off. They stay in the fucking dark."

My capos nod at me and my eyes sweep the restaurant. Over their heads I see something that almost gives me a heart attack.

Maya stands in the foyer, looking more than a little lost. I can make out her fantastic ass from over here, because her black jeans wrap around her like a second skin. She doesn't call me in a fucking week, and then she just decides to show up like this? Where any of her father's people can see her?

Christ, I don't need this right now.

But I can't pretend it doesn't give my ego a boost to see her wave off the hostess and march toward my table. Male heads turn as she walks past tables. She wears a slight frown as the guards stop her before she gets to me. And I wave them away. My captains glance at her. And then they look again. My mood lifts to the sky.

Yeah, that's the girl I'm fucking.

"Well, look who's here. I guess this means you finally figured out I'm not a bar owner."

"Oh, *Maddon!*"

A chorus of laughter erupts around me as Maya takes a timid step forward, her eyes dark with eyeliner. She wears a white tank top that puts her tits on display, and I think I can make out one of the bruises I gave her with my teeth, still yellow on her skin.

Down, boy.

"*We need to talk.*"

I raise an eyebrow as the guys seated around me give me knowing smirks, because that's basically code for, I'm pissed off.

"This isn't the best time, hon."

She crosses her arms over her chest. "It's urgent."

I roll my eyes, but inwardly I'm uneasy. What made her desperate enough for her to come all the way here?

"All right. Guys, give me a couple minutes."

They stand up and scrape back their chairs as they move away. Maya shakes her head when I pat the seat next to me.

"We need to talk in private."

It has to be about her fucking father, right? Now I'm pissed off at myself for allowing this stupid affair to continue the moment I found out who she was. It was fucking risky. I'm endangering my relationship with *Les Diables*, but I couldn't help it. Just *had* to have her. Even now my blood pounds through my veins as if I've had too much wine. She has that effect on me.

"Okay, let's go into my office."

So that I can fuck your brains out.

I stand up from the booth, unable to tolerate another

147

second of being next to her and not touching her. I palm the small of her back, and she stiffens.

Goddamn it.

She knows who I am for *five fucking minutes*, and her attitude toward me does a 180-degree turn. It pisses me off. We walk past the kitchens, and then I open the door to the manager's office.

Maybe she's still down to fuck. It's the perfect place, really. I could bend her over the desk, or have her straddle me in my chair. I realize that I can see the outline of her bra against her tank top. My mouth is dry. Jesus Christ, this girl turns me on without even trying, but she doesn't look like she's in the mood.

Her whitened face turns toward me and she takes a big, shaking breath. "Okay, first of all, I'm sorry for everything I said. I didn't know who you were."

So that's what this is about?

She jumps when I grab the head of her chair, my hands on either side of her. Her nostrils flare and her pupils turn into pinpricks. I'm used to this. Used to people being fucking terrified of me, but I hate seeing it on her.

"*Stop.*"

"You have to believe that I wouldn't have said any of those things. Please, don't take it out on my father."

A sick feeling roils in my stomach. As much as it's

amusing to see the proud, shit-talking girl grovel at my feet, it's also—sad. "I liked you better when you didn't know who I was."

It's a fucking cold thing to say, but she doesn't flinch.

"Now get the fuck out of my office."

I'm sick and tired of meeting the same woman everywhere. I liked her when she talked back to me. It was so much more satisfying to win her submission from her, than to receive it immediately like a fucking tribute.

"No! I haven't even told you what I came to tell you."

"Well, fucking say it."

She opens and closes her mouth. "You—you should sit down."

Now she's got me keyed up. I don't like the way she's looking at me. It's as though she expects me to smack her around. A small shock runs through me when her eyes well with tears. They're like two dark pools. Tears streak down her face.

Jesus.

The energy goes out of my limbs. I sit down next to her and squeeze the back of her neck.

"*What is it?*"

But she just can't say it. She can't even look at me. Her hands cover her face and she shakes her head.

"What the fuck is it?"

Then she uncovers her face and shoves her hand through her purse. I'm bewildered at her antics. She grabs my palm and shoves something plastic in my hand.

"What the fuck is this?"

There are two of them. They're rectangular pieces of plastic with positive pink signs. They look like—

Oh fuck.

It feels as though I'm falling. There's no ground at my feet. The office doesn't exist. I can only see my shaking hand, holding those two pregnancy tests. Both of them positive.

"You're pregnant?"

"Yes."

"It's mine?"

Her voice seems to come from far away. "Yeah."

"You're sure?"

"Yes, I'm fucking sure. You're the only guy I've been with in years."

The tests tremble in my hand. I'm shaking. I *never* shake. I can count on my hand the times I've been afraid in my life, but nothing comes close to the threat of actually becoming a father.

"How the fuck did this happen?"

"We didn't use a condom that first time."

Oh Jesus. She's right. I was so worked up—we both

were—and I came inside her without wrapping my dick first.

Fucking moron.

"Does your father know?"

"Of course not!"

A look of terror flashes over her face. I can only imagine the shit storm that would cause. To hell with that. What am I going to do?

First, make sure she's actually pregnant. Maya doesn't come off as a crazy chick, but she could have easily swiped the tests from someone else.

I wouldn't even be angry if that's what happened.

"Come on. Let's go." I toss the tests in the trash and take her hand.

"Where are we going?"

"To get you tested by a doctor."

I'm barely quelling the panic building up inside me. I might have knocked up a girl I barely know, a girl who is the daughter of my strongest ally. He'll never forgive this. Jesus Christ, how could I be so fucking stupid?

I lead her back into the restaurant and my men look for me at once.

Be fucking cool.

"Chris, I need my car. I won't need a driver."

"'Course." Chris slips from his stool and sweeps away

without another word.

The rest of them give me curious looks that I ignore. Even though I'm the boss, this is the sort of gossip that would spread.

Johnny Cravotta knocked up the princess of *Les Diables*.

You don't know that for sure yet.

I grip her hand so tightly that I'm sure it's painful, but she doesn't make a sound until I lead her outside. The fear in her eyes makes my heart gallop.

"We don't know anything for sure, Maya."

She closes her eyes and two bitter tears squeeze from them. The wind almost takes them away, but I wipe them with my thumbs.

"I think it's pretty fucking certain."

Fuck.

"You can fucking panic when we get the actual results."

* * *

Fifteen minutes.

That's how long it takes for the results of a pregnancy test with ninety-nine percent accuracy.

I can't sit down and wait. I pace the small room as Maya sits on the bench in her paper gown. Even though there's only a thin piece of paper covering her naked body, I'm in no fucking mood.

She clenches her fists. "Will you stop pacing?"

I stop in my tracks and throw a glare at her. "Oh, so now you grow a pair of balls?"

"You're making it worse."

Maybe I'm being an asshole. I should be sitting down at her side, holding her hand or some shit. I don't fucking do the handholding shit. That's just never been one of my needs. I like to fuck, but I'm not affectionate.

As I stand there, though, the guilty feeling burns like acid. Like too much tequila sitting in an empty stomach. I can't just let her sit there alone.

Her lip trembles as I walk closer to her, and I lay my hand on her head. I bend my lips to her forehead and I kiss her. It levels out my nerves. She inhales a gasp as the door creaks open and even I dig my fingers in her hair, heart pounding.

The nurse walks in with a sheaf of paper, and in two seconds I rip it out of her hands.

"Sir, *excuse* me—!"

My eyes scan the massive sheet of text—

POSITIVE.

There it is in big, bold letters.

Maya stands up. "What the fuck does it say?" She grabs for the page, but I'm still holding on to it and she tears it in half.

The nurse clucks in disapproval. "I was going to tell you that yes, you're pregnant. Congratulations!"

A strange feeling goes through me as I keep staring at the piece of paper. I'm going to be a father. A father, for Christ's sake. This is what I wanted, isn't it?

And then a voice sighs in my head.

Finally.

Relief floods my veins. I've spent years chasing pussy after my two failed marriages, and a family is what I always wanted. This was never how I imagined it.

The sound of crumpling paper snaps me out of it. Maya inhales a huge gasp and hurls the paper from her, and then she breaks into loud sobs.

At least one of us is happy about this.

"I'll—er—leave you two—"

"Get the fuck out!"

I rake my fingers through my hair as Maya screams at the nurse, who gives her an extremely offended look.

Fuck. I'll pay her off, later.

The nurse slams the door behind her and I turn toward Maya. I step forward and she backs away, tears streaming down her face.

"No!"

I grab her before she can take another step and pull her into my arms. I smooth the back of her head as she finally gives in and slides her hands around my middle. Another throbbing stab of guilt hits me, and it's horrible because I rarely feel bad about the shit I do. This has got to be one of the worst things I've done. She's going to get so much shit.

"We have—we have to get an abortion."

I curl my fingers into her hair, suddenly hit by gut-wrenching nausea. It's what I've wanted—*for years*—and it's about to be ripped away from me.

I pull back from her. "*No.*"

"Why not? Give me one good reason why I should keep it?"

Her shrill voice rises to the ceiling, stabbing my ears as she glares at me.

"Because I want this baby."

"No, you don't."

"Yes, I do." My heart slams against my chest. "I'm older than you, sweetheart. This is something I've wanted for a long time, but I could never find the right girl."

She shakes her head, looking miserable. "I'm not the right girl."

"I don't care. You're pregnant with my kid, and I'm going to take care of you. I will support you."

"No, this is a disaster waiting to happen."

Something painful twists inside my chest.

"It doesn't have to be."

"I'm going to get an abortion. You can't stop me!"

That's right, *I can't*.

No matter what I say or do, she can do whatever the fuck she wants. It kills me, and the venom in her voice makes it worse. I'll fucking admit that it hurts me a little to hear that violent reaction from her.

Disaster.

A baby isn't a disaster. It's a gift.

Maya's hand reaches for my face and she touches my jaw. "I'm sorry, I didn't mean to—"

"Do you want this because the baby is mine? Or because you don't want kids?"

My hands tremble as I watch her open mouth, waiting for her answer.

"This isn't about you. He'll kill me. M-maybe if I say that someone else got me pregnant—"

"Are you trying to piss me off?"

"No!"

"I *will* be the baby's father. I am not going to fucking hide like a coward."

I push myself off from the wall, disgusted that she'd even suggest pinning the pregnancy on someone else. I'm no fucking coward.

"He'll never be okay with it if you're the father."

I clench my fists so hard that I can feel my nails digging into my palms. "We'll get engaged. We'll tell him together."

Her mouth drops open. "Are you *insane*?"

"I'm trying to save both our relationships with your father. Marrying you is the right thing to do. He'll be even more pissed if I don't take care of his daughter—"

"I'm not fucking marrying you. I don't even know you."

I'm not sure I even like you.

"I hate to break it to you, but that doesn't mean shit. You get a girl pregnant, you marry her. End of fucking story."

"What century do you live in?"

"The century where you are *fucked* without me."

She backs against the wall, her chest pulsing as I trace the edge of that stupid paper gown, following the neckline as my finger sweeps over the tops of her breasts.

Could I have let her go, even if she wasn't knocked up?

"That's not what everyone else does."

"You and me are not like everyone else."

A row of goose bumps spreads over her skin. I lean into her body, my cock stirring to life as her curves press against me. My lips find her neck and I kiss a hot trail, feeling her heartbeat. She sighs when I kiss the shell of her ear.

"Your dad is going to disown you when he finds out, and you'll have nowhere to go but my house. I won't let you in unless you agree to get engaged."

I soften my words with a kiss to her cheek. It blooms with color as she jerks her head to the side, away from my face.

"I'm not going to marry someone I barely know."

"You think I want to get married *again*? It's the way it is."

Her lip curls, and I take her jaw in my hand. "Face it, Maya. You belong to me now. You were your father's, and now you're mine."

My mouth falls on those pouting lips that swallowed my cum the other night, and I reach up to her neck where there's a little tear in her paper gown. The tear drives me nuts, and I yank it. It makes a loud, ripping sound, and I keep yanking until two ripped halves hang from her shoulders. The paper drapes over her tits, hiding her nipples. I see her thighs glistening, and then I tear the rest of her gown so that it falls into pieces on the ground.

I'm going to fuck her. Right here in this doctor's office.

She crushes her mouth against mine, her tits flattening against my chest. Her hands rip my expensive jacket from my shoulders and it falls to the floor like the cheap paper gown.

"We can't—she could be back any minute!"

"You think I care?"

I wrap one arm around her back and lift her legs with the other, carrying my woman to the examination table. The paper crinkles as I lay her down, and my cock jumps as I see her laid out like that for me. She really is gorgeous. I love the way her tits sit on her chest, and I get up on the stool to grab them.

"I'm going to fuck you hard and fast."

I yank down my slacks and pull my cock out, fisting it. No need for a condom anymore. I grip the base as her legs wrap around me. Then I slip my length along that pink cunt, massaging her clit as my hands run up her sides.

"How do you like that?"

Maya shuts her eyes. "You're insane."

It's true. I've never been this crazy for pussy. The last few years have been all about getting my dick wet, but never the same woman. Never would I have considered tracking a girl down to fuck her again.

I take it slow. My head pushes its way through, her walls squeezing me tight, already wet and ready to go. I grab her hips and bury every inch of me inside her. I love the gasps she makes when I'm all the way inside. I love the way her tits bounce when I start to thrust.

She lets out a shout and I clap my hand over her mouth as she looks at me, horrified.

"I love it when you scream for me, but this isn't the right place."

She moans into my hand as her body jerks with every hammer of my hips. Her cunt is perfectly wet and tight. It grips my dick as though it doesn't want me to pull out.

I pound her hard, keeping myself there for a moment as her eyes glaze over. Then I move my hand so that my fingers play with her lower lip.

"*Johnny.*"

Fuck. The way she says my name.

My heartbeat pounds through my dick so hard that I'm sure she can feel it. It's a constant ache, and I'm slowly losing myself. It's such a relief to just let everything go. The only thing I want to concentrate on is getting my cum inside my woman. Yes, there's no question about that now. She belongs to me. She'll complain and fight, but she'll come to me. Her father won't give her a choice.

I can't take the sound of her groans, which we aren't bothering trying to keep quiet anymore. My hands find her tits and grope them. I drag my tongue over them. She twists my hair and pulls so fucking hard that I wince.

"Harder!"

Then I bury my face in her tits, my legs straining as I

thrust once. I'm shoved over the edge, and so is she, judging by the way she rips out my hair.

"Oh my God."

I feel her pussy clenching around my dick as I come inside her. The hot jets burst into her as euphoria fogs my brain. I breathe hard against her skin and kiss her over and over. Her chest keeps shuddering with huge gasps as her muscles spasm around me.

"Why the fuck did we do this?"

I get the feeling that she's not just referring to me nailing her in a doctor's office. I raise my head, grinning at her.

"You came to *me*. You wanted me? Well, now you have me."

"This doesn't change anything."

She struggles to sit upright and I wrap an arm around her back, her face growing pink as I stare at her.

"What do you mean, it doesn't change anything?"

She sets her lips into a firm line. "I haven't decided what to do yet, but I'm definitely not going to marry you."

"I think you'll change your tune once you realize how badly your dad will react to this."

"I don't care. I'm not ready to get married. I'm only twenty-two."

I grind my teeth as she sets her jaw stubbornly. "This

isn't about whether you're ready, or love, or any of that shit."

She bends over and snatches her clothes from the ground. "I'm glad to see that my feelings matter so much to you."

You're right, they don't matter.

"Our feelings rank pretty low on my priority list. You really want to start a fucking war because of your pride?"

That holds her gaze for a few moments. "I'm not going to say anything to my dad, and neither will you."

"Yeah, how long do you think you're going to be able to hide this? You need doctor visits—"

"Stop it," she says through her teeth.

"Ultrasounds, prenatal care, all that shit. I'm going to be there with you."

Maya shoves her legs into her jeans, muttering to herself. I slide myself back in my slacks and zip them up.

"I'll call you and let you know whatever I decide."

Maya grabs her purse, and I take her forearm before she can straighten up.

"When am I going to see you again?"

Christ, I hate not being in control.

Maya shrugs and licks her lips. "I don't know."

A beautiful flush spreads over her chest as I reel her in and wrap my arms around her waist. She touches the damp skin of my neck, both of us smelling like sex. Then she raises her head and gently kisses my lips. Her mouth is soft, and it makes my skin tingle. A mere ten, fifteen minutes since I came inside her, and I want her again.

"Don't make me come after you."

* * *

My patent-leather shoes crunch the dead grass over the silent graveyard. It's Sunday. Family day. I'm supposed to be at my ma's, but instead I'm drinking a bottle of bourbon like a fucking drunk degenerate as I think about my old man.

The knowledge that I'm going to be a father really fucks with my head. I'm cautiously optimistic. The sane part of me is screaming to the sky. WHAT THE FUCK ARE YOU DOING? YOU'RE GOING TO RUIN YOUR LIFE!

Just like my dad, eh?

I come across his grave. It's a flat piece of stone, and I spit out a stream of alcohol. It splatters on the date.

He died just before I became boss. My old man was a captain.

I worshipped him.

It still burns, even after all these years. I died that night. I made him kneel and put my gun against his head. He didn't beg. He knew what he had done, what would have happened to me. His fucking son.

I shot him. I watched his brains splatter the pavement and immediately felt unsatisfied. He went so quickly, and I didn't feel anything. Just rage. Then I pretended to grieve with my ma, even when everyone in the family knew what I had done.

When your own father puts a hit out on you because you're getting too big, you lose faith in humanity. He was my hero and he betrayed me for the scared, weak old men who couldn't handle the fact that a young made guy was a rising star. Bringing in millions of dollars a week. Attracting media attention. I was smart. Most guys are good earners. I was the best.

Take it from me: being the best makes you a target. Not just from men—women, too. They want a piece of you.

The wind howls a bitter sound in my ears as my eyes burn, staring at that fucking plaque.

I wish he was alive so I could kill him again.

Then I upend the bottle of bourbon and let it splash all over the grave. It spills over the grass and soaks into the dead blades.

"See you later, *Papa*."

Fuck him.

I walk back to my car, where Chris waits outside. "Let's

go to Tony's house."

Then I enter the car without another word and Chris drives off. My stomach bubbles angrily. I'm going to be a father. I just know Maya won't have it in her to get rid of it.

As much as I hate to admit it, I need to talk to someone. He won't be happy to see me. I let Tony Vidal leave the family to save face. It's a long story, but he knows exactly what I'm going through.

And I'm a little bit drunk.

We stop in front of Tony's house in the suburbs of Terrebonne half an hour later. I get out and tell Chris to wait in the car, and then I walk up the neatly trimmed lawn. My fist hammers on the door, and in a few seconds I hear a feminine voice. "Coming!"

Shit. His wife. She hates my fucking guts.

A slight woman wearing a summer dress yanks open the door, her face falling into disgust when she recognizes me.

"You're not welcome here."

Fuck.

"Elena, I just want to talk to Tony."

"*He left the family.*"

"This has nothing to do with the family. I just want to talk to him, I swear."

165

Suddenly a baby's squalling voice echoes in the house, and Elena looks over her shoulder toward the noise. A tall hulk of a man walks into the hallway, carrying the baby in his huge arms.

Surprise registers in his voice. "Johnny."

"Hey, Tony. Do you mind if I come in?"

He frowns but nods in approval, earning him a glare from his wife. I step inside and give Elena a jerk of my head as I walk toward Tony. The baby waves its fat fists in the air and gurgles at its father, who smiles.

"Amy, say, 'Hi!'"

She gives me a toothless smile and I can't help but return it.

"She's beautiful."

"Thanks."

Elena walks up to her husband and takes Amy from his arms, glaring at me as she walks upstairs.

Sigh.

Tony gives me an apologetic smile. Whatever. I can't fault her for hating me. He jerks his head and I follow him into his office. The moment the door closes, he rounds on me.

"So what is this, John? Why are you here?"

Can't he just look at me without the fucking judgment in his eyes?

"I fucked up pretty bad."

Tony tenses as I sink into his leather couch. He sits across from me and licks his lips.

"What happened?"

A painful grin stretches across my face. "I knocked up a girl."

"Oh." He smiles at me. "That's it?"

"I knocked up the daughter of the president of *Les Diables*."

My words hang in the air for a second and Tony's mouth stretches into a smile, as if he expects me to burst out, "Kidding!"

"You're serious?"

"Yeah."

"*Holy fuck*—"

"Yeah."

"That's really bad."

I give him a pointed look.

"And you gave me so much shit for knocking up a made guy's girl. Remember?"

My face heats up at his grin. "Completely different circumstances. I didn't know who she was at first."

His deep laughs rebound loudly in the small room. "At first?"

"I was thinking with my dick."

A huge hand covers his mouth as he tries to stifle his laughter.

Laugh it up, prick.

"It's not really that funny."

"No, it's just very déjà vu for me."

I sigh loudly.

"Well, what's done is done. The question is, how are you going to handle it?"

My fingers tap the leather on the arm of the sofa. "I don't know."

Normally in these situations, with a hostile person like Carlos, I'd just kill him. Get rid of him. But I can't just fucking kill the president of *Les Diables* without someone noticing. Without war.

"Do you think getting engaged would cool him off?"

Tony grimaces. "I don't know, John. You should talk to Sal."

"Sal hasn't been through this."

"He's your consigliere. Everyone is going to find out anyway."

"She wanted to get an abortion. I think I talked her out of it."

"What? Why would you do that?"

I look up from the sofa, incredulous. "You have a daughter."

"Yeah, but—"

"I want this kid."

I want what you have.

"Well, then you don't need to explain yourself. You're the boss. You do whatever the fuck you want."

True, but there are limits. Like don't-fuck-my-daughter limits. And I just fucking bulldozed over that one.

"Do you like the girl?"

I look at him. "I barely know anything about her." Other than she's a great lay and I can't get enough of her body. I think about harnessing that wild, proud girl. Putting a ring on her finger. Getting to fuck her whenever I want. Doesn't sound so bad. It's the other shit that I'm worried about. Her father's reaction to knocking up his precious daughter.

"I'll probably have to meet him with her. Explain what happened."

"Do it on neutral ground. He'll blow your fucking head off in that fortress."

"I'm not an idiot."

Meeting Carlos doesn't scare me, but I'm vaguely worried for Maya. I'm not sure how free Carlos is with his hands, and she's carrying my kid. Every cell inside me wants to drive up to Sorel-Tracy right now and take her to my apartment, where I know she'll be safe. I don't know much about her, but the thought of her being in pain because of me makes me fucking sick. I need to protect her.

Tony gives a beady look. "Things might go south with *Les Diables*."

And if they do, I might have to kill Maya's father.

MAYA

Lined-up cigarettes burn like candles as I hold the flame to them, lighting up the whole row. The white paper wrinkles, turning a smoky, dark color as the small fire licks the head.

At first I thought I'd have a cigarette. It's been years since I kicked the habit, but something about an unwanted pregnancy with a Mafia don made me want to inhale a lungful of cancerous smoke. I held it up to my lips and thought about the tiny life growing inside me that I just couldn't make a decision about. I couldn't draw a single breath of that shit because of one thought running through my head.

It'll hurt the baby.

The baby. Not the soon-to-be-aborted fetus. Baby.

I look across the neatly trimmed lawn of *Parc Mont Royal*, staring at the cigarettes quietly burning on the blades of grass.

The best, *sanest* course of action would be to get a goddamn abortion. Get rid of it before Dad finds out about it and raises hell, but I just can't bring myself to do it. There's no rhyme or reason behind it. I just can't.

What the fuck do I do now? Marry that crazy asshole?

Hell no. You can take care of this yourself without him.

Across the field, a man wearing a leather cut makes a beeline toward me, his steel-toed boots obliterating the grass. He treks right through happy couples sitting down, having picnics, his heated eyes trained on me.

Here we fucking go.

There's no point in running.

I stand up and extinguish the cigarettes with my shoes, picking my purse off the ground. Heaviness settles in my chest as I recognize Chuck through that dirty blonde beard and his shoulder-length hair. That pigeon tattoo on his shoulder is a dead giveaway, but I'm glad it's just him.

"How did you find me?"

Chuck stops a foot away from me, crossing his arms.

"I know all your haunts. Let's go, little girl."

Little girl? A ripple of anger runs through me.

"Dad must be pretty pissed," I add casually as we walk toward his bike.

I watch his face carefully, but it's hard to notice anything behind that wild beard. He doesn't say a word and a chill runs down my spine.

"He's not happy. Just like he's not happy whenever you run off."

Yeah, I'm just doing this to piss off my old man.

"I'm not trying to *run off.* I'm trying to live my life."

"You're putting yourself in danger every time you take off by yourself."

In danger? What fucking danger? From the hot guys who want to get their dicks wet?

I climb behind Chuck on his bike and wrap my arms around him, gritting my teeth when the engine roars into life.

What should I say when I get back?

Dad's going to want a reason why I left the fortress and returned much later than I said I would. Again.

Oh, sorry, Dad. I just had to meet with the guy who knocked me up, who happens to be the bane of your existence.

My arms dig into Chuck's abdomen as he bikes out of the city. My hair whips around my head as we drive on the freeway and finally take the exit twenty minutes later. Then I lean forward as he rides up the winding path to the fortress, my heart slamming against his back as the huge gates roll into view. They creak open automatically and Chuck drives into the compound, kicking up dust.

There's a small gathering of people hanging outside the clubhouse when Chuck parks his bike and I slide off the seat. They look away when I glare daggers at anyone staring at me. I'm sure they think that I'm some kind of nuisance. A waste of their resources. The bitchy daughter who's always going off by herself to do God knows what without an escort.

I walk straight into the clubhouse, ignoring those who wave to me as I seek out my bedroom. The noise almost cuts out when I slam the door shut and rake my hands through my hair, glancing at my meager possessions.

This is what my life has become. Small bits of freedom. A breather here and there before being dragged back to this place that I hate. The drugs. The alcohol. The strippers. A ball of hot shame grows inside me at the thought of actually raising my baby in this place. God, the baby.

Johnny was wrong. This *is* a disaster.

Loud footsteps crash down the corridor and my insides tense as I recognize the sound of those heavy boots. I sit up straight. Jesus, it sounds as though there's an elephant thundering down the hallway. The door smashes open and I don't even blink.

Mom crashes through the door with Dad, whose face is purpled with rage.

What now?

"STUPID FUCKING *CUNT*!"

"Carlos, stop!"

I stand to my feet, electrified. He throws Mom from his arm, and she makes a painful whimper as her head hits the wall. It's not as though I haven't seen him do it dozens of times before, but somehow it feels worse because she's defending me.

"Don't touch her, you fucking bastard!"

He whirls on me, spittle flying from his mouth. "I KNOW WHERE YOU WERE!"

I cross my arms as a thrill runs through me. "What?"

"Why the *fuck* were you at *Le Zinc*?"

So they saw me at the restaurant. Shit.

I put on a bored voice. "Some people like to eat out, Dad."

He snarls in my face, jabbing my chest with his finger. "Don't you fucking lie to me."

"I was having lunch. With a friend."

"*A friend.*"

He spits it out as if I uttered a disgusting swearword.

"You fucking stupid bitch."

"You said that already."

"You're meeting Johnny Cravotta behind my back to hurt the MC."

I slap his hand away from my face. "No, I'm not!"

"Are you going to stand there and lie to me?"

"I'm not—!"

"What the *fuck* did you tell that greaseball?"

Okay, this is a lot worse than I thought it was.

He lunges at me before I can dodge, and his thick hands wrap around my throat, squeezing hard. I scratch at his fingers as I gulp for breath, fighting back for all I'm worth. He pins me down. My head grinds against the dirty floor and my mother's screams ring in my ear as blackness pricks at the edge of my vision.

"TELL ME!"

"*Stop! Fucking stop it!*"

"Get *off* me!"

"She can't breathe!"

The screams become a distant roar. I can't see—I can't hear. My lungs burn. Fuck, it hurts. I claw at my father's face and the pressure on my throat relieves.

I roll to my side as oxygen punches my brain and all my senses return. My chest heaves great breaths as Dad crouches over me.

"Start fucking talking."

A surge of vicious hatred that I've never known before consumes everything. I don't give a fuck about what he does to me.

"I was on a date—" I gasp.

"What?"

"I was on a date with the Italian guy I'm fucking."

The look on his face is priceless. Stunned doesn't quite cover it. Shocked beyond belief doesn't either.

"You're lying."

"I'm not lying."

I've never wanted to tell the truth about anything more in my life. I want to rub it in his face and laugh at his pain.

"An Italian?"

"*Yeah*, I met a guy at a bar and he was Italian—and connected with the mob. You know what, Dad? He was a real gentleman. He told me exactly what he wanted to do with me—"

"*Shut the fuck up.*"

"I went to his house. He *fucked* me really good—"

His hand strikes my face. And again. The blows rain on my head, knocking me into the cheap plywood floor. Stars burst in my vision.

"DID YOU KNOW ABOUT THIS?"

"No!"

Mom backs away from him as he raises his fist and glares at me.

"You—you let one of those *disgusting* people touch you—"

"He wasn't disgusting."

"STOP TALKING!"

"Why should I? Since you care so much about who gets to touch my pussy, maybe I should tell you more about how amazing he was in bed."

My father can't even produce a complete sentence. "FUCKING—BITCH! CUNT!"

"I let him come inside my mouth!"

"You sick, twisted bitch."

Let the whole fucking club hear about it. I don't give a flying fuck if they know I sucked Johnny Cravotta's cock and loved it.

"I had some fun for the first time in my goddamn life, and you can't stand it. You're the one who can't keep it in his fucking pants, so don't you *dare* tell me who I can and can't fuck!" I scream at his furious face and grab the hair-cutting scissors on my nightstand.

"SHUT UP!"

I stab at him with the scissors, but he grabs my wrist and twists it painfully. The bones grind together as he grips me hard and wrenches mercilessly. A sharp pain sears up my elbow and I scream.

I need to get out.

A crashing sound pierces my ears and I see Mom cracking my ceramic vase over Dad's head. His vise grip loosens and I shove him aside.

"Fucking crazy bitch!"

I scramble to my feet and grab the baseball bat hidden behind my bed. "DON'T!"

Bits of ceramic crumble from his head as he dazedly

gets to his feet, looking at me with a hatred so poisonous I feel it turning my stomach. "You fucked a goddamn guinea. Some slick-haired, provolone, cock-sucking dago."

A small smile twitches on my face at the thought of what Johnny might say if he knew my father called him a dago.

"I did. And I loved it."

Fuck you.

It's like waving a red flag in front of an enraged bull. His screams seem to shake the walls, and I tighten my grip over the baseball bat.

"YOU'RE A FUCKING DISGRACE! I should fucking kill you!"

He reaches for his hip and I hurl the bat at him. I crash into the door, seized with adrenaline as his screams of fury follow me down the hall. My body smashes into the people hanging outside the door and I shove them aside.

"Get out of my way!"

My shoulder slams into someone. She flies from me and crashes on the floor. I skirt around her, sprinting toward the door.

Something explodes over my head and I cover my face as glass shards sprinkle down. A picture frame sizzles with a small, round hole and I can't make any sense of it. Then another blast, and a rush of air beside my hand.

I whirl around and see Dad aiming a gun at my head. Mom grabs his arm, wrenching it, sobbing and pleading. He shoves her aside like a bear batting away his cub.

The air freezes. My chest doesn't move and I hold my breath, waiting for him to pull that trigger, to end my life exactly how he ended so many others before mine.

"*Carlos*, what the hell are you doing, man?"

A gentle but firm voice rings out in the clubhouse, and my dad's head wheels toward Chuck.

"My daughter is none of your concern."

"She's a member of this club."

"Who fucked an Italian!" Red-rimmed eyes turn toward me again. "I can't believe you let one of those slimy fucks touch you."

I find my voice somehow. "They're not all bad."

"OF COURSE THEY ARE!" The gun trembles in his hand. "I can't look at you without feeling sick to my stomach."

Same here, asshole.

"Carlos, calm down."

A gunshot cracks the air, the sound splitting my head in two. I drop to the ground, because I must be dead. He was aiming the gun at me. Then I look over the dirty floor and I see Chuck lying on the floor. Screams hit my ears as the numbness fades. A dark-red pool spreads as Chuck lies in the dust like a dog. His face looks like parchment, that's how white it is. Glassy eyes search for me as his wheezing breaths echo sharply in the clubhouse.

The man who was always patient with me looks at me, his hand outstretched. He mouths something: *Run.*

Dad looks at him in disbelief. It was an accident. He didn't mean to.

My face screws up in pain. "You fucking bastard."

The gun aims toward me.

He meant to kill me.

I get up to my feet and I burst out of the clubhouse, sprinting so hard that I can't hear anything but my breathing. I head for those tall iron gates. Julien mans them, and he stiffens when I slide to a halt in front of him.

"What happened? I heard—"

"Let me the fuck out!" I bang my elbows on the gate. Any second my dad's going to come flying out of the clubhouse and fire into my back.

"I can't just—"

"OPEN THE FUCKING GATE!"

I don't bother to wipe the tears running down my face. I just smash the bars over and over again. If only I had the strength to rip them down for good. These fucking bars have kept me in for too long.

"All right. *Jesus.*"

He rolls the gate open. It seems to take an eternity for it to open wide enough for me to squeeze through the narrow opening.

"MAYA!"

My father's voice hits me like a spear to my knees, and I fall down. My knee slams into the concrete and I feel the grit digging into my flesh.

Get up, damn it.

Shit, I'm so exposed here. Nothing but sheer adrenaline makes me sprint down the road until my lungs and legs burn. I reach town after a quarter of an hour, my lungs so tight that I can't draw any more breath. Crippling nausea hits me and I retch on the side of the road.

I need a payphone, but I don't have a dime on me. All I have is Johnny's phone number because I carry that folded piece of paper everywhere I go.

And I have nowhere to go now. No wallet. No money. Nothing.

Calling him is the last thing I want to do. I wanted to be on my own for a little while, but now that my father's gone psycho—

Pain clenches my heart and my chest shakes as I desperately draw in breath. I don't know if Chuck is alive, but if he's dead it's my fault. I goaded my father, and all Chuck ever did was protect me. Hold my hand when we crossed the street. He wiped more than a few tears from my cheek.

Fuck no. I can't think about this shit.

A glint of metal catches my attention, and I bend over to scrape the shiny coin from the pavement. Nickel. It pings on the street as I drop it and walk down the sidewalk of the industrial town built around the fortress. The houses here are all low income, or they were before they were abandoned to rot. Crumbling streets. I stub my toes on the uneven sidewalks and keep my eyes peeled for a fucking telephone booth, or a diner, or something. Then a see a grubby little sports bar, and it's open. I stumble inside the dark room and my nostrils wrinkle at the faint smell of piss.

"Can I use your phone?"

The bartender takes one look at my disheveled appearance and shakes his wizened head.

"*Non.*"

I can't believe this.

"It's an emergency!"

"I don't serve biker bitches. *Va chier.*" *Go shit yourself.*

I summon all the energy in my chest. "Maybe I'll tell my father to come to this bar and shove that rifle up your ass."

I see him angling toward the rifle behind his bar, and

he freezes.

"His name is Carlos. Have you heard of him?"

The bartender relents. The threat of my father is too much for him to ignore. He grabs an ancient telephone and slams it on the counter.

"There. *Mange d'la marde.*"

Fuck you, too.

I pick the phone off the hook and dig into my jeans for Johnny's card. It's been folded so many times that I can barely make out the black text. It rings, and I release a shaky sigh.

"*Johnny.*"

"I-it's me. I really need your help."

Arrogance slides into his smooth voice. "*You called a lot sooner than I thought.*"

"I'm in deep shit."

"*What happened?*"

"He found out—he knows. I barely managed to get out."

"*Where are you?*"

"I don't know. I'm in some shitty bar down the hill from the fortress."

"*I'm coming to get you. Don't move.*"

My nails dig into the plastic as I watch the door. "What if he finds me? He tried to kill me—"

"*He what?*"

Static crackles between us. My mouth opens, but I can't force out a single word. Vivid images flash in front of my face. My mom—what's going to happen to her?

"*Just fucking stay put. I'm leaving now.*"

As soon as the comfort of his voice fades to a dull dial tone, panic ramps up behind my chest. I walk deep inside the bar and then I consider just hiding in the bathroom stall to wait for him. Yeah, that's what I'll do.

The dingy, shitty bathroom only has a cheap screw and a hook to look at, but it's amazing how much safer I feel. Even though it'd only take one kick to blast open the door.

The light flickers on and I notice the gash on my knee, bleeding freely into my jeans. I reach out to grab a handful of paper towels, but the roll is empty. So is the toilet roll. Great.

There's another line of blood on my hand, right where Dad's bullet split my skin open.

He didn't mean it.

He couldn't have.

Bullshit, you know he meant it.

My mind buzzes with a strange numbness as I turn the faucet on. The icy water stings my hand, and fresh blood spills from the wound. I splash some on my knee, gritting my teeth as I clean the dirt away.

What just fucking happened to me? Did my father really try to blow my head open, or did I imagine all of that?

"Did you see a girl?"

Jesus Christ, I'm so lost in my own head that I didn't hear anyone come into the bar. I know that fucking voice. My heart jumps into my throat as if I've been shoved to the edge of a cliff. I flatten myself against the wall as his heavy boots stomp through the bar.

I inhale my breath, knowing that any second now, he's going to give me away.

"*Non.*"

"You better not be lying to me, asshole."

The footsteps travel down the length of the bar, blood pulsing in my ears as his steps creak closer to me.

Don't go in the bathroom.

"The president is looking for her."

"She's not in my fucking bar."

I marvel at the bartender's irritated voice and wonder why the fuck he's protecting me. It's probably just his hatred of the MC.

He knocks his fist against the bathroom door. "Hey. Open up."

Oh fuck.

I look around for something in this shitty bathroom to use as a weapon, but it's completely bare.

"I can hear you breathing. Don't make me break down this door."

Fuck off!

"Leave my fucking customers alone, damn it!"

"Shut up, old man."

I inhale a sharp breath as another pair of footsteps walks into the bar. Is it him? Please, God, let it be him. A smooth voice makes my heart stop.

"Is there a problem here?"

I hear the biker's leather squeak as he turns around. "What the fuck are you doing here?"

"You better watch your fucking tone when you're talking to me."

A beat of silence.

"I'm looking for the president's daughter. She ran off."

I bite my fist as Johnny speaks in a lilting tone. "Has she?" I can just see the smirk on his face.

"You know what I think?"

"I don't give a shit, actually."

"I think that girl is in that bathroom, waiting for you to pick her up."

"Maybe. Maybe I need to take a piss, and you're in the way. Maybe go fuck yourself."

The bartender mutters a threat. "I'm calling the police."

Johnny's voice growls in response. "You do that and I'll fuck you up."

"When Carlos finds out you fucked his daughter—"

"I don't know what you're talking about."

"I can hear that little bitch in there!"

"I don't hear jack shit, and you're starting to piss me off."

"This is no coincidence."

"Are you calling me a liar?"

The man's tone wavers. "No."

Johnny's joking voice addresses the bartender. "I think he's saying that I intentionally banged the president's daughter."

"Well—"

"Why don't you get the fuck out of here before I kill you?"

Another beat of strained silence hangs, and I'm on the verge of shouting a useless warning.

"All right, Johnny, I'm sorry."

Oh thank God.

The heavy boots scrape the floor and I hear his body push from the door. I sag against the wall in relief. Seconds later my heart slams against my chest as Johnny raps his knuckles on the door.

My hands shake as I unlatch the nail from the hook and the cheap door swings inward, revealing Johnny's slim figure. He wears black slacks and a dark-green polo, which clings to his body in a way that makes blood rush to my skin's surface. A heart-stopping smirk tugs at his mouth.

"Close shave, hon." He steps inside the bathroom and his smile falls. "Jesus, look at you!"

I glance in the mirror as he grabs my face. His thumb gently caresses my neck, brushing over the angry marks where my father choked me. I hiss in pain and pull away.

"That hurts."

"I'm sorry."

His voice sounds calm, but I'm scared of the darkness brewing in his eyes when he pulls back.

"That piece of shit did this to you?"

That piece of shit is still the president of the Devils MC.

"What happened?"

I'm still racked with nerves, and I don't want to look at Johnny's hard-set jaw and tell him everything that happened. My right ear won't work properly. The gunshot was so loud that listening to him talk is like hearing a voice through a soda can.

His brows knit together. "We'll talk about it in the car. Let's go."

"Is he gone?"

"Yeah. Come on."

A warm hand slips into mine and I jump slightly, looking down at it. He frowns at me and walks. I follow him, strangely at ease. We pass by the bar and Johnny digs through his pockets.

The bartender shakes his head. "I don't want it."

Johnny slams a small stack of fifty-dollar bills. "Take it."

"I don't—"

"Just take it, old man," he says in a slightly harassed voice, and the bartender shuts up.

I follow the pressure of Johnny's hand into the sunlight. My head jerks up and down the street, looking for a hint of chrome, but I see nothing.

"Get inside, *quick.*"

I stoop down as Johnny opens the door for me, and then I collapse inside the black leather interior. The door slams shut as he effortlessly slides in next to me.

I am saved.

"Take me home, Chrissy."

Then he slams the partition shut and for some reason blood rushes to my face when he gives me that concerned look.

"What the fuck happened up there?"

The cold voice feels like a bucket of ice water dumped

on my head.

Chuck's hand was reaching for me. He told me to run. And then my own father shot me.

I bury my face in my hands. If only I had just shut my mouth and kept my fucking thoughts to myself—made up some lie about why I went to *Le Zinc*—none of this would've happened.

"Maya, I need to know what we're dealing with."

Selfish prick.

"He knows I fucked someone who was at your restaurant. He doesn't know who. Thanks for the fucking concern."

His hand tenses next to mine and then it snakes over my shoulder. I feel it like stepping in a hot bath. He pulls me into his chest like a rag doll and his heart thumps against my back.

I can't remember the last time I was held like this. Even though I know he's just doing this to placate me, my skin heats like a furnace when his lips touch my cheek.

"What happened, Maya?"

"He—he shot Chuck. I don't even know if he's alive. Mom tried to protect me."

Why am I so calm?

"They saw me going into your restaurant. He thought I was meeting with you to betray the MC or something."

"Jesus."

I look up and he irons his face with his hands. Hot, bubbling guilt surges inside me.

"It's my fault."

"What are you talking about?"

I have to make him understand the full brunt of my guilt. "I pissed him off on purpose. I was just—I wanted to hurt him. I said—"

"It doesn't matter what you said. He did this to you."

A finger brushes over the choke wounds on my throat.

It feels as though it was just another day at the MC. My dad guns down a man I actually respected, and I don't even shed a tear. Christ, what the fuck is wrong with me?

"I can't believe this shit." His voice is breathless as he takes my hand, the one with the gash, and runs his thumb underneath the wound. Then his voice turns black. "If he was any other man, I would kill him. I would turn my car around right now, and gun him down in front of his wife."

I don't think I've ever heard such a gritty voice. It's hard to believe that the sound came from his chest. There's no warmth in him, just cold rage.

"He's still my—"

"He's the president, and I owe him the courtesy of explaining what happened, but if he was anyone else he would be dead for touching my girl."

I freeze in his arms as he presses his cool cheek to mine.

"I'm not your girl."

He doesn't skip a beat. "You're carrying my kid. That makes you mine."

No, I don't think so.

"I didn't leave the MC to be possessed by another man."

"So you didn't get what you wanted. Too fucking bad."

My heart flutters as his lips touch the side of my temple. I really hate how good it feels to be in his arms. I tilt my head to the side to avoid his touch even though I crave it.

"You're just like my father. You don't care about me. You just want to control me."

"I saved your goddamn ass in that bar."

"Only because I'm carrying your kid."

His hands slip under my shirt and I gasp as his palm touches my stomach. Urgent lips touch the side of my head, making me burn as his hands glide over me. His hands make a mockery of my pride. They make my skin singe.

"You think that's the only reason?"

He kisses my neck and it's like being injected with Valium. I slump into his arms. I'm just so fucking tired of fighting all the time. It'd be nice to give in, for once. To let them win.

But I can't.

"I think you'd be crazy to risk everything for pussy."

"World-class pussy."

I feel his smile tickling my flesh.

"I haven't been able to get you out of my mind."

His hands sweep over my body, sensual and rough at the same time. They curve over the hard bones of my ribs and then his fingers slide under my bra. A thin gasp cuts through the air and my heart beats like a hummingbird's wings, instantly sent into overdrive. Warmth pulses between my legs and I close them, uncomfortably wet as he gropes my tits.

I should be pissed that the only reason he wants me around is because of how good the sex is, but how can I be surprised? We barely know each other and it was always supposed to be a one-time deal. One night became two nights plus that tryst at the doctor's office, and here we fucking are.

He slides his hand over mine and grazes the wound. He hears my hiss of pain and glances at it.

"You should have never went back. You should have stayed when I told you to stay."

I hate flinching from the anger in his voice. "I didn't

think he would find out so quickly."

"I don't care what you thought would happen. You should have listened to me."

Arrogant prick.

"I don't need to listen to you." He cuts my voice off with a gale of laughter, and I shove his chest, pushing myself away from him. "I've spent my whole life under my dad's thumb, and I don't intend on becoming your *little bitch.*"

He gives me a wide grin, trying to stifle his chuckles. "Well, you can play that game with me, but you won't win."

"Try me."

"You don't have a choice, baby. It's me or the streets."

Ruthless eyes bore into mine and his smile freezes. "Believe me, Maya. You want me in your life."

"What the fuck is that supposed to mean?"

"You're better off with me than without. You know that." His hand drops heavily over my thighs. "I won't let you go, anyway."

My insides seethe at being told that I need a man. I don't fucking need him. "I just need a place to stay for a week or two, and then I'm on my own."

"I'm not letting you in unless you agree to get engaged."

My jaw drops open. "Are you fucking serious?"

"My house, my rules."

"I only need a place for a couple weeks!"

"Until what?"

"Until I get my credit cards and money from my bank."

A strange look falls over Johnny's face and his hand falls on the back of my neck. I'm so pissed off that I want to throw him off, but instead I revel in the feeling of his fingers slowly massaging my knots.

"Sweetie, he's probably on his way to freeze your bank accounts."

"What?"

He shrugs. "It's what I would do."

Shit. He's probably right.

"C—can I use your phone?"

I just can't believe that my father would use his connections to do something so petty. The pitying look creases his eyes, but he slips his hand down his slacks and hands me his heavy iPhone.

I call the bank of Montreal as Johnny watches me unsmilingly. His hand at the back of my neck soothes me as a clinical voice cracks on the speaker.

"Hi, I need to withdraw money from the bank, but I lost all my cards."

I rattle off my personal information as she finds my

account.

"*I'm sorry, madame, but it appears that your bank account was emptied today.*"

"What? Who gave the authorization? I never—"

"*It looks like you had a joint account with your father. I'm sorry, but he withdrew all the money about one hour ago.*"

Years of work, gone in an instant. My hopes and dreams, completely fucked. Ruined. Turned to shit.

"But he can't—" I sob into the receiver and the banker's voice softens.

"*Do you want me to contact the authorities?*"

I shake my head as a ball of fury builds up behind my eyes. "No."

The banker murmurs something else into the phone, but I pull away and tap the red circle, ending the call. The screen fades to darkness, unlike the pressure in my head, which is close to the breaking point.

"It was a joint fucking account. I basically just handed him the money."

He winces in sympathy.

"I fucking hate him."

Johnny covers my shaking hand with his. "I hated my dad, too."

Is that supposed to make me feel better?

Suddenly the car grinds to a halt in front of Johnny's

high-rise, and my hands clench over my knees.

"You don't have a choice."

No, I never did. All the way back to my fucking birth, I never had a goddamn choice.

"I don't see why we have to get married," I say in a shaking voice.

"Number one: it's the right thing to do. Two: it might just save this alliance of ours."

The driver opens the door for us and Johnny gets out first, extending his hand to me. I ignore it and stand up, brushing the gesture aside. His hand finds mine as Chris drives away, and he pulls me against his chest, the grip biting.

"Don't do that again."

"What?"

Even though I know exactly *what*.

"Don't be disrespectful toward me in front of others. I'm the boss."

"You're not *my* boss."

Against his chest, I smell the fresh scent of his skin and that tantalizing male musk from his hair. His smile widens, reminding me of that predatory stare he gave me when we first met, when I knew he was the one I wanted to spend the night with.

"Why don't you say that to me again when I get you

upstairs?"

Energy shoots straight into my heart like a live wire. He grabs my elbow and leads me to the marble-floored foyer and into the elevator. All the while my heart hammers against my chest. As soon as the elevator doors close, he turns around, and I'm no match for his deadly smirk and the rippling muscles flexing his arms, which pin me against the wall. He's so much stronger than he looks.

"The moment you step through that door into my apartment, you become my fiancée."

A thrill runs through my heart as I look at the faint lines beside his eyes that wrinkle when he smiles. He's so much older than me, and I don't understand anything that's going on in his head. He shouldn't want this, but he does.

If I go in there, I'm never coming back out.

"I'm not ready." I hate how high my voice sounds.

Johnny grasps my chin lightly and runs his thumb under my bottom lip.

"This isn't about *love*, sweetheart. Love doesn't exist for people like us."

"Maybe not for *you*, but I intend to find it."

"Not with me. Get those thoughts out of your head."

Pitiless black eyes stare back at me. Just when I'm reeling from the sensations he gives me, he drives a spike through my heart.

"This is about what we both need to do."

"You can't want this."

"I do."

"You want to marry me?"

"If you're going to have my kid, we need to be married."

A growl of frustration rips from my throat. It's like talking to a fucking robot. The elevator pings and the doors open, but Johnny doesn't let me down from the wall.

"Time to make a choice."

"C-can't we wait for a few months?"

"No," he snaps.

Just tell him yes. He can't force you to do anything.

My head spinning, I give him a quick, affirmative jerk and he steps back, holding the door open with his arm. "Wise decision, Maya."

"You forced me into this," I spit as he brings me to his apartment.

There's no remorse on his face. "I will do whatever it takes to keep this alliance from blowing up in my face."

So it really has nothing to do with what's best for the baby, does it? My insides seethe as he unlocks the door. I cross my arms and walk inside, heading straight for the living room as the door shuts.

I look around at the beautiful, spotless apartment and a cold shiver runs through my limbs. It's a gilded cage, isn't it? I sink into the couch without realizing it's there.

Johnny moves swiftly in front of the couch and sits down next to me, reaching into his jacket for a small black box.

My heart jumps in my throat as he cradles it in his hand.

"It's not exactly how I proposed to my last two wives."

The breath I don't even realize I'm holding in blows out. "What happened to your last two wives?"

"I killed them." He turns his head, laughter on his face. "Is that what you want to hear?"

"What happened?" I say in a firmer voice.

"What's there to say? They didn't work out."

Yeah, I think I'm starting to understand why they didn't.

I wonder what kinds of wives would cause this extremely traditional Mafioso bastard to divorce them.

"I think I have a right to know."

His fingers close around the box and I almost flinch at the look in his eyes.

"Not now, Maya."

I glare back at him, but he looks away, back at the black box. It pops open and a diamond splinters the light into a rainbow of fragments. He gently tugs it out of the box.

I'm amazed. The tiny band glitters with a thousand small diamonds. He takes my hand and slides the ring over my finger. It's tight. My breathing quickens as though he's wrapping a collar around my neck. And I can't believe I've said yes to this man I barely know, this Italian guy who I just wanted a one-night stand with.

It's a beautiful ring. It's big and gaudy and expensive.

And it's not me at all.

"This is too much."

"You don't like it? I can get another fucking ring."

I don't want another fucking ring.

I twist it off my finger and slap it back in his hand, and then I stand up from the couch.

"I'm sorry. I think I'll take my chances at the women's shelter."

An extremely shocked look crosses over his face, which quickly darkens. "What the fuck are you talking about?"

He's too cold—too brutal, and just not enough.

"I'm sorry. I can't marry you."

Then I walk toward the door, my head completely clear. I'd rather live in poverty than marry a man who doesn't give a fuck about me. Hell, we don't give a fuck about each other.

My body snaps backward and spins around as he grabs

KNOCKED UP BY THE BAD BOY

my upper arms.

"Let me go!"

"You're not going anywhere."

"You need me more than I need you!"

He shoves me against the wall, his face red as he yells at me. "What's that supposed to mean?"

"You don't give a fuck about me. All you care about is your fucking family."

"I'm sorry, sweetheart. My head's a bit preoccupied with knocking up the daughter of the most powerful biker gang leader."

"So I'll just leave town. He will never find out and we won't have to get married."

"There's no fucking way I'd let you leave town."

"Actually, I think it's a free country—"

I shove his chest, and scream in outrage when he pins me back against the wall effortlessly. His face splits with a wide smile as he laughs at my anger.

"Maya, I want this baby. I really do."

"Have a fucking kid with someone else!"

"I tried, and they didn't work out. You will."

"Well, you have shitty judgment because I can't stand you."

I hold my breath in as my cheeks slowly burn, immediately regretting those words, but Johnny merely shrugs, looking unconcerned.

"You can't stand me, huh?"

The hands holding my wrists to the wall become sensual.

Oh no.

They glide over my skin, giving me goose bumps as Johnny's hips dig into mine. His lips just brush my cheek.

"You must hate my fucking guts."

I feel the outline of his cock, slowly starting to harden against my thigh. I clench my thighs together and feel the wetness gathering between him.

"Y-yeah."

Damn it.

It's as though he flipped a switch that makes my skin hypersensitive. His hand glides up my neck and grasps my face, so that I'm staring right into his shit-eating grin.

I wasn't lying. I can't fucking stand him.

"Asshole."

"Biker bitch."

He crushes his lips against mine and every last thread of resistance snaps. He weaves his fingers through my hair and yanks hard so that I moan in pain. This man is not fucking capable of being gentle, but that's fine.

I like it when he's rough.

Fingers claw at my dirty clothes, ripping them from my

head. He's like a fucking animal—the way he treats my body. So rough and violent, but that's probably all he knows. My bra straps dig into my shoulders as he yanks hard and then hurls the bra away from him, the cold air stinging my nipples. His mouth finds my shoulder and he utters a subhuman growl, biting a vicious mark into my skin. *Jesus.* It burns, and then he releases me, kissing the next spot. He reaches my neck and I cringe, but there he proves that he can be gentle. Featherlight kisses touch the sore skin, but he grabs my jaw and lays his lips on my mouth, cruelly devouring them.

My back hits the door of his bedroom and it slams open, banging against the wall. We're not even in bed, and I'm already soaking my panties. It's the way he treats me, like I'm his addiction and he can't help but lose himself around me.

Fuck me, you bastard.

He grabs my hand and forces it over the hard rock between his legs. I wrap my fingers around his cock as he hovers an inch from my face.

"You're going to make my cock your full-time job from now on."

Laughter bursts from my mouth as he stands back. Is he a parody or what?

"What did I tell you about laughing?"

"You said you'd kick me out, but we both know that won't happen."

He beckons with a finger. "Come here."

I roll my eyes and follow him as he drags an enormous box out of his closet. He crouches over it, blocking the contents from view as he takes this and that, shutting the box before I can catch a glimpse. He walks to the door first, and then he reaches up to the frame and slips some kind of material behind it. It shuts and two straps hang from the top. Then he walks back to me and picks up the Velcro handcuffs from the floor.

Fuck. I see where this is going.

"Give me your wrists."

The grittiness in his voice strikes a chord deep inside my body. Warmth floods to my skin as I give him my hands, and I feel as though I'm handing over my freedom at the same time. He wraps the Velcro straps over my wrists, his eyes flaying me alive as he tightens them with deliberate slowness.

Then he slides his hands down my waist and the throbbing ache between my legs pounds like a heartbeat.

"You're going to have to learn to obey your future husband."

The smile playing on his lips makes me wonder if he's fucking with me, but the more I get to know him and his bullshit adherence to tradition, the more I suspect he's serious. Is there any harm in letting him think that he owns me?

"I am."

"You're not. You're just doing what I say because you want my fat cock inside you."

Yeah.

He takes my wrists and pushes me backward, until my back hits the door. Then he takes each wrist and anchors them securely to the hooks hanging from the top of the doorframe. They pull at my wrists, my arms stretched high above my head as Johnny trails his fingers down my neck and around my tits, his thumb playing with my hardened nipples.

Holy *fuck* he feels amazing. Just a light graze of his fingers around that sensitive skin makes the air thinner. His body is inches from mine, the heat blazing but out of reach. I want his naked skin pressed against mine, but he lets me smolder. A smirk staggers over his face when I inhale a sharp breath as he takes my tits in his hands and squeezes.

"I'm taking in what belongs to me. You have no idea how sexy you look like this."

Then he unbuttons my jeans, leaning in close enough to plant a chaste kiss on my shoulder. I want more of him.

The zipper makes a mouthwatering sound, and then his hands slide underneath my jeans and panties with ease, following them all the way down my thighs and calves. The cool air hits my wet pussy as I step out of my clothes, and a blush creeps up my neck as Johnny stands back up, looking me up and down.

"Your pussy seems to know who it belongs to already." He lets out a chuckle that makes me steam. "Look at how fucking wet you are."

I know I am. I feel it running down my legs.

"Just because I want you to fuck me doesn't mean you own me."

A warm finger slides into my pussy and hooks into me. My heart slams hard against my chest as my walls constrict around his finger. Johnny approaches me with a shit-eating grin, digging his finger deeper.

"I bet I can get you to tell me that I own your body within the next fifteen minutes."

A second finger slides into me as Johnny bends his head, his tongue darting out to catch my nipple at the same time. His fingers pulse inside my aching pussy as his mouth closes around my nipple and sucks hard. Oh God.

I moan into the simmering air and I'm already halfway to saying whatever the hell he wants, so long as he fucks me.

Then a third squeezes in, stretching my walls as he takes my tits in his cavernous mouth, sucking and licking. He bites down and sucks—leaving marks everywhere just to prove that I'm his fucking property. I don't fucking care because it feels so damn good. He turns me around, fingers still inside me, so that my arms crisscross. His palm strokes one of my ass cheeks.

I know what's coming.

SMACK!

At the same time, he pumps his fingers inside me so that sharp blows of pain punctuate the ecstasy. I arch my back, my chest against the door. The burn spreads across both cheeks and he curves his fingers into me until my breathing is high-pitched, until I am on the cusp of an orgasm.

Then he slides his fingers out.

He slides them *out*.

"What are you doing?"

Another harsh slap makes me end the sentence in a yelp.

"*Don't fucking talk.* Just obey."

Yeah, whatever.

He turns me back around and holds his fingers in front of my face.

"Open your mouth and suck every last drop."

I shouldn't want to. It's dirty. It's *wrong*, but Johnny makes me want everything that I thought was demeaning. His fingers slide inside my mouth and I suck myself from his fingers. Shame burns my cheeks.

"Good girl."

He slides out of my mouth and my heart jumps at the smile on his face. "Please, Johnny. I want you now."

"It's so much fun seeing you worked up like this, begging for my cock."

Suddenly his hand burrows in my hair painfully and he yanks my head to the side, crushing his lips against mine and forcing his tongue through. He tastes me and pulls back, sucking my lips.

A growl rumbles from the back of his throat as he wraps his arms around my legs and hoists me up so that my legs straddle his waist, where I can see the thick bump of his cock.

"Do you honestly think you'd ever find someone you'd want more than me? Who can fuck you better than I can?"

Christ, I don't know. I grew up in the fortress, dreaming of a life outside. I must have watched *Cinderella* a million times, wishing I could have my own Prince Charming to whisk me away from that hellhole. I never would have thought I would've ended up with a man not so different from the ones I grew up around. Johnny's gorgeous. He makes my heart flutter with his slick smile, but he's such an asshole. He's no Prince Charming, that's for sure.

I never thought a man like him would make me feel so good, especially one who likes ordering me around. No, I don't think I'd ever find someone so disarming—someone who makes me wet with his very presence. I rebelled against men like him all my life. How the fuck did this happen to me?

"*No.*"

His smirk disappears for a moment as he lets me down and takes the shirt off his back, revealing a map of tattooed, lean muscle. There's a flag of Sicily, St. Joseph on his shoulder, and a bunch of other religious shit I don't recognize, and a cross with the word *Sempre* around it. Red, white, and green. He's a proud Italian, through and through.

My eyes linger on the huge bump right under his waist, straining against his slacks, but he makes no move to pull them down. I can visualize it in my head, see the fabric pulling down his waist and over that thick cock, beading with a gossamer strand of pre-cum.

"*Please.*"

"Fuck."

I can see the fight behind his eyes as he reaches out and

touches my breast. He wants me to grovel at his feet, but he wants to fuck me more than that.

I own you.

Still smiling, he bends toward the floor and picks up something metallic with a long wire and a clicker attached to the end. He puts the round metal object against my pussy and clicks.

A buzzing sound fills my ears as the metal egg vibrates against my clit, sending electrical shocks deep inside my pussy. Holy Christ, I've never felt anything like this.

"Oh—*oh my God!*"

"I'm not a god," he grins.

It's torture to feel that hard egg buzzing against my clit, slipping slightly as he massages me. His tongue drags a circle around my nipples and the shocks make me arch my back into him.

"Please, for fuck's sake!"

I thrash in the handcuffs he has me in, but his arm wraps around my waist, holding me still. "Say that you'll marry me."

Jesus.

The egg pushes through my folds and slips inside. His fingers curve on the back of it as he shoves it in deep, massaging my clit against the vibrating waves. I can't fucking hold out much longer. With every throb of my heartbeat, I imagine his dick shoved inside me, rutting me hard.

"Say it."

I don't have a choice.

"*Fine.*"

"No, that's not *fine*. I want to hear you—"

"Yes, I'll *fucking* marry you!"

Like I have a goddamn choice at this point, pinned against the wall with a vibrator jammed against my pussy. God, I can't stand him.

His thumb pinches my clit and the vibrator electrifies me at the same time, sending me careening over the edge.

"JUST FUCK ME!"

My legs tremble as he finally throws the vibrator aside and pulls his pants down, releasing his cock. I barely get a look at his throbbing length before he picks me up. The head slides inside me swiftly, painful and deep. It knocks the breath out of my chest as he slams his hips against me.

"You're mine. *Say it.*"

He shoves his cock balls deep. It's buried to the hilt and I can barely breathe with him pulsing inside me, my legs wrapped around his waist. I don't find that I give a shit about admitting that *yes*, I'm his, especially when he's looking right into my eyes as he's inside me.

"I'm yours."

Then he pounds my hips, his cock thrusting inside me, filling me completely as I twist my wrists in the straps. He bites down on my tits and I scream to the ceiling, unable to take the stimulation from his dick and his mouth. I got so worked up from that vibrator that I feel myself teetering on the edge, and I want to hold on to his shoulders and ride his cock.

"*Moan for me.*"

I clutch the straps yanking on my wrists as he slams into me. His left hand lets me go briefly to get in a vicious slap on my ass. My legs tighten and I squeeze, my tits rubbing against his face.

"Johnny!"

I moan out his name as I come all over his dick, and he sucks in his breath and pounds me faster, yanking my waist into his. Then he buries his face in my neck and groans out loud, releasing a torrent of cum inside my pussy. Holy fuck, it's so warm. His chest pulses rapidly as he blows air across my neck, kissing my skin between breaths. I sag against my restraints as he slowly lets me down and unhooks my handcuffs from the straps on the door, and I wrap both arms around him as he lifts me up and carries me to bed.

We both collapse on the mattress, exhausted, my body still glowing with the orgasm. He gathers me in his arms and drags me into his chest with surprising strength, as if I'm a rag doll.

"I told you I'd get you to say it."

I'm too tired to muster up the energy to hate him.

Johnny's warmth leaves my side for a second, and when he returns he slides his arms back around me. I feel safe, just content to close my eyes and feel his heartbeat against my back, his low voice rumbling through my body.

Then he takes my hand and I see the diamond ring between his fingertips. I bite my lip as he slides it down my finger, the glow bursting like a needle to a balloon.

He wants me for sex, nothing else. Or his pride. That wouldn't be too bad, except for the fact that I have a baby inside me. I'm supposed to marry this guy and have his kid, even though I barely know him. I'm not sure I even like him. He's a mob boss, for fuck's sake.

I turn around in his arms, cradling my hand with the new ring. Maybe it's because I haven't seen his bad side, but I'm just not scared of him.

"What is this between us?"

"You're my fiancée."

His voice sounds so dead and I feel as though I'm shrinking. There's no connection between us, is there?

What makes you think that he'll even be a good father?

My chest freezes as he plants a kiss on my stunned

face, rubbing my back as if to soothe me. He's very good at imitating acts of affection, but without the warmth it feels so empty. There's passion in his eyes, but it's not for me—it's for the baby.

"I don't know you."

He makes a sound through his nose and sinks into the pillow. "You never get to know someone."

"What does that mean?"

"Everybody has something to hide." A dark shadow crosses his eyes like a storm. "Like you."

"Like me?"

A smile tugs at the corner of his mouth. "You didn't tell me you were his daughter. You could have if you wanted to, but you didn't."

"Then you wouldn't have fucked me."

"Wrong."

Strong hands reach around my head and pull me closer so that his breath billows over my lips.

"I was fucked the moment I saw you. Nothing in the world would have stopped me from chasing you."

It's the perfect thing to say, even if it's a lie.

His lips fall against mine, softer than they've ever felt before, and then I'm not so sure.

I don't care. I need to be able to hope.

JOHNNY

She pretends to sleep as I get dressed, even as I sit next to her head, admiring the view of the sheets only partially obscuring her gorgeous tits. The more I look at the rather perfect image of her soft brown hair splayed over her cheek, fluttering with every breath and the swell of her milky breasts, the more I feel my cock getting stiff. I already fucked her this morning, and goddamn it, I want her again.

I grab the edge of the sheets and drag them over her shoulders, pretending that I don't know she's faking it, and then I give her a kiss on the cheek. Guilt stirs inside me for the things I said last night that I didn't mean. I whispered sweet things that she needed to hear from me, that women like to hear, but I feel nothing but a burning desire for that pussy and a need to protect what's mine.

My fiancée.

My baby.

It's hard to feel close to them yet. I feel *proud*, as though I'm finally a whole man, with a fiancée and a baby on the way. It's what I always wanted, but she's going to want more. That's why I do these little gestures—covering her while she "sleeps" and telling her that I'm crazy about her. If it makes her a happy wife, what's the harm in it?

I stand up from the bed and start walking toward the door.

"Where are you going?" she calls out after me, as clear as day without a trace of sleepiness in her voice.

Maya sits upright, the sheets gathered at her waist. I'm distracted by how gorgeous she looks topless, and how badly I want them in my hands again.

Maddon.

"I'm going out for a while."

She raises an eyebrow. "For what?"

"Work."

"Where?"

I let out a long sigh. "You're going to have to get used to me going out at all hours, and not knowing what I'm doing at those hours."

She throws the sheets aside and slips out of bed. I clench my teeth as my fiancée walks toward me, completely naked. Maya stands inches from me, her tits in grabbing range.

"So, are the same rules extended to me?"

"What?"

She smirks. "I get to go out whenever I want, for however long I want and I don't have to tell you jack shit?"

I smile back. "No."

"Well, that's bullshit."

"I'm a boss, sweetheart. I don't get run around by anyone, not even my future wife."

Boy, does that piss her off. Her nostrils flare and she jabs her fingers at me.

"Listen to me, you sexist asshole—"

"—You better stop there."

"I'll say whatever the fuck I want."

Goddamn it, she's a hotheaded little spitfire. She's so beautiful when she's pissed off. No one looks at me the way she does. She actually meets my gaze and holds it.

"I love the way you are, Maya, but you can't act like this in front of other people. You can't say whatever the fuck you want all the time."

"Why not?"

"Because there are consequences. Bigger ones than getting my hand across your ass, I mean."

"Oh, is that a threat?"

Will nothing I say work on this broad?

"You need to understand that my reputation is at stake if you're running your mouth at me in front of other men. It makes me look *weak*."

She crosses her arms in front of her chest.

"People have gotten killed for less."

"You seriously think that could happen?"

Finally I see fear widening her eyes. I take her jaw in my hand. "So far, I've been very patient with you. *Nice*, even. I'm never nice."

"You're demanding a lot from me."

"I know, and that's why I've been patient. You get the special treatment because you're the mother of my child."

"Whatever." She rolls her eyes at me, seeing through the honeyed lies on my tongue.

It still boils my blood.

"I still want to know where you're going."

Jesus Christ.

"There are certain aspects of my job that you don't want or need to know."

"*Where are you going?*"

Just tell her.

"I'm going to meet your dad."

She blanches and wraps her arms around herself, suddenly sitting back down on the mattress, and I feel a surge of triumph.

"I told you that you would be happier not knowing—"

"You're not meeting him at the fortress, are you?"

"I'm not a fucking moron."

The air stills as she sits there in silence, twisting her

hands in her lap.

"Maybe—maybe I should come with you."

"No," I say flatly. "I don't know how it's going to go."

Maya bites her thumb and nods, looking extremely nervous. To be frank, I'm not relishing this meeting either. Who wants to tell a colleague that you banged his daughter and got her pregnant?

I walk past her, but she grabs ahold of the tips of my fingers. I look at her.

"Be careful. Seriously."

There's genuine concern written all over her, and it puzzles me. She has nothing to worry about.

* * *

Listen, Carlos. I accidentally fucked your daughter. She tripped and fell on my dick. I didn't know who she was at first, but when I found out I decided to see her again—

No.

Your daughter is pregnant and I'm the father. By the way, the engagement party is on Friday.

I barely suppress a smile as the dialogue runs through my head, even though it really isn't funny. I should have more respect for the man, but I don't. Not after hearing about his prejudice and how he nearly gunned down his own daughter.

Worthless piece of shit reminds me of my own father.

I drum my fingertips on the wooden table as Sal keeps his hands clenched on his thighs. Everyone in my crew knows about it now.

"All due respect, John, what the fuck were you thinking?"

"I didn't know who the hell she was."

Frustration screws up his face. "No, I meant not letting her take care of the baby."

Take care of the baby? An abortion?

Redness sears across my vision, and for a moment I imagine myself standing up and clocking Sal across the face. "It's not a fucking option."

"All right."

"Don't bring it up again."

"I'm sorry."

Simmering, I sit back in the chair. We're in a hotel suite. Neutral territory. My entourage surrounds me, and Carlos' will be joining us soon.

Things could get heated.

They could get dangerous.

Luckily it's standard procedure to collect weapons at the door, so at least he won't be able to blow my head off the moment I tell him what I did.

Shit.

There's a knock at the door and the faintest edge hits

my heart. I nod to Chris, who opens the door and frisks the men.

Carlos already looks pissed. That dirty old bastard walks into the room as I stand up and extend my hand.

He ignores it.

Strike one.

"Where the fuck is my daughter?"

So we're getting right to it, aren't we?

"Have a seat, Carlos."

He doesn't look like he wants to sit down. He looks like he wants to smash his fist across my face. Can't say I blame him.

"I know she's been to *Le Zinc* to see you and I know you picked her up from that bar."

"Sit the fuck down."

His heated voice puts me on edge, and my soldiers tense against the wall.

Defuse the fucking situation.

Carlos backs off, venom in his gaze as he sits down on the chair as though it has pins. I take my seat and fold my hands into steeples.

"Couple weeks ago, I met a girl in my bar," I tell him, staring directly into his eyes. "I took her home. We had a good time and that was that."

"You son of a bitch—"

223

"I had no idea who the fuck she was until she came into *Le Zinc*."

Carlos doesn't say another word. He just stares at me with the most poisonous, rotten hatred I've ever seen in my life.

"My daughter came to you and you fucked her like one of your whores?"

Heat slowly builds up in my chest. "I told you, I had no idea who she was. I would have never touched her."

That's a lie.

"I want my daughter back home—"

"No."

He stands up from the chair, biceps rippling. "No?"

"Sit back down."

"I will fucking—"

"She's pregnant, and it's mine."

For a moment there's stunned silence and his jaw goes slack. Then he lets out a scream of outrage and the table flips over, crashing to the side of the wall. I saw it coming a mile away. One wrong look and he'll come after me and I'll be forced to kill him.

I stand up and grab the head of my chair, watching his pacing body as he desperately tries to keep it all together.

"You fucking insult me by fucking my daughter and getting her pregnant—"

KNOCKED UP BY THE BAD BOY

"Carlos, I had no idea who she was, but I want to make it right. I never meant to disrespect you."

"You disrespected me the moment you put your fucking cock inside her." He spits on the floor and Chris makes a violent gesture, but I hold out a hand.

He's allowed to be pissed.

"We're engaged. I'll make her part of my family—"

"NO!"

My hands turn white. *"I'm trying to do right by your daughter."*

"I'd rather see her *dead* than watch her get married to an Italian."

"What the fuck did you just say?"

The ugly words hang over our heads like a grand piano on the verge of crashing down. There it is, out in the open. Carlos sucks in his bottom lip, bursting to tell me off like the dumbass he is.

Say it again, you piece of shit. And I'll grab the shotgun hidden behind the couch.

"You want to make it right?" he says in a cooler tone.

"Yes."

He points a finger in my face. "She gets an abortion and she comes back to me."

Hell fucking no.

"I am not killing my unborn child."

225

"Then she is fucking dead to me, AND SO ARE YOU!"

He lunges at me, but his men grab his arms and yank him back. "Carlos, come on!"

"NO! He knocked up my daughter and I'm just supposed to fucking take it?"

"I apologized to you," I say through my teeth. "I am trying to be respectful even though I'd like to put a bullet in your head for suggesting that I force my fiancée to abort my child."

"Why don't you fucking try it, *dago*!"

I'm seconds away from hurling my chair in his face and beating him down until his legs stop working. I want to hear him scream, for his ribs to break because he just used that word against me.

"Get him the fuck out of here before I kill him."

What a disaster.

Tensions are taut, stretched beyond their limit. Like a flickering match in a gasoline-soaked room. Everyone's ready to explode.

"This isn't fucking over!" he screams over his shoulder as his men drag him outside. "That fucking guinea touched my daughter—"

I kick the chair aside, and I can't see anything but red as I lunge at the door. Sal tackles my chest before I can get to the door, and then the others help pin me against the wall. My throat is ripped raw from my screams.

"FUCKING COCKSUCKER!"

"Johnny, calm down."

"I'll fucking kill him!"

The roar of motorcycles drowns out my voice. There's still a chance—I can still fucking get him.

"Let me the fuck go!"

Their arms finally loosen their hold on me, and I shove Sal's chest. I want to smash his face to a pulp.

"You should have let me kill that piece of shit. He has to go."

Of that, I'm certain.

Sal squeezes my shoulder. "You just told him that you knocked up his daughter. Let him cool off."

"No one calls me a fucking guinea. I should rip out his tongue and feed it to the pigs—piece of shit!"

"I hear you, but he's the president of *Les Diables*."

Yes, he is.

He's also my fiancée's father.

I try to let those facts sink into my head, even though I want nothing more than to climb into my Audi and run him over. It would be satisfying to see that prick launch from his stupid bike, and the police would probably thank me for it.

"This is my opinion, but I think you should give him another chance. I don't think his people want a war, either."

That's what'll happen if I make a move on their president. A lot of people will die, and there's still the matter of the airport heist. It can't be derailed, no matter what.

* * *

I park my car and slam the door shut. When I get into the elevator, I pace around the small box, hating my reflection, because it reminds me so much of my own father. Then I jam the keys in my apartment and wrench open the door, slamming it so hard that the walls shake.

I see her hanging against the doorframe, her arms crossed. She pushes off slightly and makes a beeline toward me, her long hair swaying behind her shoulders. Dark makeup makes her eyes look mischievous, but I'm in no mood for her shit right now.

"So how'd it go?"

I don't say anything. I'm not the fucking type to open up about my goddamn feelings. I'd rather just bury it. Forget about it.

"That bad, eh?"

An apologetic smile lifts the corners of her mouth and some of the steam cools off my chest.

"You look really pissed." She bites her lip.

"I am fucking pissed," I finally snap.

"What did he say?"

I march past her, torn between the need to rant and rave, and what my mother would say if she knew I was badmouthing my fiancée's father in front of her.

She won't leave me alone. Maya's footsteps echo behind me, even as I enter my study. The one place she shouldn't fucking follow me.

"What do you want?"

"I want to talk to you."

"You don't want to hear me trash your father, so please just leave me the fuck alone."

I'm appalled at my tone. It's not her fault. She doesn't deserve this.

Maya steps inside my office, bold as brass. Her hands glide over my shoulders and slide my jacket from my arms. What the hell is she doing?

"Johnny, there's nothing you could say about my dad that I haven't thought of already."

"He's a miserable prick. He insulted me. Called me a fucking *dago*."

Her brown eyes slide to mine. "He calls you that all the time behind your back."

My heart pounds against my chest. I hear my blood

229

roaring in my head.

She bites her lip again. "I shouldn't have said that."

I sigh as she loosens my tie and unbuttons my shirt. Her hands soothe me. It's nice to feel them flattening over my muscles. Hell, just looking at her makes me feel better.

I want to stew. I want to go after that son of a bitch, but Maya's fucking hands are all over me. Her right hand slides down my waist and anchors over my cock. She gives it a squeeze.

And then I wonder why the fuck I'm pissed when I have a smoking-hot fiancée, standing right in front of me, fondling me. Just begging for it. She gropes me through the fabric and a low growl escapes my throat.

"That first night with you."

"What about it?"

She's making waves of blood pound through my dick. "The way you just stripped off your clothes in front of me to distract me." My muscles stretch into a smile for the first time. "That's what it feels like you're doing right now."

"Is it working?"

You know damn well it's working. It made me come inside her without protection, which knocked her up.

I don't regret it.

And I don't regret what I'm about to do to her either.

She hisses in pain as I grasp a handful of her hair and pull.

"I don't want to fuck you while I'm angry—"

"Why not?"

"I don't want to hurt you."

But it's already too fucking late. I grab the neckline of her t-shirt with both hands and rip.

"Johnny!"

I tear it all the way down and then I fling the discarded pieces away from her. She whirls around, her eyes widened.

I take her jaw gently and sweep my thumb over her parted lips, which sigh against me. "For your own good, you should tell me to stop now."

She should walk away right now, except she reaches behind her back and undoes her bra. Her tits spill out as the bra slides down her arms. Fearless eyes.

"I want you."

How can I resist that?

"I want to own your body."

My blood simmers as she bends over and pulls her jeans and panties all the way down. Her shaven pussy gleams with wetness. She is so beautiful. I don't want to hurt her, but I fucking want her.

I fist her hair and arch her neck over my arm as though

I'm about to slit her throat. Then I make her walk to the desk in my dark study. I've never fucked anyone on my desk.

I kiss her throat as her chest pulses, and then my mouth drags over her skin, all the way to her ear. Her body responds to my touch by turning a bright red color.

"I wanted to tell your daddy that I would have fucked his daughter even if I knew who she was."

I palm her back and force her to bend over my desk.

"Lay your arms in front of you."

She obeys like a perfect little fiancée, already obsessed with pleasing her man. What a fantastic view of her pussy. It's mine, along with every other part of her. I'd like to spank that swell of her ass over and over and feel the blood rush to my palm and her skin heat up, but I don't have time to play with her. I unloop the belt at my waist and shove my slacks down, loving how she jumps when I lay the leather strap over her ass.

Thwack!

The imprint of the belt slowly swells red as I crack it over her ass. The rage flows down my hand, pulsing into that belt as if it's an extension of myself. I lean over her, my thick cock flattening against her ass as I loop the belt around her neck and pull it back with my fist. My heart pounds at the sight of her bent over the desk for me. The way her back curves and her tits kiss my desk. Holy fuck, it's a hot sight. Then I sink my cock into her, pulling on the belt as she lets out a sharp hiss. Her warmth swallows me whole. I dig my fingers into her ass as I watch my cock slowly sink between her lips. She moans, pressing her ass against mine. My fingers make red marks in her skin and I yank back on the belt, watching her hair spill over her back. I bury myself balls deep inside her, transfixed by the image of her hair over her naked back. She screams as I rut her hard, the contents of my desk spilling to the floor as she splays out her hands.

I lean over her body and slide my hand under her chest, squeezing her round globes. She turns her head, the belt tight on her throat.

"Johnny!"

I want to see her come apart as I fuck her brains out. The belt makes a loud sound as I hurl it away from me. Then I pull out of her, my cock pounding with the need to release. I wrap my arms around her ass and lift her onto my desk so that she sits on the edge.

She digs her fingers in my hair as her chest heaves. I push her down so that she lies flat on my desk, her knees spread apart with her pussy open for me.

No one calls me a fucking *dago* to my face.

My dick slides back into her and a low moan trembles

from Maya's parted lips. She wraps her legs around me and screams. My hips slam into the desk, fucking her cunt so hard that I have to force myself to slow down because of the edge of pain in her voice. Her tits bounce on her chest as I bang her, and I bend over her body, overcome with a need to mark her as mine. Her fingers thread through my hair as I touch my lips to her gorgeous tits and suck. I bite her fucking hard and she yanks on my hair. The red mark swells and I find another area of smooth skin to defile. She doesn't tell me to stop. She digs her heels in my back and arches her body into my mouth as though she can't get enough of it—enough of me.

My mouth finds her nipple and she twists under me, moaning. I love seeing her like this. It makes my cock pulse with blood. I feel myself getting close, and I think how hot it would be to come all over her body, to see her tits dripping with my cum. It's filthy as fuck.

"Johnny!"

My beautiful fiancée is close. I can see the desire screwing up her face. My mouth finds her lips and she crushes them against me as I bury myself balls deep. She nearly chokes me with her tongue and I bite down on it. Her moans vibrate through my lips.

"Keep going!"

She digs her fingers in my back so hard that I know I'll

have marks. No matter. I gave her about a dozen on her tits. I nearly come when I think about defiling her pretty body, and taking a picture of it and sending it to her asshole father, but I would never do that, of course.

I thrust my hips harder as she clings to my back and moans into my ear. She squeezes my cock and convulsions rip through her body.

"Oh my God!"

I pull out my dick, so close I can feel it building up inside my shaft, and then I fist the base of my cock. A rope of cum shoots out, draping over her tits. I pump my shaft as three more ropes shoot out, the energy leaving my body as I stroke my dick. It's as perfect as I envisioned. Thin streams of white lie across her body, over her breasts and the marks sprinkled all over. Goddamn, it's beautiful.

"I want to remember the way you look right now."

She turns her head, too tired to respond.

You're completely and utterly mine.

I bend over, my legs shaking as I take my discarded shirt and wipe the cum from her body.

She sits up on the desk, her eyes narrowed at me as I hold my shirt.

All of a sudden my balance is off. She shoves my chest and she's on her feet, and then her palm rips across my face. She slaps me so goddamn hard my head whips to the side. A vicious sting makes blood rush to my cheek.

What the fuck just happened?

My cheek burns as she looks at me as though I'm scum, and I touch her shoulder. She flinches from my touch, and that alone makes me swallow hard.

"Did I hurt you?"

"*No.*"

"Then what is your problem?"

"*You.*"

Arrogant eyes flick toward me and away as she walks to the door.

"Is this some kind of pregnancy hormones, mood-swing *bullshit*, or do you have a reason for slapping me?"

"*You* might have fucked the anger out of your system, but I've been pissed off for days."

Fine, I get it. She's used to getting what she wants, and she's upset that she can't go off on her own anymore.

"I'm stuck here all day, and I'm getting married to a man, who, well…"

Her voice trails off and I cross my arms, my temper flaring again. "Who…*what*? Finish your sentence."

A pink blush spreads over her cheeks. "Never mind."

I reach out and touch her cheek. "Tell me."

Her eyelashes flutter against her cheek and then she looks back at me with that challenging stare. "You're a cold bastard."

I've heard it a thousand times before, of course. My ex-wives loved to hurl it at me, and each time they did I never felt anything but cool indifference. This time there's a tiny pinprick of pain, like a splinter in my heart.

"You have the emotional range of a teaspoon."

Don't get angry.

She's just plain wrong about that. I used to feel joy, instead of a numb detachment. It's hard when you don't even remember what it was like.

"I'm not a hearts-and-flowers guy, Maya."

But my heart rips in half when her eyes suddenly bead with tears. "This is *never* going to work."

"I'm not calling this off."

"Then maybe I'll have to."

"I don't think so."

"I'll want a divorce!"

A knife twists in my heart. "Good luck finding a lawyer who will represent you against me."

Her eyes widen as I take her arms and gently pin her against the wall.

"I'm not letting you go, sweetheart. You were mine the moment I laid eyes on you."

"Is that supposed to make me feel better?"

"It's supposed to make you stop fighting against me."

A gust of air leaves her mouth. "Fat chance."

Fucking hell.

I grab her chin, anger flaring up inside me again. "I might not be what you want, but I'll treat you better than any man ever has in your life. I promise. You can have anything you want. Just ask, and I'll give it to you."

Maya stares at me for a long time, as though judging whether she can trust what I say. Then she walks away from me.

Goddamn it.

I stalk her, heat rising in my chest when she ignores my footsteps. She spins around when I grab her elbow.

"*What?*"

"Did you not hear what I fucking said?"

My chest caves in when her eyes swim with tears. She turns away from me and wipes her face, a sob shaking from her throat. I've seen a lot of women cry in my time. God, the screaming fights with my ex-wives, and the wailing at funerals. The sound made me inwardly cringe, but the noise coming from Maya—that desperate intake of breath—is like a knife to my chest.

"Please don't—I'm sorry."

I'll do anything to make her stop crying.

"Don't!"

She pushes my attempts to hold her—to stop her from

making that awful sound. I hold her against my chest even though she shoves me, because it's the only thing that I can think of that'll make her stop.

"I don't want to live like this."

"Like what?"

Then her tears stop and her reddened face snarls at me. "If I'm going to be your *wife*, you need to start treating me like one."

What the fuck is she talking about?

"I am treating you like my wife." My fingers spread over her back. "Anything that's mine is yours, Maya—"

"I don't want your fucking things! I want *you*."

A grin spreads across my face. "Not fifteen minutes ago, I was balls deep inside you. I don't know what to tell you."

"I want intimacy. I want to *know* you—"

She wants to go on fucking dates. To hold hands and walk down the street and hear sweet nothings whispered in her ear.

"All you had to do was ask."

Her eyes flutter when I run my fingers over her flushed cheek.

"I didn't think I had to."

Snarky little spitfire.

She leans into my hand and lets out a sigh. It's one of

those painful sounds. Every instinct tells her to hate me, but she wants me—feels hurt at the idea that she's only a piece of ass for me.

I bend down and suddenly pick her up. She throws her arms around my neck as I lift her into my arms.

"What are you doing?"

"Taking you to the living room."

"For what?"

For a fucking date, that's what.

"To watch a movie with me."

Deep down I know that I've been an asshole to her. It's the stress of so many things going on. I've had no time to make sure she was happy. She's having my kid. The least I can do is make sure her needs are met.

She smiles when I sink down into the couch with her in my arms. Maya nestles in my chest as I turn the TV on.

"What do you want to watch?"

"*Legally Blonde.*"

Oh Christ.

Somewhat regretting my idea already, I choose the channel and prepare myself for an hour and a half of Reese Witherspoon's ridiculous face. But it works. Maya laughs at the screen, the sound shaking through my body. The movie is boring, but I'm content just to hold her and watch the mirth on her face. The couch squeaks as she moves her body. She rests her head against my chest and her eyelids flutter.

"So tired."

"Go to sleep."

She murmurs something and I'm just content to stroke her arm, my eyes heavy. I lie there, my fingers slowly kneading her until I'm lulled to sleep, too.

MAYA

The warm, humid air clings to my skin as I walk down the street in a short cocktail dress. I take Johnny's hand, forcing him to slow down and walk by my side. The night hums with the slight buzz of packed bars and happy voices. We pass by a closed restaurant and he grins at me before pulling me behind a privacy screen of the outdoor seating.

"What are you—?"

The backs of my legs hit the wooden bench next to the folded-up chairs, and he climbs on top of me, silencing me with his lips pressed against mine.

Damn it—it's instant heat between us. Or at least, I feel it burning my chest. The heat is right above my heart, which flies like a bird.

He pulls back with that crazy, animalistic look in his eyes and bends swiftly to kiss the swell of my breasts—and bite.

"Johnny!"

A growl rumbles in his throat and then he sucks in air, straightening from me. He pulls me to my feet effortlessly, and I bump into his chest. Then he reaches a hand under my dress and gives my ass a squeeze.

Jesus Christ.

"You look hot."

His voice creeps inside me as his hand lingers on my ass.

"Tonight's for going out."

"Yeah, *yeah*."

He promised he would take me out so we could get to know each other a little better before our engagement party, although I doubt he really gives a shit about getting to know the finer details of who I really am. Still, I can't be mad with him. He's making an effort.

My insides simmer as we walk down the street, hand in hand. According to Johnny, my father's people would snatch me the moment I strayed from his presence. I know they're here, watching me, but I don't really mind. I'm desperate for news about my mom, and Chuck.

I follow Johnny without really seeing where I'm going, full of doubt. Weeks ago I was following my dreams. The classes for beauty school started a week ago, and it's hard not to feel a pang for what I've lost.

Now I'm just a pregnant mob fiancée destined to become the don's wife.

Johnny stops walking and I nearly crash into him. I look at the tiny hole in the wall. *Napoletana.*

"This is one of my favorite places."

I'm skeptical as he leads me inside, eyeing the amateurish painted mural on the wall and the plastic green-checkered covered tables.

"How'd you find this place?"

"My father took me here all the time."

We squeeze through the narrow entrance and Johnny heads toward an open table in the side room where it's a little quieter. He pulls back the chair for me and I sit down. Then he circles the table and sits across from me. A passing waiter notices him immediately.

"*Bonsoir, Monsieur* Cravotta."

He gives him a little nod of his head and the waiter returns with two menus and a bottle of wine. The waiter pours just a small amount of wine and Johnny tastes it, nodding in approval. Johnny looks at me across the table and smiles as the waiter pours him a full glass. When he goes to fill mine, Johnny makes a stopping motion with his hand.

"She can't drink."

That's right. Shit.

My hand unconsciously curls around my stomach. "I keep forgetting that I'm pregnant."

"I haven't."

He surveys me across the table, the low visibility

obscuring half of his face in shadows. Then the waiter lights one of the candles and softness flickers over his tanned skin.

"Are you—are you scared of becoming a father?"

I know I don't feel ready to become a parent. Johnny mulls it over with a slight smile and shakes his head.

"No. I've wanted this for a long time."

It just doesn't compute. Why would a sex-crazed mobster want anything to do with kids? Why have anything get in the way of fucking as many women as he wants and going out all night?

"Why?"

"I don't know," he says, shrugging. "I guess I just didn't feel like a whole man. There was something missing—a void."

His black eyes blaze with restless hunger as I curl my hands over the table. I can't identify with that. I was just trying to have fun, to get out a little bit, not sign up for a lifetime of domestic bliss.

"But you don't even know me. I might be a terrible mom."

He shakes his head, smiling.

"I might smoke and drink while I'm pregnant—beat the kid or something."

"I don't get the crazy vibe from you."

I don't get any kind of vibe from you.

"What makes you think that a baby is going to fill this void of yours?"

The intensity in his eyes drops to a low simmer. "I didn't know how badly I wanted a family until your dad threatened to take it away from me."

A small thrill runs through me when I feel the protectiveness of his words, but it's not just that. He wants a family—he wants to possess me.

"I know it doesn't make sense. I can't explain it."

I never thought I would keep a baby from a one-night stand, but here we are. I don't know why, but I trust him. He'll take care of me and the baby. He's a fucking Italian, for fuck's sake. It's practically encoded in their DNA.

"All I know is that I just need to protect what's mine."

My heart jumps in my chest. "You're mine, too."

A small smile curls his lips as he slides his hand down the table and takes my hand, intertwining his fingers with mine. "Yes."

"I mean it, Johnny."

"I don't plan on getting another wife."

"You know what I mean. No fucking strippers, cocktail waitresses—I'm the only one who gets to touch your dick."

A smirk staggers across his face. "I find the fact you

think that I chase hired pussy *insulting*—"

"I saw you staring at that cocktail waitress' ass the second time we met."

His smirk refuses to disappear and my insides boil with heat as he leans across the table, his hand stroking my knee underneath. "You're already fucking jealous, huh?"

It's not exactly jealousy, but I can't deny that I'm worried. He has a crazy sex drive, and what'll happen when I'm huge and there are hot waitresses and strippers strutting around him all day at work?

"You don't need to be jealous, Maya."

"My stomach is going to swell and I'm going to get fat—"

It feels ridiculous to admit these stupid, insecure fears of mine as he inches his hand up my thigh.

"You'll be sexy."

His dark eyes seem to glow at me from across the table, and I can tell that he means it. Maybe he's even looking forward to it. It brings a smile to my face.

"My child is inside you, and you're wearing my ring. Why would I want someone else, when I have you all to myself? All I want to do is fuck you until my cock stops working."

Greedy fingers squeeze my thigh and a sudden flare shoots between my legs, sending heat to my face. No one's ever looked at me the way he does. He makes me feel like a prize. It's the way his eyes linger on every inch of my skin, and the way he strokes my body after he fucks me, as though he still wants me. I'm addicted to that. The more I look into his eyes, the more I just want to call this whole dinner off and go home.

"Have you thought about names?"

"A little bit," he admits. "I like Matteo, for a boy."

Thinking of the baby sends my heart racing.

"I worried about becoming a mom."

"*It'll be fine.*"

"I have no one to look up to. You don't understand what it was like growing up in that place."

"That's exactly why you'll be a great mom. You survived that shit-hole."

Confidence blazes from him, but I can't help the trembling of my hand. I wish I could be that sure of myself. I only know what I know.

"You've been there?"

"Many times." He clasps his hands on the table. "Bikers have no fucking class, no offense."

He's right, but it's a little rich to hear him say that.

"Your opening line to me was, 'I want to fuck you.'"

White teeth flash at me as he lets out a short laugh and shrugs apologetically. "I was just getting to the point, sweetheart."

"Nothing gets to a girl's heart faster."

The corners of his lips turn. "You didn't seem to mind any of the filthy shit I said to you."

"Well—"

"You definitely didn't mind that filthy shit when I did them to you."

Cocky bastard.

"If you've been to the fortress, then you know what it's like there."

"I guess."

I lean in across the table. "I don't want our kid to be surrounded by violence."

"That's not going to happen."

My voice lowers to a whisper. "But your job—"

"Unlike your father, we don't involve our women and kids in the family business." He slides his hand along my arm. "I don't bring my work home."

My eyes search him, the handsome, dark suit, his hair neatly swept, the deep, earnest eyes. He's not lying. How could that be possible?

"Sounds too good to be true."

The smirk lifts to his eyes. "It probably does after living in that place for so long. It may come as a surprise to you after hearing your father's bullshit, but we respect our families."

His hand slides away from me as I slowly digest that. It sounds like a fantasyland.

"What's your family like?"

He makes a face at the question, quickly hiding his discomfort under a smile. "Can't complain."

The guy can't stand talking about himself, can he?

"Was your dad like you?"

At the mention of his dad, Johnny compulsively grabs his wineglass. "He was in the life, yeah."

I'm startled by the grittiness in his voice. "What was he like?"

His eyes cut into me as every trace of warmth recedes from his body. I feel it like a wave of frost curling around my limbs. He gives me a look as though it's none of my fucking business.

"I'm just trying to get to know you."

"You don't need to know anything about my dad for that."

He looks like he might snap the stem of his wineglass. Fine, I'll drop it. It's not worth him getting pissed off, but he changes tack with lightning speed.

"What did you want to do before you met me?"

A sagging feeling makes me slump over the table. The hair salon. Beauty school. Both dreams, crushed. I can't stand to talk about it now.

"It's stupid."

"Tell me."

"No."

"Come on."

Fine.

"I wanted to go to beauty school, and I worked at the café because I was going to save up money to move out and work at a hair salon. Maybe have my own business, one day."

It was a stupid, modest dream, but it was mine.

There. Go on. Laugh at me.

But he doesn't laugh. "That's not stupid. Lots of my guys' wives work in hair salons. Who gives a fuck?"

Seeing him shrug it off lightens a huge weight sitting on my chest.

"My dad said it was a waste of money. He wanted me to stay in the compound, date a biker, and watch everyone's kids. Anyway, he made me quit my job and refused to pay for the school." I shrug hopelessly. "And now I'm here."

And now I'm depressed.

"What was it about it that you liked so much?"

I stare at the small hole in the plastic tablecloth, avoiding his gaze because I don't want to see how sorry he

251

feels for me.

"It doesn't matter anymore. I was supposed to go to college, and then that fell through because my dad thought it was a waste of time, so I shouldn't be surprised that he thought beauty school was a waste of time, too."

He frowns at me as the waiter drops a deep-red pizza in front of us, the cooked tomato aroma hitting my stomach immediately. Shit, that smells delicious.

"My father said the same thing to me."

"What?"

"He never really gave a shit about education. He just wanted me to start working for him. You know, help provide for the family."

We're quiet for a moment as he cuts a slice for me and slides the wedge onto my plate. He cuts one for himself, slicing into the plate with a knife so loudly that the ceramic shrieks and I wince.

I guess he still hates his dad.

He picks up a knife and fork, cutting into the slice.

"You seriously eat pizza with a knife and fork?"

He looks at me, his utensils raised. "What?"

I sputter with laughter as he gives me a serious look. "I never took you as a prissy guy."

"I get my hands dirty all the damn time."

Then he winks at me and my heart squeezes.

"So pussy juice is okay but tomato sauce isn't?"

"Don't talk like that here—"

"I seem to remember you laying on filthy lines at me at that sausage place."

"That was different. People know me here for being—"

"—For eating your pizza with a knife and fork."

"Come on."

"I *promise* you that they gossip about it."

He drops the knife and fork and grabs the slice with his hands, tearing off a piece with his mouth as he stares at me, chewing. "Are you done breaking my balls?"

"Why? It's so much fun."

Hell, I'm actually smiling for the first time in days. We eat the rest of the meal in comfortable silence and I feel as though a little weight has been lifted off my shoulders. I still don't know much about him, but I learned a few bits. At least he has a sense of humor.

"Mr. Cravotta, thank you so much for coming. I hope you have a pleasant evening."

Johnny gives the waiter a genial smile as he stands up, slapping a bunch of bills on the table.

"Do you ever get tired of people sucking up to you?"

He lets out a long sigh as he guides me out of the restaurant. "Why do you always say whatever's in your head?"

I slip my hand into his as we walk down the street, and a smile pulls at his lips.

"Do you want me to be a sycophant like everyone else?"

"*No.*" He stops in the middle of the sidewalk and tugs my arm so that I fly into his chest, and then he looks down at me through smoldering eyes. "I want you to shut up and kiss me."

The moment I feel his breath on my lips, I lean forward because I'm tall enough in these heels to catch his lips. Something more than desire heats up inside me as he curves his arm around my waist and kisses me back right in the middle of the sidewalk. It feels as though there's something leaping inside my stomach and a breathless wave of happiness hits me as he pulls back and smiles.

* * *

"It's so nice to meet you!"

A woman I've never seen before in my life embraces me and bumps her cheek against mine. I get a strong whiff of perfume and for a moment I'm dizzied by the smell. She looks like a richly decorated tree with her golden bracelets and necklace. All I have is my gaudy engagement ring that still needs to get sized. Her manicured nails seize my hand as she catches a glimpse of it.

KNOCKED UP BY THE BAD BOY

"Oh my God, it's gorgeous! You must be so excited!"

"Uh—yeah."

I'm practically bursting with excitement.

"Have you set a date?"

I resist the urge to glance at Johnny. "Not yet."

"Well, I can't wait. Lovely to meet you!"

My head spins as the next person sidles into view, her teeth nearly cracking from her fake smile. "It's such an honor."

An honor? I'm only here because we didn't use a condom.

"Thanks for coming."

Then the next one comes along, and the next. They treat me as though I'm a goddamn queen, but I'm just waiting for my dad to show up and cause a huge scene. I stand at Johnny's side like a prop as a line of guests greet him one by one, sucking up to the don.

"Hey, there he is!"

Here we go again. *Another one.*

One of his captains wraps his arms around Johnny and gives him a kiss on both cheeks.

"Congratulations, Johnny," he says, giving me an admiring look. "You're a lucky guy."

"Thanks," he says, beaming.

"So what's the plan after this? You're going to get married right away?"

"That's what I'd like, but I'd prefer to get her old man's approval."

Never going to happen.

"Isn't he here?"

"Not yet."

He turns his head, looking at the small group of people, and then I recognize him as François, the man who hit on me in the bar right before Johnny cock-blocked him. François shrugs and turns back toward his boss.

"Do we have time to talk a little business?"

"What do you have for me?"

François bends his head, his grin splitting his face into two. "Really fucking good news. We've got the keys. We're going to be *fuckin' rich*."

The boss' face remains impassive at the news. "Good."

"We got one of the girls to fuck him upstairs while Tommy and I took his keys and made a copy. He won't have any idea."

"Keep your *fucking* voice down."

What the hell are they talking about?

"Right, this isn't the time."

Whatever it is, it's got my fiancé on edge. I don't know much about his work, other than what everyone else already knows: construction scams, extortion, the ubiquitous money-laundering Salerno cheese, etc.

"No sign of my future in-laws so far."

He should be glad they aren't here.

It's a peaceful, quiet party. Pristine white dishes sit on the rustic tables, the waiters slowly gathering them as I sit in one of the wooden chairs of the outdoor garden of *Le Zinc*. I'm possessed by a sleepy lull brought on by a full stomach, and darkness slowly descends over the party. Soft lights in the trees illuminate the tables.

A tall man with rugged good looks walks into the courtyard, a baby in his arms. Johnny's small circle breaks to greet him, "Tony!" A small woman, who I'm assuming is Tony's wife, gives Johnny a scathing look and heads for my table, ignoring him completely. She looks unhappy to be here.

She's my new favorite person.

The men crowd around the baby, and a huge grin lights up Johnny's face when it reaches out and grabs his finger.

"She has a strong grip."

Smiling, I turn back to the woman, who watches her baby anxiously. She notices me and smiles reluctantly.

"Hi, sorry, I'm Elena."

"I'm Maya."

We shake hands and she falls back into her chair, looking at me curiously.

"I'm the one who got knocked up."

"O—oh!"

My face heats up. "Sorry. It's been a long day."

Elena's anxious face breaks into a smile. "No, it's okay. Are you—*ah*—excited?"

Everyone keeps asking that, and I don't know how to feign excitement. I am nervous about it, but everyone expects me to scream about how *lucky* I am to marry Johnny Cravotta, the boss of the family. The king of Montreal.

"I don't know."

Elena's voice lowers so that I can barely hear her. "You don't have to marry him."

Well, that's a first.

My skin crawls and I look around for Johnny, but he's still playing with the baby. No one is within earshot.

"I don't have much of a choice," I say in an undertone.

But I find it bothers me less than it did a couple weeks ago. He's *not* a horrible man. I'll be treated well, far better than any of the guys in the MC would have treated me. It's just not every girl's dream, you know? Marrying the guy who knocks you up—who dreams about that?

"You don't have to be with him if you don't want to."

I look at her, wondering who this woman is and why she has the courage to say such things to me. Johnny would go nuts if he knew one of the guests at his engagement party was trying to convince me not to marry him.

"Maya, I know you don't know me, but you don't know *him*."

"You do?"

She drags her arms across the table and raps on the wood with her fingers, debating whether to tell me or not.

"My husband used to work for Johnny. He almost got both of us killed. He's a self-righteous, arrogant, cold bas—person," she amends quickly, turning a brief shade of red.

Cold bastard. Even I've called him that.

My heart rattles against my chest, and my gaze flickers toward him. "He's been okay to me so far."

Her deep-brown eyes bore into mine. "You barely know him."

"Yeah, but—"

"You have to get out of this Mafia shit. It won't end well for you or your baby."

My heart thuds against my chest. I don't want to hear this kind of crap—not now, when I'm already in too deep.

"Ladies, having fun?"

The scream catches in my throat as Johnny's voice cuts through the tension. He leans with one hand on the table, clutching the edge as his eyes smolder with an indeterminate amount of cool rage.

"We're fine," Elena says, standing up without speaking to him and walking back to her husband.

Johnny watches her leave. "Bitch."

What just fucking happened?

The bench creaks as Johnny sits down beside me and lays his hand on my leg. "What did she say to you?"

I don't know why I'm so unnerved by that woman, who is already hanging by her husband's side.

"She doesn't like you very much."

He sneers in her direction and gives her a little wave. Elena tugs her husband's arm, giving him a frightened glance.

Jesus.

"What the fuck is that all about?"

Johnny gives my concern a dismissive gesture.

"She's just trying to start trouble because she hates me."

"Why does she hate you?"

"I made a mistake and put her husband's life at risk. It's a long story."

Well, that explains her hostility, but it still doesn't explain why she was practically begging me to get away from him.

His eyes follow the direction of my gaze. "She's not the

first person you'll come across who won't care for me."

"Well, *Jesus*."

"People don't like the man in charge. You should know that better than anyone."

My mouth twists. "I don't like him because he's a bastard, not because he's in charge."

He looks around the small courtyard, at the men milling with drinks in their hands and guns strapped to their waists. "I don't care if they don't like me. They just need to respect me."

"What about me?"

A heart-stopping smirk reappears at his mouth and he grabs my chin between his fingers. "You like me."

"Yeah, but what if I didn't?"

His head turns suddenly so that he whispers right into my ear. "I can live with you hating me so long as I have your pussy available to me whenever I want."

A violent shudder runs through my body when his lips kiss the shell of my ear.

"Carlos!"

"Get out of my way, asshole."

Oh shit.

The blood drains from my upper limbs as Johnny pulls away from me, his head perking up with the air of a hound scenting a rabbit. A small group stands at the entrance of the courtyard, their dirty leather cuts at odds with everyone else. I recognize Tanner and Blaze standing next to my dad, who pushes aside an older woman with raven-black hair—*Mom*!

They're actually here.

Oh God, this is about to get ugly.

Through his grizzled mane of hair, he spots me sitting down at the table, Johnny at my side. Hair swinging wildly, my dad walks across the courtyard, making a beeline straight toward me.

François heads off my dad before he can take a couple steps, placing both palms on his chest as the rest of Johnny's men frisk my dad's entourage. They back away, finding nothing, and Johnny slowly rises to his feet.

"Stay here, Maya."

My legs lock together as he walks away to meet Dad, but I just can't get over this impending sense of doom. Shit is going to get bad, really fast.

It takes seconds for me to jog up to Johnny's side, and he gives me a stern look that I ignore. Whatever. He doesn't know how to handle my dad. I do.

"Carlos, I'm glad you could come."

Dad looks as though he hasn't shaved in about a week and his eyes have a permanent red tinge. My ball-busting mom stands behind him, looking wrecked. Her hair's a mess and her makeup is half made up, as though she forgot about it halfway through applying her mascara. Her pale lips tremble when she sees me, and suddenly I can't hold back the dam.

What has he fucking done to her?

"Maya!"

Suddenly what I want most in the world right now is just to feel Mom's arms around me. Am I fucking crying? I take a step toward her, but a cold, clammy grip holds me in place. Johnny's hand curls around my elbow, his face grim.

"Let me go!"

"I need to talk to my daughter alone."

"That's not going to happen."

Johnny speaks in a polite tone, but Dad reacts by spitting on the ground, dangerously close to Johnny's feet.

"I don't take orders from you anymore, *John*."

"Our business arrangement still stands."

"You fucked over our alliance when you decided to stick your dick in my daughter."

A small crowd gathered nearby erupts into scandalized gasps, and Johnny glares at me, jerking his head.

No, I'm not fucking leaving!

Johnny steps in Dad's space, their faces inches from each other as rage ripples off my father's body. "Shut your fucking mouth."

"I told you, I don't take orders from pieces of shit like you."

Jesus Christ.

"I let you run your fucking mouth at that meeting—I won't let you do it here at my fucking engagement party."

In slow motion, I watch as Dad lifts his hands and shoves the boss' chest. Johnny stumbles back, which seems to be just what his soldiers were waiting for.

Everyone knows that you don't get physical with the boss. You don't touch him.

They draw their guns, and Mom and Dad are right in the line of fire.

"Do you have a fucking death wish?" one of them screams.

"STOP! That's my mom!"

I shove one of them aside and sprint into the thick of that circle, ignoring Johnny's outrage. "*Maya!*"

She wraps her arms around me, and I squeeze her middle, breathing in the smell of her clothes—smoke and gunpowder. God, I missed her.

"Back off!"

Over my mom's shoulder, I watch as they lower their guns. Blood pounds through the veins in my head. I hear the roar almost drowning out Johnny's voice.

"Let's go somewhere private to talk."

Johnny motions with his head and two of his soldiers follow Dad as I trail behind with Mom. We walk inside the empty restaurant and Johnny sits behind his usual table. It's pleasantly cool inside, but dark. Mom sits beside me.

"Are you okay, baby?"

"I-I'm fine. I missed you."

"I missed you, too."

God, having her here makes me realize that there are a lot of people back home who I care about.

"What happened to Chuck? Is he all right?"

Mom's eyes lower and she gives me an almost imperceptible shake of her head. Then I feel a gaping void in my chest. That poor man was just about the only decent guy in that place. The only fucking man who stood up for me is dead.

Suddenly I hate everything about my father, from his grizzled face all the way down to his shitty, steel-toed boots. All he ever did was wear me down and make me feel less than human, and now he's a murderer.

"You killed him."

Johnny's hand finds my knee under the table and squeezes it. *Shut up.*

I won't shut up.

"He never did anything wrong, how could you?"

His voice explodes as his fist smashes into the table.

265

"How could you let one of them touch you?"

"I wanted him, and he wanted me. It's that simple."

"They're the enemy." He points his finger at Johnny's face. "This guy doesn't give a *shit* about you. The moment you have his kid, he'll throw you aside like garbage."

Blaze puts his hand on Dad's shoulder as Tanner winces at his comments.

God, even *they* think he's fucking nuts.

"I'm going to ask you to shut the fuck up one last time, and if another insult comes out of your fucking mouth, I'll cut your fucking hand off." Johnny squeezes me so hard that I can't feel my circulation. "Put your anger behind you."

My father's face turns a nasty shade of puce. "You destroyed my only child."

Johnny releases my hand and folds his arms, looking indifferent, but I can see the vein pulsing in his neck. He's a lit fuse, about to explode.

"You insulted the club by seducing my daughter and getting her pregnant, but I'm willing to let things slide if you meet my terms."

Oh Jesus.

"Which are?"

"We want a thirty-percent reduction on your wholesale prices, and we want to regain our territory."

Johnny's teeth look like they're about to crack. "And?"

"And my daughter gets an abortion—immediately."

The air stills as my father's voice rings across the restaurant. I don't dare look at Johnny's face, but Mom clenches my fingers in my lap. I don't dare breathe.

"I will kill you if you suggest that again."

"*Johnny!*"

I've never seen him like this. It's scary. His lips are white and shaking, like a wolf curling its lips over its fangs.

"She is mine. Our child is mine. I will not let anyone come between us."

"Then we're going to have a problem."

Flecks of spit fly from Johnny's mouth as he yells across the table. "You're the one with the *fucking problem*. I want the Devils and the family to continue our business arrangement. We're running a fucking business, not a pissing contest."

"You fucking Italians think you can do whatever the hell you want—"

"Dad!"

He leans over the table, staring at Johnny's whitened face. "Go ahead, fuck my daughter. Do whatever the hell you want with her. *Salute.* Is that what you want me to say?"

"Carlos, shut up!" Mom tries to grab his arm, but he

267

rips it out of her reach.

"You fucking animals nearly tore us apart in the '90s—"

"Without the support of the family, you wouldn't even be president. I own you and your fucking club."

"Not anymore! We're fucking done taking orders from—!"

"From what?" Johnny stands up, his screams stabbing my ears as one of his soldiers holds him back. "From what, you fucking coward? Say it!"

Horrified, I glance at my father, who remains tight lipped. He can't—he'll be killed for sure. Beside me, my mother moans. "Please, don't!"

"Say it so I can blow your fucking head off, right here. Right now."

"If you do, you're dumber than your father."

Johnny's arm moves and then two deafening shots explode in my ears. Something wet showers over my face and I look at a fine sprinkling of little red drops, all over my hand. Tanner and Blaze crash over the table, blood spilling from their heads like two cracked eggshells.

"Oh my God!"

Mom screams as we both stand from the table as blood creeps over the wood. My heart seizes in my chest as I watch Johnny calmly stand up, the silence ringing in my ears as he grabs the scruff of Blaze's shirt and yanks him from the chair. His body makes a meaty slapping sound as it hits the tiles, and then I see the back of his head, blown open and black, with chunks of pink in his hair. His brains are all over the floor.

The color faintly reminds me of the charcuterie we had as an appetizer, and the rich meal I ate suddenly rises in my throat. I turn away from the carnage and slap my hands over my mouth, swallowing it down.

Johnny sits on the chair vacated by Blaze, his suit ruined, and aims his gun right into my father's stunned face.

"Johnny, what are you doing?" One of his older men speaks up behind him.

"Getting rid of this asshole."

"NO!" The scream rips from my mother's throat and Johnny's head turns toward us as if sensing our presence for the first time.

"Get them out of here!"

"DON'T KILL MY HUSBAND! NO!"

They grab my arms, and I'm still shaking when I'm outside. Mom fights tooth and nail, screaming.

"Mom!"

"He's going to kill him!"

I know that. It sinks into my head as she grabs both of

my shoulders and shakes me.

"Do something!"

Why should I?

A second later I feel sickened with myself. It's not enough that my mom obviously would be devastated if he died?

"He's your father."

I search within myself for a scrap of pity for him. He shot at me. Killed Chuck. He ground my nose against the dirt to the point of desperation.

"He's all I have!"

Even she would be better off without him.

Mom's face falls, and then she goes in for the attack. "What about the people at the club? Don't you *care*? This is going to start a war. People will die! Your cousins will get hurt."

I think about Beatrice and her long blonde hair. Doing her highlights every couple months, talking about guys, convincing her to come with me to a connected bar. There were small rays of sunshine in the fortress, and she was one of them.

I can't just abandon them.

Do nothing, and you might as well pull the trigger yourself.

"Get out of my way."

I shove at the two men guarding the restaurant's

entrance, but there are multiple entrances. I run down its side and they take off after me. My shoulder slams into another door and I stumble through the kitchens, where Johnny looks at me as though through a mask of blood. My dad kneels on the tiles, staring straight at Johnny. I realize they moved him to the kitchens because it would be easier to clean the blood from the floor.

"Don't kill him!"

A chill descends over me as Johnny's handsome face turns toward me, his eyes detached. They're endless, black tunnels. Nothing. Jesus, there's nothing there.

"He needs to go."

"Johnny, *please.*"

"This was never going to work out."

The harsh sound of Mom's voice grates in my ears. "Maya, stop him! Oh God!"

"He's the president. *You're going to start a war.*"

I scream his name, but it's like yelling at a brick wall. His men grab my shoulders and rip me backward, and my heels connect with someone's shin.

"Fucking bitch!"

Johnny gives his soldier a deadly look and eyes me with the same deadened expression. "It's too late now."

Blood runs from my dad's nose, which looks broken. "Pull the trigger, you son of a bitch. Watch what happens."

Johnny digs the muzzle in my father's skull. "What'll happen is this bullet will go right through your fucking head!"

"No!"

I shove his arm away and he grabs me, rage contorting his features as he attempts to shove me out of the way. His face tightens under my fingers as I grab him.

"Please, Johnny."

"Why? Give me one good reason why I shouldn't kill him."

I search for reasons inside me, anything that might spare my drunken asshole of a father for the sake of my mother's tears. I just know deep down that killing him will make things worse.

"Two dead bikers is bad enough, but their president? You'll have to kill every last one of them."

"Then that's what'll happen."

"He deserves a chance—"

The restaurant echoes with his hollow laughter. "You don't know me very well. I don't give second chances."

He smiles against my hand, and it's his smile that makes my throat tighten and tears slide down my cheek.

"Give him one. For me."

Then slowly, little by little, he lowers the gun from my dad's head, his haunted eyes never leaving me.

* * *

From here on out, we're done. You stray from your territory, I'll kill you. You make an attempt to contact my fiancée, I'll kill you. You so much as suggest to her that she should get an abortion, and I'll take my time pulling you apart, limb from limb.

The sodden rag I'm holding drops into the dirty dishwater.

Pink mist.

Like the suds of this dishwater, except blood red, flying through the air in fine water droplets.

He just killed them. Two men from the MC. Foul bastards, but still. They had wives. And he just blasted them as though they were nothing. He was going to do the same to my father.

My heart pounds a wicked beat as I wash the dishes.

Just keep him happy. Keep him content.

Or he'll kill your father, and that'll be enough to start a war between the bikers and the mob.

I don't want anyone else killed for me. I wanted so badly to get out of there that I wasn't prepared for how much I'd miss my mom. My cousins.

And now it's all turned to shit. What's going to happen when Dad goes back to the MC and tells them that the boss of the Cravotta family gunned down two of his men?

It'll be a long, bloody war with casualties on both sides.

273

So how the fuck do I stop it?

I need to control him.

There's no fucking controlling Johnny Cravotta, you idiot.

I have to try.

A key scrapes in the lock and I jump to action, washing the rest of the dishes and hurriedly putting them away.

He steps inside. I hear the hollow sound of his footsteps and a chill runs up my spine.

I'm not weak.

I barely hear my own footsteps as I walk toward him. A smooth dark-navy suit glides over his body like silk, and he glances up at me even though I'm not making a sound. I feel as though I'm balancing on a tightrope the closer I get to him. Looking at him feels hot and cold. His smile makes my skin break out in a hot flush, but his eyes clench my insides with a cold grip. I can't look at him the same way I did before. I force myself to step closer to him. My hands tremble as though I'm trying to tiptoe past a lion. He stares at me as though I'm meat. I hook my fingers under his jacket and I pull it off his lean shoulders. His lips stun my cheek and I feel a glow burn into a sudden flare, but I turn away toward the closet.

My feelings toward him are so fucked up.

I hang his jacket in the closet, and when I turn around he's still staring at me.

What did I do?

"What's that I smell?"

"Oh, I made dinner."

"Huh."

I never make dinner, because I can't cook for shit.

He walks into the kitchen and grasps the edge of the dining table, looking at the neatly laid silverware and dishes. A smile tugs at his mouth.

"What is all this?"

"It's dinner."

"I can see that," he says, pushing off the table and stepping into my space. "You can't cook."

"I've just never tried."

He takes a look into the sink filled with suds, the pans blackened. I should have just ordered something, for Christ's sake. He lifts the lid off the pan on the stove and raises an eyebrow at the fish.

"Are you trying to kill me with all this black shit?"

The smirk in his voice sets me off. "I took all the black shit off. Don't be a baby."

A shadow crosses over Johnny's eyes and my heart leaps. Then he threads his fingers through my hair and yanks my head back, and the two men he butchered in front of me are tugged to the forefront of my mind. I never saw so much blood in my life.

His breath hisses over my neck.

"All of this *reeks* of desperation."

I am desperate.

"Johnny—"

"Stop it," he snarls. "Stop being so fucking scared of me."

But I am scared of him. He could end this fucking war if he wanted. Only he can ensure whether the people in the fortress live or die, my mom among them.

He reaches under my shirt with his other hand, smoothing over my back. My bra snaps against my skin as he lifts the strap. My muscles contract at the small sting.

Then his voice rolls over me, smooth as velvet. "You have nothing to fear from me."

"You killed those men right in front of us—"

His eyes are like lead. Seductive fingers twist my strap, slowly loosening the hooks. The skin around my straps starts to tingle and a flush spreads over my chest.

"I'm sorry you had to see that, but I'm not sorry for killing them."

All this time I never saw the darkness. I knew it was inside him somewhere, deliberately hiding out of sight. Now it's staring at me in the face, talking to me through his remorseless tone as he removes my bra with a loud snap that makes my legs clench together.

His hands smooth over my bare back, bringing me within his intoxicating embrace. The dimples curving into his face tell me that he knows exactly how affected I am.

"You didn't have to do it."

"I'm the boss of the family. "

"He mentioned your father, and you went berserk."

Johnny's eyes blaze. "He pissed me off beyond endurance. It set me off."

What if he does the same thing to me, someday?

His fingers slide out of my hair and the smile disappears. "Don't look at me like that."

"You're going to start a war!"

The apartment rings with my voice before I remember that I'm supposed to be playing the demure housewife role. Oops. Too late.

All smiles again, he descends on me, his hands soothing my shoulders, my face. "Is that what's got you so worked up?"

"Of course it is."

His voice is like honey. "Everything's going to be fine."

"Are you fucking kidding me?"

"I'm the most powerful man in this city. Nothing's going to happen to you."

But I can't say the same for your family.

"You *killed* two of the MC's men. If you think they're

going to sit back and just—"

Johnny takes both of my hands suddenly and walks backward with a huge smile on his face. "I got you something."

"Got—what?"

I'm distracted by the excitement in his voice, my heart still beating fast.

"A little engagement present."

He slips his hand inside his back pocket and removes a long, thin envelope, which he hands to me, smiling.

"You can't just distract me with a present."

"Open it."

He looks so fucking pleased with himself. I stare at it for a long while. He can't just fucking bribe me like this.

What's in it?

I stick my finger inside the envelope, but it's already open. I can't imagine how a piece of paper is going to make me happy. A folded, pink paper falls out.

It's a letter from the Robertson Beauty Academy.

"Read it."

"*Dear Maya, on behalf of the Admissions Committee, it is my pleasure to welcome you into the Robertson Beauty Academy for the Hairdressing Program.*" My voice trembles and breaks. "How did you do this?"

"Turns out, I know a guy who knows a guy whose wife

works there."

The paper shakes in my hands as I reread that sentence over and over. It's one of the best schools in Montreal. The curriculum is better than anything I could've ever dreamed of.

"I can't believe it." Tears fall from my nose. "Why would you do something like this?"

Warmth glows from his hand, which smooths my cheek and wipes away my tears. "I want you to be happy."

No one's ever said that to me, even my own mother. Happiness was valued last over the MC and family.

"Why do you care?"

It's just such an alien concept to me. I'm so used to seeing people treat their wives like crap that part of me believes this has to be a trick.

His gives me a chaste kiss on my forehead. "I want our kid to grow up in a happy home."

He wants me to be happy.

I can't believe he actually bought the courses for me— he remembered what I told him at the restaurant and got the classes. It's such a sweet gesture that I have a hard time reconciling this with the man who blew away two men in front of me.

"Now you can follow your dreams."

JOHNNY

Four a.m.

My favorite time of the day.

When midnight blue lightens into a color that reminds me of a deep coma, washing over the bed and the walls. Covering her skin in that coolness. My arm is snug around her waist, my palm resting over her smooth belly, just underneath where my kid is growing.

I shouldn't have let him go.

It nags at me constantly. It's the fucking reason I'm wide awake at this time, as she sleeps, oblivious. I prop my elbow on the pillow, watching as a strand of hair flutters over her nose. The ethereal blue light makes her look like stone, but she's warm in my hand.

Sal says I fucked up by killing his two men, but how long was I supposed to tolerate his disrespect? The fucking bastard wanted my child dead. I wanted to kill him. I should have, but she begged me for her father's life. The splinter in my chest aches like an infection. God, her loyalty reminded me of mine. I almost forgot what it was like to feel a sense of duty toward your father. He said jump, I jumped. Would have done anything—killed

280

anyone for my dad.

My arm tightens around her waist, my hand anchoring over her hips. What would he say if he were alive right now, and he knew I fucked up the alliance he worked so hard to build?

Who gives a shit, right?

I look at her instead, and the rapid pace of my heart doesn't exactly slow down, because it can't when I'm around her. The hand around her waist dips lower, until I stroke the slit of her pussy, because she's always naked in my bed. She stirs, smiling when she feels my hand between her legs.

Maya makes a bone-cracking sigh and turns around, giving me a nice view of her tits. Jesus. My cock hardens, blood rushing to it immediately.

"Go back to sleep, hon."

She smiles when my arm curls around her back, her body sliding over mine. Fuck. Her hair is like a dark halo, and her lids open slightly. My skin tingles when she plants a kiss right on my neck and pulls back with a smile.

"I'm crazy about you. I even dream about you."

"Yeah?"

She makes a sound and lets her head fall on my chest. I keep running my hands down her curves, my cock growing thicker. It wasn't hard, making her fall for me. Those classes did the trick. I gave her what she always wanted, and she loves me for it. I can tell.

Sometimes I'll be sitting down at the couch, and she'll bring me a beer without me asking. Shit like that. I realized how much I missed this. Not just having someone do things for you, but also having someone to come home to. Someone to fuck all night, every night.

Maya's still awake. I know it because she reaches down and grabs my cock, which is hard as a rock. Then I flip her over and nudge between her legs, and I'm thrusting inside her, slamming it home. Her screams echo in the apartment like music, and I just want to do this for the rest of my life. I fuck her until her throat tears as she begs for more. Her breath shakes out of her lungs with each thrust.

You're mine. You're mine.

I'm determined to coat her womb with my cum, just in case anything happens. I'd fucking knock her up again— and again. I want a family, and she wants me. She's wrapped around my finger and I've got my dick wrapped in her cunt.

She arches her back and I finish inside her, euphoria slamming into my shoulders. The bed creaks as I fall forward, propped up by my elbows. The way she looks at me makes me feel weak, and I hate that fluttering feeling when she presses her lips to mine. Fuck, she's beautiful.

She traces a finger over my chest, her eyes not quite meeting my gaze. For a few minutes there's nothing except the sounds of our breathing. Hesitation makes her open and close her mouth.

Just fucking say it.

"What is it?"

It takes a few false starts before she finally looks at me and speaks.

"I never said thank you." Anxious eyes slide over to mine.

It takes me a couple seconds to realize she's talking about the classes I bought for her.

"You don't need to thank me for that."

"Yes I do." Her brows furrow. "You've done so much for me without me even asking."

Because I have selfish motivations. "You look like that bothers you."

"It feels like you're paying me off."

I am, but another part of me can't deny that it makes me happy to see her smile. I want a devoted wife, not a prisoner.

I lower myself so that my nose touches hers. "I'm not just here to fuck you into oblivion every day."

A smile twitches on her lips. "No?"

"I want you to be happy. Why can't you believe that?"

A slow burn fills Maya's cheeks. "I don't know."

"I like the way you are." I kiss the side of her head and hear her sharp intake of breath. "I like that you speak your mind, that you're not afraid to give me shit. I like that you have dreams. Any normal girl in your position would've just given in to your dad, but you didn't."

She looks at me with fire blazing in her eyes. I know that I should tell her that I love her.

Just do it. You don't have to mean it.

I should love the woman I'm marrying, but I don't even know if I believe in love. Fuck, I can't just lie to her face. A guilty, poisonous feeling spreads inside my chest when two tears slip down her cheeks.

"I'm sorry I didn't believe you."

She slides her hands around my neck and kisses me hard, her tears transferring to my face. Her kisses become lighter as she tires, and then I pull her onto my chest as she falls asleep. The wheel in my head keeps spinning as she falls asleep. In the past, I would have never bothered with any of this. I would have bought her jewelry, or given her a thick wad of cash for her to buy whatever she wanted. I want her to be mine, but putting a ring on her finger isn't enough.

Her loyalty needs to be mine.

* * *

I have better shit to do.

My muscles tighten as I impatiently sit in the small bakery, only half-listening to the owner prattle on and on about this flavor or that one. Several trays of slices of wedding cake lie on neat ceramic plates. The owner takes them off the tray and explains the flavors *in detail*, one by one.

For God's sake just shut up.

Then I look at Maya, her eyes widening at the choices, the big smile on her face.

This is her first wedding. It's special.

"We have a lavender vanilla, a chocolate rose, maple bacon—"

"Bacon?" The word catches my attention.

The owner points out the small slice of cake, a medium-brown color with a sticky glaze. I stab it with my fork and taste the caramelized bacon and maple syrup. Shit, it's not bad.

I turn toward Maya with a piece of my fork. "You've got to try this."

"I'm not going to have a bacon-flavored cake at my wedding."

"Just try it!"

"Fine!"

She opens her mouth and I slide the piece inside, unable not to think of blowjobs when I see her throat moving as she swallows.

Fuck, not now.

"Yeah, it's good, but I'm still not having a bacon cake."

After all the cakes are laid out, the owner stands up. "I just have a bit of paperwork to do in the back, so I'll let you guys try the cakes while I do that."

Good, get out of here.

Her heels click on the tiled floor as she disappears behind the glass counter and through an office door. I slide my arm over her shoulders and my fingers disappear into her hair.

"Whichever one you like, we'll get."

Seized by a sudden desire, I bend over her chair and kiss her head.

Maya's face flushes with pleasure. "No, you have to help me choose. Try some of these."

She takes a few plates and drops them in front of me. I'm really not into sweets, but I try them anyway. There's so much shit I have to do, but pleasing my future wife comes first.

"They're all good."

"I would have thought a boss would be more decisive."

Sensing that tone in her voice, I take a handful of her

blouse and pull her toward me. "I am about things that matter."

Earlier this morning we went to the doctor, who gave us the baby's due date and a list of things to do. I couldn't believe how happy she looked.

"All these details matter, Johnny."

"Then you decide. I'll marry you if there's a fucking maple-bacon wedding cake, I don't care."

A slow smile spreads across her face, and then she picks up a small piece of strawberry cake with her fingers and holds it against my mouth.

The feeling of her fingers on my lips makes blood rush to my cock. It swells and hardens into a rock and I don't know why, except that this woman gets me so fucking worked up that I feel like a teenager again, getting hard-ons in the middle of a bakery. I swallow the piece of cake without tasting it, and then I grab her wrist, sucking every clinging bit of sweetness from her fingers. A blush rises in her cheeks.

I slide her fingers out of my mouth, digging my hand into her hair as I crush her soft lips against mine. My heart leaps in my chest. I sweep my tongue across her sweetness and stand up, pinning her against the wall. Her stomach twitches when I slide my hand underneath her shirt and she gasps into my mouth.

"You feel how fucking hard I am?"

"We're in a bakery!"

It doesn't matter where we are.

"I don't care. I want you."

"She's going to come out!"

The part of my brain that listens to reason is turned off. She sighs when I kiss a trail down her jaw to her neck, using my tongue to suck. She wears a boat-neck t-shirt, which teases at a hint of cleavage. I bend my head over it and suck, biting hard when she digs her fingers into my scalp.

"Did you pick something?"

I almost laugh at Maya's horrified face as the cheery voice echoes loudly in the bakery. She pushes my chest desperately and I sit back down, pulling Maya onto my lap so she can feel how hard I still am. My cock rides against her ass as the baker walks in the room with a big smile on her face for the happy couple.

"I don't know. Maya?"

"I-I think we need a bit more time to decide."

My smile is buried in the back of her head.

* * *

A low series of beeps plays in the background as I gaze down at a white hospital bed holding a man so badly beaten that only a few square inches of his face are visible.

Wedding cakes and this in one day. I can't take this shit.

"They found him in the street, outside *Napoletana*."

Tommy, one of my newer soldiers, grips the railing of the hospital bed and bares his teeth. "I couldn't fucking do anything. There were too many witnesses, John."

My icy tone hits the air. "What happened?"

"I was still inside the restaurant, getting the money. I saw six of them drive up on bikes. He ran across the street and they caught up to him."

That is no fucking excuse for letting this happen to one of our own. "You didn't do anything to stop it?"

His voice rises from the judgment in my tone. "I was outnumbered and the cops were on top of them two minutes later. Like I said, there were too many witnesses."

His fingers whiten around the railing as I walk closer to him. "So you let those assholes get away with this?"

Tommy's hazel eyes shine as a grim smile stretches his mouth. "Not all of them."

"What the fuck are you talking about?"

I turn around as he strides past me, closing the door to the room as he faces me with an ear-to-ear, hair-raising grin.

"I got one of them. Pulled him right off his bike and bashed his head in—"

"Why the fuck didn't you just say so?"

289

Tommy inches closer and bows his head to my ear. "He's in the trunk of my car."

Jesus fucking Christ. This is the problem with having too many hotheaded type A assholes working for you. They make stupid decisions. I can't believe this shit. I want to smack him around—the stupid fuck.

"*Are you out of your mind?*"

"He's still alive," he says in an undertone. "We can get information from him."

Tommy's new, but he came to me straight from New York. He was no longer welcome there after killing two made guys. Vincent always sang praises for him. Apparently he was quite effective at getting information out of people.

I don't trust torture. People will say anything when there's a pair of pliers and a blowtorch in their face.

"I want to see him."

Sal's voice cuts through. "Johnny, we can't let this slide."

"I've something in mind."

The idea grows in my head, festering like an infected wound, coursing vengeance through my veins.

Carlos knows damn well that I would have been well within my rights to kill him, but I didn't. I spared his worthless life.

You're becoming weak.

Not after tonight.

* * *

The air feels thick, almost as if it's soaked with blood.

He lies like a slab of meat in the backroom of a deli where we play poker, sometimes. The wooden table slowly soaks with his blood as Tommy, that fucking maniac, carves him up like a turkey.

The boy screams, and the sound punctures my ear. Fucking loud. Tommy barely flinches. He moves his knife over the biker's skin like an artist. A stroke here, digging it in the ribs there. He knows exactly what he's doing.

I place my hands on the edge of that blood-soaked table and look into his eyes, which are very blue. "We can end it now, if you want."

"What do you want? I don't know anything!"

He's a younger guy than the rest of the bikers I know. Tears well up in his eyes and spill down his dirty cheeks, and Maya's face flashes in my mind.

It's the way it is. They fucked up one of my men, I kill one of theirs.

I didn't get to be the boss by playing fair. I need to know what Carlos is planning, to protect the family. To protect her.

Another loud scream punches my head as Tommy

twists his knife, his face impassive as the boy's face streams with tears. He's ready to crack. I can see his sanity splintering in his eyes like broken glass.

"He knows about the airport heist!"

His chest heaves and his eyes go dark as if he immediately regrets what he said.

A thrill shoots into my heart. "What? What the fuck did you say?"

His face screws up in pain. "He knows—someone inside told him that you're planning something."

My insides turn to ice as Tommy shares a worried look with me. Then I seize one of the knives on his tray and wrench that fucker's hair, the tip of the blade right next to his eyeballs.

"I'll take your fucking eyes out if you lie to me."

"I swear to Christ, I'm not lying. He wants you dead."

"*Saint sacrament de tabarnak de marde*!" I slam the knife back on the table and try to keep my emotions in check. All year—all fucking year I've been developing this thing. It's the scam of all scams. The biggest in Canada's history. And Carlos fucking Lemyre knows about it.

"He thinks he can fuck with me?"

"I don't know."

Tommy looks at the boy and then back at me with a firm nod. He's telling the truth.

Then I have no more use for him.

I don't even bother lowering my voice. "Kill him, but don't get rid of his body. I need it."

I have a plan in mind, and I won't deny that it turns my stomach a little, but it needs to be done.

"NO! PLEASE, DON'T!"

Tommy nods in affirmation and quickly ends his screaming with a slice. The boy's gurgling gasps hit me harder than the screaming, and I walk out of the room, breathing hard. I have a fucking headache.

This cannot be fucking happening to me right now. Millions of dollars are at stake.

One crisis at a time.

Send *Les Diables* a message they'll never forget.

* * *

"It's just a dead guy, for fuck's sake."

François and Chris give me a look as they hesitate in between grabbing both rigid arms and hoisting the body onto the truck.

"Are you sure about this?"

That's the second time he's questioned me in front of my other men. He drops the man's arm as I approach him, energy seething through my body. He can probably see how pissed I am.

"Yes, I'm fucking sure, and I don't remember having to

explain myself to any of you. I'm the fucking boss. Shut up and do as you're told."

We're right in the middle of biker territory, and I don't have time for this shit.

"Put his fucking body on the car."

They jump at the sound of my voice and hoist the broken body over the car's windshield. The dead body's arms splay over the windshield like a cross. Chris winds ropes around his wrist and wraps it inside the car. The dead biker's head lolls onto his shoulder as his other wrist is tied.

"Jesus Christ," Tommy says as he stares at it, hands deep in his pockets.

"The fucking cocksucker deserved it."

We're down the hill from the fortress in Sorel-Tracy, but I'm going to ride with them all the way to the top.

Tommy opens the door to the truck as Chris prepares to light the fuses leading to the barrels of gasoline.

"This is so fucking dangerous. I can't believe I agreed to do this shit."

The spark flies and Chris runs to our car, diving behind the wheel as I slide into the passenger seat.

"Go!"

The truck lights up like a bonfire, and Tommy floors it for the twenty or so seconds that it takes to reach the fortress. The whole thing explodes into a bright fireball as Tommy crashes it right into the gates, denting them as the blaze quickly rises, crawling up the walls of the fortress.

In all my life, I've never done something so fucked up. It's a bright, furious sign. A warning to those fucking jerkoffs.

Fuck with me, and I'll destroy you.

The orange flames quickly crawl over the body sprawled on the windshield, and I hear shouts from inside the compound, its lights flickering on as the guards scream for fire extinguishers. Fucking dumbass.

The second gallon of gasoline explodes, rocking the ground as Tommy stumbles toward us, hidden in the dark. He coughs as he approaches me.

"You all right?"

"Yeah—just the gasoline."

"Let's get the fuck out of here."

I don't give a shit if the bikers see me. Let them watch. They'll know exactly who sent what was left of their patched member, Julien.

I slide inside the backseat of my car with Tommy, and the other men start their cars, rolling down the hill.

"Take me home, Chris."

He starts the car, the orange ball burning in his windshield mirror.

"Do you think they'll fuck off after this?"

My honest opinion is no, but sometimes you have to send a message to keep appearances. This will escalate things.

"If they're dumb enough to retaliate after this, I'll hit them harder. As many times as it takes."

Tommy regards me thoughtfully, nodding, talking to me in that New York accent that I hate. "Making a move on their home was pretty ballsy."

"Do you have something you want to say?"

My icy tone doesn't seem to deter him.

"We shouldn't have hit them where their families live."

"I hit the fucking gate."

"They won't see the distinction. To be honest, John, with all the risk we're taking with this airport heist, why do this?"

"We're up against one of the biggest groups of organized crime besides us. We needed to make a bold statement."

"After what that kid said, can we still go through with the heist?"

I don't even want to think of the possibility of a year's worth of work gone down the drain.

"We need to get rid of the people he has on the inside."

"I'll take care of it."

Now that we're no longer allied, I don't give a fuck about disposing of any of his people.

"I'm getting married next week."

"Jesus."

Chris stops in front of my apartment complex and I get out of the car. The walk to the elevator and the ride up doesn't seem to happen. It's been a long fucking day, but my muscles are tense when I walk into the apartment. The flames still burn on the backs of my eyelids. I feel the heat when I enter my apartment and swiftly lock it behind me. The television blares in the living room and I grit my teeth against it. I wanted to come home to peace and quiet, but she's watching some kind of news channel. Fuck, I don't even give it a second thought.

Then I see bright-orange colors that light up the whole screen. Maya's face is illuminated by it. She turns around, her beautiful face electrified.

"My home's on fire."

Fuck.

MAYA

"On fire? What are you talking about?"

He shrugs off his jacket and lazily hangs it on a chair, and then he loosens his tie and tears the first few buttons of his shirt, clearly eager to get rid of his clothes.

I try to shrug off my fear, looking at the TV anxiously. "The news said there was a fire at the fortress in Sorel-Tracy. They didn't say how bad it was."

"I'm sure it's not that bad."

A sudden suspicion hits me as he turns away.

But those fluttering butterfly feelings kick up in my chest when he faces me again and gives me that I'm-tired-but-I'm-happy-to-see-you smile. He walks around the couch and sits down next to me. His lips briefly press against the side of my head, and I catch a strange whiff.

Gasoline.

My insides feel like steel.

"How was your day?"

"Eh, you know. Usual shit."

No, I don't. That's why I'm asking.

"You?"

I shrug again, still preoccupied with the TV.

His fingers graze my shoulder as the towel slips down, and I slide over his lap, linking my hands around his neck. The heat of his skin glows. I always get a strange feeling when I look into his eyes. Then he slides his touch across my back and a swooping sensation hits my stomach.

God, I'm falling for him, aren't I?

Is it one sided?

I rest my head into the crook of his shoulder, watching the screen as it changes back to the news program. A marquee scrolls on the screen: *SYMBOL OF BIKER POWER UP IN FLAMES.*

"Holy shit!"

I try to stand from his lap as images of bright-orange flames surrounding my home burn on the dark screen. Jesus Christ.

"Good evening. Earlier tonight, a fire broke out at the gates of the notorious Sorel-Tracy fortress. Firemen are currently on site, fighting the fire. Reports indicate at least one casualty—"

"I need to leave."

I stand up from the couch, ripping his hands from my waist. I pat my jeans. Where are my things? My wallet—

"No, you don't."

Johnny's clipped voice sends a wave of fury crashing through me. I've listened to his fucking demands, even the most outrageous ones that I never thought I'd go through, but not this one.

I just can't fucking do it.

I turn around, looking at him calmly seated on the couch.

"*Excuse me?*"

"I said, you're not going anywhere."

"Why is that?"

He grits his teeth.

"Because it's been a long fucking night, and I'm tired."

"I'll go—you stay here."

"*No.*"

I hate that fucking word.

Then Johnny stands up from the couch. I belly up to my fiancé, who towers over me, sending sparks through his unyielding gaze.

"I'd like to see you stop me."

"Easy."

His hands snap around my wrists and then suddenly I'm being dragged to the bedroom. My heels dig in the floor, but it's so smooth that I fall down.

"What the fuck are you doing? Let me go!"

"I'm in no mood for this right now. I'm fucking exhausted."

"My mother's in there, you piece of shit!"

He yanks me upright so hard that I bounce off his

chest. His body seethes with barely restrained energy. "I'm getting really tired of this name-calling shit. If you do it again, I'll gag you."

"You can't just expect me to stay here while my home is in flames!"

"This is your home."

"Do you care nothing for me?"

He softens, running one hand through his hair. "Baby, she's fine. It looks like it was just the outside structure."

"I know you had something to do with this!"

There it is, finally. Johnny gives me a black look as my voice rings down the hall.

"I had nothing to do with this."

"That is bullshit!" I can see the lie right there in his eyes. "Let me go!"

"*No*. I'm going to be your husband in a week, Maya," he says in an increasingly frustrated voice. "Seeing your family right now is way too dangerous. Stay the fuck out of it until this blows over."

"She's your family, too."

There's no fucking way he'll keep me away.

Johnny's frown becomes more pronounced. It's as though he can smell the defiance blazing under my skin. He grips my arms and manhandles me into the bedroom, laughing as I twist in his hands and try to shove him back.

My efforts to get him off amuse him.

"I'm worried about my mom, and the other people there who I'm close to."

"I understand that."

"Do you?"

I fall onto the bed as he pins me down, his body moving above mine. My heart hammers as his tie tickles my skin. I've met his mother briefly, but I still know nothing about his father, other than that we're not supposed to talk about him.

He reaches across my body and opens the drawer to his nightstand, pulling out a shiny pair of handcuffs.

Oh no.

Then a grin tugs at his mouth as he slaps each handcuff around my wrists, and attaches them to the headboard. I yank on them, and he catches my wrist.

"You're going to hurt yourself."

Fuck, he's right. The metal digs into my skin. Johnny's bubble of laughter ignites a furious wave of heat in my chest. He sits up, straddling my waist.

"Are you seriously handcuffing me to prevent me from seeing my mother?"

The laughter dies on his face. "Maya, please just trust me on this. You can't see your family. Not now. They just put one of my men in the hospital."

"What happened?"

"They jumped him and beat the shit out of him."

"Jesus. Is he all right?"

"He's probably never going to walk again."

I sink back into the sheets as all the energy drains from my body. *Hell, you shouldn't be surprised.* Violence was a way of life back at the MC, but I always did my best to stay out of it. Now I'm in the thick of this madness.

How many other people are going to get maimed because of me?

A smooth feeling on my cheek makes me look into Johnny's softened eyes. "Don't do that. It's not your fault."

Is he right? Or did I condemn the people I care about just because I wanted a little bit of fun? Now it sounds like Johnny retaliated by setting the MC on fire, although the images only showed damage to the outside structure. They might be all okay.

Still, another voice says. *That's pretty fucking bad.*

Unpleasant warmth heats up my cheeks, the skin on my eyelids, everywhere. The bed sinks as he lowers himself and kisses my nose.

"I caused it."

"You didn't do anything except try to have a good time. There's no crime in that."

303

And now my hands are stretched above my head, tied to his bedposts.

"If you're going to blame someone, blame me."

"If I did, I'd hate you so much that I'd never be able to look at you again."

I can't blame him anymore. There were so many things I could have done to avoid strife between the family and the MC. I could have just not fucked around with Johnny. I could have left town, but the thought of leaving him now rips me apart. It's like one of those metal hooks in meat lockers, yanking hard right under my ribs. He started out as everything that I wanted and couldn't have and he ended up being the only good thing in my life—the only man who ever cared about what I wanted. The painful part of it is that he would see the whole MC *dead*. There's not a remorseful bone in his body, and a part of me is ashamed to admit I love him for that.

I love him, and it hurts. "Just fuck me."

The grin falters on his face. "What?"

"*Fuck me.*"

I need to feel him inside me. That sweet release is the only thing that'll make me feel better, but more than that—I need to feel pain.

Johnny's face stretches with a primal smile, the one that makes my heart race as fear slowly raises a row of goose bumps over my skin. He digs his hand into my hair and I taste his breath before his teeth sink into my bottom lip.

"I need you."

My stolen whisper drives him wild. He kisses me and rips himself away, and then he curls his fingers around the waistband of my jeans. They're tight jeans and they pull on my skin, but he rips them off, rolling them all the way to my feet. Then he bends his head, smiling, and kisses my mound right through the thin fabric of my panties before sliding his hands down my body and taking them off, too.

Thoughts of the fire at home creep into my head and clench my teeth together, willing the thoughts out.

"Please, Johnny. No games. Just fuck me."

He climbs back over the bed, still dressed as he snakes his hand behind my head. His heavy body presses into my chest as he seals his lips against mine, kissing me with a frenzy that seems brand new. I'm lightheaded when he sweeps his tongue across my bottom lip.

"I fucking need you, too."

The space between my legs clenches hard when he hisses in my ear, and then he rolls up the bottom of my shirt, sliding up my bra so that both of them act as a blindfold over my eyes. My gasp hits the air when his warm tongue suddenly licks across my nipple, making it contract. Then his mouth descends over it and he sucks hard. I can't see him, so every movement he makes sends a shock to my pussy, as if his fingers pinched my clit.

Just fuck me, already.

But I love feeling his mouth on my tits, the wetness suddenly hitting the sensitive flesh.

"Please."

His groan hits my stomach and I flutter as he kisses right below my ribs. "I can't control myself when you beg like that, baby."

The sound of his belt loosening from his slacks is another throb to my pussy. My mouth waters and I strain against the handcuffs. I want to feel his muscles gliding under my hands. The fabric slithers from his hips and drops to the floor, and my heart pounds as his weight makes the mattress bounce.

His hands touch my legs, and he guides them around his waist, and suddenly something hard shoves inside my pussy. A male sigh slides over my ears as he painfully shoves through me, my legs riding up as he sinks into me.

I can't see shit, but I don't need to when he fucks me this hard. The chains rattle and I can hear the sounds his cock makes as it slides, and that thrilling noise Johnny makes when he buries himself completely. His breathing rises to a crescendo, and so do the slapping, wet sounds. He thrusts hard, letting out primal grunts as I tighten around him. It feels so fucking amazing—he always makes me feel so amazing.

His hips thrust into me, driving his cock deep as his face nuzzles in my neck. Warm breath billows over my skin as desperate sighs break out from his lips. He holds me tight as he rams deep. It hurts me, but I need the pain. I need him gasping into me as he fucks himself into exhaustion. He silences my moans with his mouth, groaning into my lips as he pounds me hard. Then he comes. I feel his cock jumping inside me and the torrent of warmth as he lets out a long, drawn-out groan, followed by desperate breaths. His lips seal against me and I feel his fingers rolling up the t-shirt so that I can see his flushed face.

My legs tighten around his waist as he reaches down and pinches my clit, pulsing his length so that I can get off, too. Within seconds I scream, wishing that I could claw his back as my pussy contracts over his cock. The tightness in my chest finally loosens as I lie there with Johnny's body over mine, still buried deep inside me.

It's the best feeling in the world.

* * *

The TV hums and flickers to life, blowing up a huge display of smoldering metal and yellow firefighters walking in the background.

"Good afternoon. This is Michelle Fox reporting live from Sorel-Tracy where last night, a tanker truck filled with explosives crashed into the gates of the notorious Sorel-Tracy fortress. Police recovered one body from the fire and suspect—"

Blood pounds in my ears, drowning out the rest as the camera pans over the wreckage of the blackened truck. A truck full of explosives? And they found a body.

This has Johnny Cravotta written all over it.

Then an intense heat grips my heart as rage sears through my veins, and then I shut the TV off. How fucking dare he? He came home—he knew exactly what happened and lied to my face, and then he prevented me from seeing my own mother.

Don't act so surprised. You knew what he did.

I grab my phone from my purse and call her number, my hand shaking as I hold it to my ear. I haven't spoken to her since the engagement party.

"Hello?"

"Mom, it's me. Are you okay?"

"We're at the hospital right now." A whimper crackles through the speaker. *"Waiting for Julien's fiancée. He's dead."*

Oh my God.

Julien. The newly patched member, who I actually liked. I imagine him faceup on a gurney with hollowed cheeks, and a violent feeling rushes up my throat.

"What the hell happened?"

"*What the hell do you think happened? Your fiancé killed one of our own and sent his body back to us.*"

The air leaves my chest. "He—he wouldn't do that."

"*Of course he fucking would!*"

Her scream rings in my ears as two tears slip down my face. She's right, he would. Especially after one of his guys was put into the hospital.

"Listen, I'm coming to see you," I say as I walk around the apartment, gathering my shit.

"*Maya, stay where you are. Your father is—*"

"I don't give a shit."

I hang up the phone and glance around the empty apartment guiltily, as if Johnny's somewhere out of sight.

It'll just be a quick trip. There and back. I'll get to see my mother, and Johnny will never find out.

* * *

A cold, air-conditioned breeze cycles through the building, making me bury my hands under my arms. My heart beats a violent tattoo as I spot the crowd of leather-clad men lounging in the chairs outside the ICU. A few of them look up as I approach. One of them nudges Dad's shoulder and he looks up from his chair. Mom freezes on his lap when her eyes pass over me.

A dozen pairs of hostile eyes focus on me as I slowly

309

VANESSA WATLZ

edge into the room, feeling so awkward that I wish I could vanish on the spot.

Dad strides toward me with Mom hot on his heels. "Carlos!"

My stomach clenches at the furious, hateful look he throws at me, and then he actually lunges at me. I cross my arms, protecting my face as Mom screams at him.

"Stop it!"

My back slams against the wall and his yellowed teeth snarl in my face. "You did this, you stupid slut. You fucking killed him!"

I feel my skin burn as though he slapped me.

"What happened?"

"They burned him. His fiancée can't even do an open-casket funeral—that son of a bitch!"

I hear his words like a series of physical wounds. One after the other.

"But y-you hurt one of his men."

"What the fuck did you say to me?"

"You badly hurt one of his men. What did you think he was going to do?"

He grits his teeth and then slowly pulls his lips into a gruesome smile. "You can suck his cock all you want. You're dead to me."

Mom shoves his chest as he points a finger in my face,

and I tremble as I listen to him denounce me in front of everyone I know. My cousins—my uncles.

"I hope you have a miscarriage. No!" he screams, turning to my mom. "She's one of them now!"

"What the fuck is your problem with Italians?"

"You wouldn't understand," he spits.

"I do. You're just a dumb redneck—"

He shakes his head, laughing, and then something strange shines in his eyes. Something that almost looks like pity. "You don't know what the fuck you're talking about. Italians have been ruining our lives for decades—controlling our drugs, extorting local businesses, making this city's infrastructure a shit-hole. At least we don't fuck with civilians. They kill people and they don't give a damn. That's what you've chosen, little Maya. You chose a rotten man—"

Even though my heart pounds so fast, I can still hear myself barely whisper, "He's been good to me."

"He killed his own father to become boss. Did he tell you that?" All the blood pools to my feet as Dad smiles humorlessly. "No, of course not."

"Dad, I—"

"I would have set you up with a nice life. Any one of the guys in the MC would've treated you well, but instead you chose this piece-of-shit man who will throw you out the moment you're used up."

Then his eyes glance behind me and I turn instinctively, right into someone's chest. He grabs my arms and I try to jump away, but it's only Johnny, whose face is stony.

"Carlos, I'd appreciate it if you stopped sending your guys after my men. Things could get a bit—*hot*."

Jesus.

"You *fucking* cocksucker!"

One of his men slams Dad's chest as he drags my father, who only has eyes for Johnny.

"*Take it easy,*" he hisses in my dad's ear.

Johnny watches him and mutters under his breath. "Yeah, take it easy, *criss de tabarnak.*"

I barely feel his arm curling over my shoulder, and I don't fight back when he turns me around. I feel Johnny's burning heat right through my skin. His anger pounds through his feet. His fingers scratch me through the thin t-shirt I'm wearing.

He's fucking pissed that I came here. Well so the fuck am I. He lied to me.

"How did you know I was here?"

"I keep tabs on you." His voice is tight.

"Oh, so now you don't trust me?" I yank my arm out of his grip and Johnny's eyebrows rise.

"What the fuck is wrong with you?"

"You're a lying, cold bastard."

He lunges at me, and I'm so surprised at the pain crushing my arm that tears spring to my eyes. We're standing in the middle of a busy hallway, but he doesn't give a shit.

"I don't want to hear this shit right now. You came here when I told you not to—I told you it was dangerous."

"She's my mother! What did you expect me to do?"

"I expect you to be smart."

The vicious burn seethes in my chest as he pulls me down the hall, and I'm bursting to scream at him. How dare he admonish me?

He stops suddenly when we go outside and I bump into his back, swearing. Johnny gives me an icy look.

"I don't want to hear a goddamn word from you while we're in the car. I'm serious. It could be bugged."

This time he leads me to his car, hardly sparing me a backward glance as he walks across the parking lot. My head still pounds with everything my dad said, and he opens the car door for me. I pause and think of what a mess I've made with my life.

"Get in."

The car ride is tense and my fists clench whenever he takes a sharp turn, or puts his foot on the gas, flooring it. I dare to glance at him and immediately regret it. His whole face burns red, but he stares straight ahead.

"I can't fucking wait—"

"Maya, don't—"

"You lied to me about everything."

I feel so fucking stupid. The things my father said chilled me to the bone, and I can't pretend that I'm not really fucking worried that he's exactly what Dad said he was.

Julien is gone, and they actually strapped his body to the windshield and lit it on fire. *God.* I can't even imagine.

"Wait 'til we get home."

"*No.* Let's talk about this now."

"Fuck!"

He slams the brakes in the middle of the street and the car grinds to a halt. I feel my insides lurch as he stops the car, smoke billowing around the tires. My hands slip against the leather, chest pulsing as I realize we've come to a full stop.

"Maya, *please fucking wait* until we get home."

I'll wait 'til we get home, and then the gloves are coming off.

He parks the car and slams the door, but I get out before he can reach my side. Fuck him.

I march past him, hardly giving him a glance, and he catches my arm, pulling me to his side effortlessly.

"What the hell?"

"Don't treat me like a jerk-off, Maya. I don't care how pissed you are with me."

And then that bastard plants a soft kiss over my lips, and it's so sweet that it almost distracts me from my anger. It makes me cling to him a little bit longer when I just want to smack the smile off his fucking face. Then I remember how pissed I'm supposed to be, and I rip away from his side. His chuckle raises my hackles and I stalk into the elevator, pounding the button so I don't have to look at his face.

As soon as the door closes, Johnny tries to pull me in his arms. "*Hey.*"

"Don't fucking touch me!"

I slap his hands away and stare into the mirror, watching his deepening frown.

"You lied to me."

He approaches me close enough to hiss in my ear. "If I didn't, you would have headed for that fucking place and gotten yourself killed."

"You killed Julien and he was just a kid. Barely younger than me—"

"That *kid* was the part of the crew that bashed Michael's fucking brain in. My soldier captured him, and we killed him. An eye for an eye."

The fucking indifference.

"So they hurt one of you, and you react by killing one of them and setting his body on fire?"

"Yes," he says, deadpan.

He looks like nothing in the world could possibly be wrong with that. The elevator pings and he exits first. I trail after him as he unlocks the door.

"I have a question for you: how fucked up are you?"

I'm marrying a fucking monster.

He grabs my arm with a frustrated sigh and yanks me inside the apartment, slamming the door shut. Then he locks the door and I stumble backward, startled from the noise.

"I'm not a monster, Maya."

"You strapped him to that car—and you burned him."

That pretty much makes you one.

"He was already dead."

"What the fuck is wrong with you?"

He pins me against the wall with his eyes, which are shrouded in the darkness of his apartment. "There's nothing wrong with a man trying to defend his family."

"What family?"

"*You*, goddamn it!"

My back hits the wall sharply as he starts forward, grabbing my shoulders. The emotion twisting his face stuns me into silence.

"I'll do anything—*kill anyone* to keep my family safe."

"That kid—"

"—was a fucking degenerate, just like the rest of them. He knew what he was signing up for. What, I'm supposed to roll over and let them fuck me in the ass?"

Tears build up behind my eyes, and I don't know why. I know he's right. There are all these feelings burgeoning inside me, and I don't know where they're coming from. Maybe it's just that I'm having a fucking baby with this man—this beast of a man who can't even tell me anything real about himself.

"My dad told me things."

His hands slide up my shoulders, disappearing around my neck. "I'm sure he did."

The dismissive tone makes me fire back.

"He said you killed your father to become boss!"

I expect him to pull back in disgust.

I expect him to deny it.

A smile staggers across his face.

"Yeah, I did."

Oh God.

"And I'd do it again, and again—and again. That miserable prick had it coming."

"Oh my God."

He cups my face, but I worm away from him, backing

into the pitch-black living room. He won't let me go. Swift hands wind around my waist and pull me closer, right up against his chest where I can feel his heart beating.

"Don't look at me like that."

"I don't know how to look at you anymore. You're not the man I thought you were."

"I'm the same man you met in that bar, hon. I'm just— *more.*"

My hands are pinned against his chest, and I can barely draw in breath. Soft eyes look down at me.

"You won't tell me anything about yourself."

"That's not true."

"You killed your own father to get ahead. Why?"

His body leaves my side as a shadow descends over him like a shroud. "That's not exactly what happened."

Johnny walks away from me, looking back as though he expects me to follow, and I do. I follow him all the way into his study, where he walks behind his desk and opens a drawer, fishing out a dusty picture frame. He blows air over the glass and hands it to me.

"That's me and my dad."

An older, balding man with vague good looks throws an arm around a small boy with dark hair and eyes. The same eyes staring at me right now.

"I told you he was in the life with me. He groomed me,

you know? Raised me in the mob so that one day I could take his position after he retired."

"Did you get along?"

He smiles. "Yeah. I worshipped my dad. To me, he was a goddamn hero."

How the fuck do you go from there to killing your dad?

The smile disappears. "The problems came in my midtwenties, when I started making millions of dollars for the family a month. I surpassed all the captains—surpassed *him*. At the time, my dad was a capo and I worked under him. I was getting a lot of attention in the papers for how successful I was. Basically, I was getting too big, too fast."

The pain tightening his voice makes me want to reach out to him, even though I don't even know what happened.

"They pulled me in for a meeting and everyone was there. They asked me all kinds of questions and my dad said nothing to defend me. I think they were nervous about me. Young kid, lots of money—I could have made stupid decisions and gotten the family under fire. Anyway, I left that meeting knowing that my time was limited. Sooner or later, one of them was going to pop me."

Then his whole face clouds over. "I just didn't expect it from my own father."

Oh my God.

"Several of them ordered hits on me, including him."

"Jesus."

Johnny looks tired as he walks to the couch and sits down, his head in his hands. My heart clenches in my chest at the sight of him in pain. I sit down next to him and touch his thigh.

"How did you—"

He lifts his head and snaps at me. "I found him and blew out his fucking brains. Then I gave the boss a choice. He could resign or me and my crew would pick them off, one by one. He resigned."

"I'm so sorry."

I can see Johnny still fighting to swallow down the pain of his father—his hero—betraying him. He lifts his head.

"Karen left me right after that. She didn't want to be with me anymore. It was too much for her."

Is it too much for me? Something about the way he looks at me says that he doesn't give a fuck. His hand slides over mine, still resting on his thigh.

"I'm sorry for what I said—"

"Maybe I am a monster," he says, turning around to look at me. "But I don't give a fuck if I am."

I squeeze his hand. "I can handle it, Johnny."

"I know," he says with a smile, sliding his arm behind my back and dragging me into his arms. "That's why you came to me in that bar. You wanted to fuck around with a wise guy."

His smile intoxicates me, more powerful than booze or drugs. It slowly weakens me and an explosive spark ignites somewhere inside me when he bends his head and kisses me. I kiss back, yielding to his soft pressure. Shit, I already want him. I slide my hand around his neck, loving how warm he is. He pulls back, just hovering over my lips.

"I'm crazy about you, Maya. I think if I don't fuck you every single day for the rest of my life, I'll go insane."

For the rest of my life.

"You always get me so fucking hard, baby."

He gently nips at my collarbone as desire floods my veins like strong liquor. "If we get married, will you ease up on the MC?"

"If? You mean, *when*. We're getting married, Maya," he ends with a rough edge in his voice.

"I could change my mind," I say in a dry voice, although it's hardly a threat.

He smiles as though I've said a cute joke. "You're not going to change your mind. Like I said, you need me, and I'm not letting you go anyway."

* * *

A question trembles on my lips.

A question I can't fucking ask while I'm wearing a

wedding dress.

I always assumed I would marry for love, not for politics. Not because I got knocked up. There are so many unanswered questions between us, but I still say "I do" when our vows are read. His head bows and catches my lips, and I try to kiss him back, but the roar of the crowd distracts me. And then all of a sudden, just like that, I'm married. He grips my hand and we walk down the aisle in a shower of lavender petals. I move slowly in the dress his mother helped me pick out, my legs shaking so hard that if it weren't for him holding my hand, I would have collapsed. We make it to the limousine waiting outside the Catholic church, and then I finally have a few moments of blessed silence.

My husband slides into the limousine and shuts the door, giving me a mildly amused look.

This is fucking real. We're married. He's my husband. That's it. I'm bound to him for life.

It terrifies me. Did I make a mistake?

"Maya, you look beautiful in that dress."

It takes me a second to appreciate what he said, and a weak smile pulls at my lips. He looks mouthwatering himself. He wears some kind of dark-gray designer suit that I've never seen before, but it's probably expensive enough to pay for a dozen of his regular suits. It fits him perfectly. The fabric glides over his lean muscles and tightens around his legs when he sits down. A smile breaks his handsome face.

"What, are you shy now?"

My heart beats in my throat as I stare at him. I want to ask him. I need to ask him.

But I'm afraid of the answer.

"Do you love me?"

His eyes widen slightly and he sucks in breath, looking stunned at my question. It hangs between us, making the air thin.

"You said, in the beginning, not to expect anything, but I can't."

I can't because I'm in love with him. The thought of him not feeling the same for me twists a knife in my guts. Then I see the hesitation on his face and I know that my worst fears have come true.

The fucking man I married doesn't love me.

"Maya—"

"I love you!"

My hands shake as a pained look crosses his face. It's that look that absolutely kills me. Like a dagger to the heart.

"I love being with you. I love fucking you—"

"—but you're not in love with me," I finish, my throat

already thick with tears.

God, it fucking hurts. It's not his fault. Hell, he made it perfectly clear that he wasn't going to have feelings for me, but it still hurts.

He touches my face. "Maya, I can't promise you to be everything you want me to be, but you'll have me forever. I'll be a good father to our kids."

A thrill shoots up my chest. *Kids?*

Then a wry smirk makes my heart flip. "You didn't think I'd stop at one, did you?"

He gathers me in his arms, almost crushing me with the force of his embrace. "I'll be good to you, Maya." His palm instinctively smooths over my womb as he plants a kiss on my head. "You're my wife, now. You're the most important person in my life."

Just believe him.

I do believe him.

JOHNNY

My wife walks into the kitchen wearing nothing but one of my white t-shirts, which barely covers her pussy. Her nipples are like dark circles on the semitransparent fabric, and my dick gets hard as if I didn't fuck the shit out of her last night and this morning. She yawns and I watch the t-shirt ride up her ass as she leans over the kitchen counter.

That's one place I haven't fucked her.

I stand up, hard-on blazing against my slacks as I approach her from behind. She doesn't hear me coming and jumps a little when my arm curls around her waist. She leans into my embrace, her curves soft against my body. Maya turns around, smirking as I hook a finger in her dangling neckline and sneak a peek of her tits. Not that I can't see them already.

She looks down and sees my hard-on. "Again?"

I slide my hands up the backs of her thighs and I squeeze her ass. "If you're going to parade yourself like this in front of me, you better get used to it."

Her tongue wets her lips and my mouth waters at the thought of having those beautiful lips wrapped around me. She reaches out and grabs my cock, curling her fingers around it. I feel it jump in her fingers.

Then my hands sweep around her waist, just under the hem of the t-shirt. I cup her mound and reach back with a finger, finding her nice and wet. I plunge inside her, and her eyes become round as she lets out a small gasp. Jesus Christ, she's wet. So fucking wet.

"Please, Johnny."

I remember the first time I fucked her—how easily she manipulated me by throwing her tits in my face. I reach around her back and tighten her shirt, admiring how it wraps around her. I bend my head and sink my teeth into her curves. I grab the little nipple with my teeth and bite, and then I play with my lips.

"You signed over your pussy to me."

We married a week ago in a church. I saw the love in her eyes when we kissed on that altar, and I see it every time she looks at me. I feed off of it—need it just as badly as I need her body.

A small chuckle escapes her lips even as I'm thrusting in that wet cunt. Her cheeks burn red as I stop. I want to laugh when the color drains from her face. I gather her thick hair in my hand into a ponytail and I yank her head backward.

"You've got something to say?"

"No."

"You laughed. You think being my wife is a joke?"

"No," she says in a tremulous voice, still smiling.

All right, then.

I lead her to the kitchen table and push her back so that she bends over. Then I flip the t-shirt over her skin, exposing her beautiful ass. Keeping a firm grip on her hair, I use my other hand to smack her. Her muscles jump as I lay my hand down on her and a slight red tinge blossoms on her cheeks. The sound cracks across the kitchen as I do it again. The red color deepens, rising to her skin as my palm cracks over her again. With my thumb, I spread her cheeks apart and look at her glistening pussy.

For the love of God, take your pants off and sink your cock into that.

Fuck.

I pull on her ponytail slightly so that she arches her back and looks at me with a pained expression. My hand soothes the burn, and then she makes a moan that seems to stroke my cock. I shove my slacks down and my boner stands to attention. Then I sink into her streaming pussy and her walls swallow me, letting me into her deep heat. God, it's fucking amazing. A long sigh shudders from my lips as I anchor myself, keeping my hand on her hip. Her tits kiss the kitchen table as I nail her from behind, and I relish the sight, reaching forward to grab a handful. Then my hands glide down her arms and I drag them behind her back, holding her wrists with one hand. I use her wrists to yank her back as I thrust my hips hard enough to make her body lurch forward, then wrench back. It's not long before her screams echo all over my apartment.

"Spread your legs. *Wider.*"

I slap her ass again and she adjusts her feet. I want to feel my balls flush against her body. My cock throbs, aching for a release, and I slam my hips into her with a loud, wet slap. She moans with a guttural sound as I hammer her cunt, yanking back on her wrists. So fucking close.

Then I let go of her hands and lean over her body, snaking my arm underneath her tits as I grab her shoulder and bury myself deep. I hold it there and a moan rips from my throat as energy runs through my groin like electricity. I pinch her clit and thrust a few more times as her pussy milks me dry. Then I feel her orgasm gripping my cock, and utter another sharp groan. I pull out of her and slide the t-shirt back down, the aftershocks still rippling down my legs.

My chest tightens when she wraps her arms around my waist and kisses me, still slightly out of breath.

Then I lower my mouth to her ear. "Get dressed, baby. I've a surprise for you."

"What is it?"

"You'll see."

* * *

Keep the wife happy while I'm working… Check.

I park my car, rolling up against the side of the curb in the busy street. Maya gives me a curious look as I shut the engine off.

"What is it?"

I say nothing, opening the door and watching her face as she gets out. She looks around, confused, and I take her hand.

"Where is it?"

The excitement in her voice makes me smile. "I'm taking you to it."

I bought it as a sort of apology for not being able to go on a honeymoon right after the wedding. With everything going on, it would've been impossible. I lead her down the sidewalk until I find Sue's Hair Salon written in fading lettering on the glass, and then I open the door. There's a row of sinks and mirrors, a receptionist desk, everything she'd need for her own business.

"What—"

"It's yours, Maya."

She wheels around, her face suddenly red as she stares at me. "What?"

My laugh echoes in the room. "This place is yours."

"Oh my God!" She claps her hands over her mouth and screams. Then she tackles my waist and squeezes my middle.

Happiness swells inside me to see her so ecstatic. I hold her to my chest and press my lips to her head. "It's my wedding gift to you."

In tears, she gazes up at me, shaking her head. "It's too much."

"Everything that's mine is yours. I want you to have everything you want."

I just can't get over how beautiful she is—how she always looks so amazing. Her hair sits on her shoulders, featherlight. Her lips flush with color as she bites them, trying to keep herself from crying.

"I love you."

And I mean it. For the first time in my life, I mean it. Like her, I don't understand why or how—I just know that she's the one. She gave me what I'd been wanting for so long.

She clings to my shirt and wraps me in a hug that somehow feels different from the ones she usually gives me. Warm air gusts over my neck. "I love you, too."

The words give me a thrill. I wanted that, too. Someone devoted to me because they love me, not because I'm the boss. She's the only one who stands up to me and calls me out on my bullshit. I love her for that.

Happy tears leak from her eyes. "But what about you? I didn't get you anything."

"I have everything I want. Now what do you say?"

"Thank you, Johnny. I can't believe this—can I change the name?"

"You can do anything you want, baby. It's your business."

She just lights up at that, and then I call out to the girls waiting in the back. "You can come on out."

Six girls walk out of the back room with big smiles as Maya looks at me curiously. "These girls are going to be working for you. They'll help you get clients and get this place running."

She greets them enthusiastically, and I pull her aside. "I've got to go, but you can call Chris when you want to be picked up."

"Okay!" Her lips tremble as sadness overcomes her again. "Thank you so much."

"You're welcome. Bye, hon."

I kiss her cheek, a glow filling my chest when I watch her smile as she checks out the place, and then I walk out of the hair salon and back to my car.

I've been up for hours, obsessing over every detail of

what we having going on later tonight. Tonight's the night of the biggest robbery I've ever planned. Everybody's ready to go on my command, but what that kid said to me still grates against my conscience.

He's planning something.

I've got my guys out on the streets, looking for Carlos to bring him in. I'm not fucking around anymore. The burning message I left at the fortress wasn't enough. Things are too damn quiet.

I run through the list of things in my head as I pull away from the curb and drive toward the meeting at St. Joseph's Deli. We've got the keys to every door, we know the exact procedure to get in and out of there, we know all the guards by name, even that you have to shut the door before opening the safe, otherwise it trips a silent alarm. I have a guy who will dispose of the van at the junkyard after I transfer the money at the garage to another car. If this goes perfectly, we won't have to fire a single shot.

Common sense tells me to stay the fuck away, but I can't shake that I need to be there. It's the biggest robbery ever attempted. I've *got* to be there.

You're putting yourself at risk.

Fuck.

* * *

Waiting's the hardest part of my fucking job. For years

I was a soldier, getting my hands dirty while my father sat on his ass, waiting for me to bring home a thick wad of cash. Dick.

Now I'm the boss. I delegate things, which is hard when you like doing everything yourself. I sit in the back of the car. We're parked near the cargo terminal of the airport.

Distant screams of jets vibrate the ground and I clench my teeth as I check my watch. The fifty-minute window rapidly approaches, and there's no sign of my men.

Something's wrong.

"Fuck!"

Sal clenches his fist at my outburst. "Take it easy."

"We have a small window, Sal. I was very fucking clear about that. It only takes them ninety seconds to seal this whole place."

Dark shapes fly out of the cargo terminal, and Chris immediately starts the car.

"What the fuck are they doing?"

I see the duffel bags on their shoulders, and then I see them heading for bikes.

"GO!"

A white, consuming rage shakes my hands as I grab the pistol strapped to my waist. Chris cuts off the motorcycles with the car and I see their rat fucking faces. One of them swings a shotgun at the window.

BAM!

The shotgun's blast kills my hearing as it blows a hole the size of my fist in the window. I slam the door open and fling my body behind it, squeezing off shots that I can't hear. The biker's head whips back, the blood like a slingshot behind his head as several sparks burst on the door next to me.

Carlos' people are already fucking here.

"John!"

A heavy weight slams into my back, and my chin hits the cement. Then I hear a scream and Sal's body rolls off me, blood bursting from his chest. I see movement and my arm jerks instinctually. I pull the trigger, but not before he squeezes off a shot. I dive to the right, and my jacket rips open as a bullet grazes my shoulder. *Shit*. It stings.

Motorcycle engines roar all around me and I scream into the air as Sal clutches his chest. I know that look draining his face. He's not going to fucking make it.

A bike slows down and I jump back behind the car door. A deep voice laughs over the roar of the engine and I realize that I'm out of ammo. And I'm staring at the end of a double-barreled shotgun.

Oh God. Maya—

It's him. Carlos. He laughs his fucking head off and

anger bristles inside me. His fucking face is going to be the last thing I see.

"Eat the road, *fuckface*. I'm bringing my little girl home, and I'll kill you and any other motherfucker who gets in my way. Thanks for the cash."

Then he aims his gun at the tires in my car, blowing them out in a series of deafening blasts.

My scream dies in the guttural roar of his engine as he throttles away.

Maya!

This has to be a nightmare. I'm just cracking up a little. There's no fucking way *Les Diables* made off with my score, killed Sal and I don't know how many others, and is en route to rip my wife and baby from my arms.

I stand up, leaving Sal to die on the pavement because nothing matters to me more than getting to my wife as quickly as possible. Blood roars in my ears as I see several more bodies.

"Chris!"

He limps toward me as the rest of my crew sprints out of the airport terminal. François and the others grind to a halt, shock all over their faces.

"Jesus. What happened to the money?"

Who the fuck cares about the money?

"He's going after my wife! Where's your fucking car?"

Sirens cut through my voice, and François gestures to the car. I sprint toward it, but François and the other men hesitate. "We can't just leave them."

"GET IN THE FUCKING CAR!"

My family—my real family—comes fucking first. He doesn't try to argue with me a second time. I sprint toward his car, the footfalls of my guys behind me. We pile into the car and a pang hits me as we roll beside Sal's body.

I've got to end it. He should've been dead weeks ago, and now I'm paying the price.

The tires screech as we drive the fuck out of there. I try to think of where Maya might be. Home? There's no way he'd make it to my apartment.

"Where is she?"

"Try the hair salon."

It keeps playing over and over in my head as hot blood slides down my arm. He cut us down like dogs, and then he took my fucking money. Now he wants to take my wife, too.

What if he does the same to her?

A horrifying image of Maya surrounded by a pool of blood makes me pound the dashboard until my knuckles bleed. My mind goes red when François drives on the street where my wife's hair salon is. Chrome glints in front of the place. Three, four bikers. They raise their weapons.

SMASH.

The windshield splinters like a spiderweb.

"RUN THEM OVER!"

He slams it and the car screeches as metal folds underneath, their bodies flying over the cracked windshield. There's a huge bang, and he loses control of the van, crashing into a parked car. My body slams into the dashboard as he hits the brakes, but immediately I open the door and get out, the world swimming in front of me.

I have to save her.

Gunshots crack at me, exploding next to me as bits of brick fly. My shoulder smashes into the salon's door, and a female scream hits my ears.

"I'm not going—LEAVE ME ALONE!"

"You're coming with me if I have to fucking drag you back. We'll get you some doctors—we'll fix the—"

"NO! JOHNNY!"

My wife screams my name as I draw my gun. He has her hair fisted in his hand, and I can't see anything but my father. My vicious, backstabbing father.

I took the black bag from his face—

I sneak up behind Carlos and with the hand holding the pistol, I crack it across his skull.

He sneered at me, his hands cuffed behind his back.

He lets out a deep moan as I do it again, and again.

There are screams all around me, like a chorus of demons. I make the bastard kneel on the hard floor.

Dad kneeled on the shitty floor as I held my Beretta against his head.

He looks at me with hatred.

"What the fuck is so wrong with me?"

I screamed the question to him. It was raining. Big fat drops all over my skin, as if I were crying. It felt like it.

I see my old man, staring up at me. "WHY ARE YOU MAKING ME DO THIS?"

I waited, but he said nothing.

Then I raise my gun to his head, and I pull the trigger. I kill him all over again. Dark blood vomits out of the back of his head, and his eyes immediately roll up into his head, but this time a woman screams. His body crashes to the floor, blood spilling over the brand-new tiles.

"You're going to die alone, surrounded by your riches."

I loved him.

Now he's dead. He's fucking gone and I killed him. My feet give way and I sink to the ground, clutching my head as the pool of red touches my feet.

"JOHNNY!"

Maya's shaking arms pull me into a hug, and I'm ripped to the present. I'm kneeling in her father's blood. Technically, my father, too. She's my wife.

She's all that matters now.

MAYA

Time heals all wounds.

Whoever invented that phrase was full of shit. It absolutely does not heal all wounds. The unopened invitation to my son's birthday party is fucking proof of that. Mom wants nothing to do with me. I haven't healed from that. The pain doesn't go away, it just gets easier to deal with.

Live and let live, Johnny says.

Time won't heal the fact that he killed my mother's husband, the president of the Devils MC. It also won't make the MC forget the bloodbath that followed the botched robbery at the airport.

Yeah, I know all about it. The whole world does.

"*Papa*!"

Matteo runs on two uncertain, wobbly feet as the door opens, signaling the arrival of his father. The rambunctious toddler attaches himself to Johnny's leg, and his deep laughter echoes into the kitchen as he stoops down and picks up his son, hoisting him in his arms.

Even after all this shit, I still melt when I see him holding our son.

"Hey, little man."

"Johnny, it's time for his nap."

"Noo!"

A wide grin splits Johnny's face as Matteo protests. "I'll put him to bed."

"Okay."

I don't think I've ever seen him so happy as when he first held his son in his arms. Tears of joy swam in his eyes. There's a bounce in his step that wasn't there before, and I wonder if it's because his void is filled.

I walk to the living room and settle on the couch, grateful for a minute of peace and quiet after spending the whole day with Matteo. I lean against the cushions, almost nodding off, and then I feel his presence behind me. Hands suddenly caress my shoulders, and then he walks around to join me.

He pins me against the cushions with his body as his hands light a trail of desire on my skin. They find my neck, and I turn my head, tasting his breath. He kisses me and a rush of heat hits my groin as he slides his tongue across my mouth, and then he pulls back.

"I want another one."

Another baby?

"Are you crazy?"

"He should have a brother. Or sister." He leans in and nips my ear. "It's time to get you knocked up again."

Why don't you get knocked up?

At the same time, I can't deny it doesn't appeal to me, especially when his lips kiss the vein throbbing on my neck. Even though I'm exhausted, a thrill hits me right between my legs.

"I want another kid, Maya." He palms my womb again and slides his hand between my panties and jeans, forcing it all the way down. "And you're going to give it to me."

Then his finger dips, stroking my wetness.

Fucking hell.

It doesn't take me long to shed every stitch of clothing, his mouth greedily sucking every available inch of flesh. I cry out, my gasp hitting the air. Then he flips me over the couch and grabs my hips. I feel the heat of his thighs against my ass. Then it slides in, the head pushing my walls apart. He fucks me until I'm gasping for breath, until I think I'm going to collapse from the sheer ecstasy of his cock's relentless pounding. Then he empties his seed inside me with a huge groan and I come with him, both of us climaxing together.

I want to pass out.

He kisses my back, his chest pulsing, and even when he pulls out he keeps his hand inside me. The thought of actually trying for a baby gives me a thrill I've never felt in my life.

"You're an amazing father—better than I even

could've hoped for."

He glows when I say that, unable to contain the wide, ear-to-ear smile. He's the love of my life—father of my kid.

"Then you'd better get ready. I'm not stopping until that stick turns pink." He kisses me. "I love you."

Everything falls into place when he holds me. I know that I'm supposed to be with him. We have each other. And that's all that matters when you're in love.

# # #

ABOUT THE AUTHOR

Vanessa Waltz is a Bay Area transplant addicted to writing steamy romances with filthy bad boys. She lives with two crazy cats and can be reached at waltzbooks@gmail.com

Made in the USA
San Bernardino, CA
05 February 2016